The

Awakened

by
AC Colins

This book is dedicated to my real life muses.

To my daughter, who inspires joy and belief in the impossible.

To my mother, who motivates hard work and perseverance.

And to Mrs. Shutzer, who taught me the power and magic of words and how to wield them wisely.

—*Prologue*—

Well?

"Go away." A small girl sat cross-legged in the depths of an icy underground cavern, her breath appearing in visible puffs of frozen air. Somewhere far above was Midgard, the realm of mortals. Lena would never have the misfortune of experiencing such a place firsthand. She was a creature of the Margins, a shadowy world of half-truths and incompletes where the Forgotten were cast away and left to their own devices. The frigid underground cave was Lena's domain, her Cair, and it was there that she sat contrite and very much alone day in and day out, keeping her silent watch. Vigilant dark eyes stayed trained on the frozen walls while images only she could See flashed across the ice at blurring speed. It was her gift and her curse.

Lena was the only Oracle left.

What do you See, girl?

Lena ignored the ghostly Voice that whispered in her ear, urging her to answer. She was in no rush to be helpful. Jaw clenched, her black eyes dropped down to the frosty shackle that was sealed tight around her dainty ankle. Her most recent escape attempt had been a spectacular failure and the Voices decided that the restraint was a necessary precaution to discourage a repeat performance from their stubborn little Seer. Lena was forbidden to leave the Margins. The insulating ice of the Cair was the only thing that protected her from the full force of her gift. Were she to leave the cave, Lena would be crushed beneath the weight of the visions that plagued her every moment. For an Oracle to leave the cavern was to die. She was a prisoner to her own power and to the meddling Voices that kept her like a pet.

Child, you try our patience!

Another bodiless Voice prodded at the little girl's mind and Lena sighed. Their questions were unending. The only way to make them go away was to give them what they came for. She chewed on her bottom lip a moment. Yes, she had an answer to their query, though she feared it wouldn't be to their liking. "I see danger," Lena said at last. Her young voice echoed throughout the empty cave. "A war is coming."

Well, of course there is, a third Voice joined the others, gruff but warm. *It was only a matter of time. What we want to know is what we're to do about it.*

Lena shifted and her chain scraped as it pulled over the ice. "There is nothing for you to do." Her tired tone was void of emotion, far too jaded for one that appeared so young. "It's time for you to stand aside." There was a moment of stunned silence.

It didn't last long.

Outrageous!

You don't know what you're saying!

You want us to…step down?

"I never said step down," Lena replied with disinterest. She knew how this conversation was going to play out. She'd Seen it already, like a rerun. "I said stand aside." That did nothing to soothe their displeasure and they let the little Oracle know.

Are you mad?

Of course she's mad, she lives in a cave!

We have ruled for thousands of years, little one. How can we just stand aside?

Lena grimaced down at her frosty bare feet. She should have known better than to tell the all-powerful that they had become obsolete. "Correct," she said pointedly. "You *ruled*. Past tense. Your time is over." There was a discontented mumbling amplified by the ice that she ignored completely. "The Mortal Realm has changed since your reign. To that world you are nothing but stories for children and fables, weakened by idle centuries. I have Seen the future if you choose to ignore my words and it leads to emptiness. You must stand aside."

Stand aside for who, little one? The insistent Voice warmed the air around Lena, somewhat soothing her chills.

"There are younger—"

Younger? Three Voices boomed in unified, horrified shock. *We barely survived the quest at our strongest and you want us to step down for some inexperienced children, damaged from the Fall?*

The Fall.

Lena suppressed a shudder that had nothing to do with the ice that surrounded her. "Why do you come here and bother me when you refuse to listen?" she demanded, folding her arms across her chest with a small indignant sound. She glared around the empty cave, fixing her heated gaze on nothing in particular. "Either you want to hear what I have to say or you don't. Make up your minds, though, because you're beginning to annoy me. I may as well just keep my mouth shut and not talk to you anymore for all the good it's doing me." She meant it, too. Lena had once gone centuries without uttering a single sound. It had driven her keepers mad, but it made her point.

She could hear the Voices conferring amongst themselves, weighing their want of information against the aggravation of dealing with a cranky Oracle. Finally one of the Voices cleared its throat. *Show us.* The command was gentle and Lena nodded.

"That's more like it." With a slight gesture to the wall, the frozen room exploded with color. It sped through the ice, twisting and darkening. Gradually, Lena slowed the visions to allow her unseen companions an opportunity to See as she did. It was one of the few magics that the little Oracle had to offer. The Voices finally fell silent while they lost themselves in Lena's Sight.

The sound of crashing waves and carnival music filled the cavern. Lena made a face as the strong smell of salty, ocean air tickled her nose. A teenaged girl sat in the sand, the setting sun at her back. She stared out over the darkening waves, her anxious expression nearly obscured by the chin-length strands of limp, red hair the wind blew across her gaunt face. Restless and dusty blue, the redhead's eyes were in constant motion, darting to every gentle swell of the water as though expecting something monstrous to appear. She was a bundle of nerves, fit to panic, and Lena shook her head.

She did not care for this vision.

Is that... Is that a boardwalk? There was a flurry of movement and noise behind the wreck of a girl while she sat rigid in the sand with her long arms wrapped about herself protectively. Flashing lights and raucous music drew a deafening crowd off of the beach and streets, luring them toward the garish display on the pier. A Ferris wheel twinkled in the distance and the crash of bumper cars disturbed the sea gulls that were on a constant alert for scraps. The scenery seemed to completely overwhelm the girl, shrinking her down with its excess and gaudiness. *It is. That is most certainly a boardwalk.*

An ethereal sigh ruffled Lena's hair. *Not just a boardwalk. I believe that's New Jersey. The Fates have not lost their sense of humor.*

I fail to see what's funny, another Voice said dryly. *Is this the best you can do, Oracle?*

Lena's expression knotted into a childish scowl. "It's hardly my doing," she informed darkly. "That one has been in my visions for some time, now. No matter what version of the future I See, she is the one left standing at the end."

Her? There was more than a little skepticism laced in the Voice and Lena growled, her breath freezing midair. *How?*

"I don't know *how,*" Lena threw her hands up in frustration. She was just a vessel for the Sight. The 'hows' hardly concerned her, but somehow she knew that wouldn't be good enough for her Voices this time. "That girl will determine the fate of the Three Realms. That's all I can offer you."

But she is alone, a Voice said quietly. *How can that be, little one?*

Lena heard the affection in the Voice and a small smile turned up the corners of her glower. "It will start with her. She will be the one to set everything in motion. The others will reveal themselves in time," she gestured to the image in the ice where the redhead was staring intently at the water. "She is the beginning."

Is she capable? a Voice demanded, unimpressed. *She doesn't look like much.*

Lena rubbed her tired eyes. The images continued even in the darkness of her mind, flashing nonstop, too quick to make sense of. "Neither do you." There was a scandalized huff and a low chuckle. "And I may as well tell you that she's lucky. *Very* lucky." Her words were laced with significance. "And I'm not the only one that's been watching. There are forces both above and below keeping a careful eye." An ominous silence filled the cavern and Lena took the time to truly study the young woman that haunted her Sight.

There was nothing remarkable about the young woman in her vision. No more than seventeen or eighteen, she had a thatch of limp, fiery hair and dull, blue eyes. Even seated, her limbs seemed far too long, boney and thin. Her shoulders were hunched as she sat, silent and apprehensive, watching the surf pound at the sandy shoreline with her knees drawn up under her chin. Every few moments she seemed to twitch, but her expression never changed. Whatever unseen thing blighted the girl, she was long used to it.

Lucky... It was said with a touch of awe and Lena smirked. That had gotten their attention. *Does she know? Does she know who— what she is?*

Lena chose her words very carefully. "No. She doesn't remember. She has a new name now, a new life, but I would tread gingerly. Once again she's managed to retain very powerful friends."

There was no response and Lena knew that the Voices had gone. The little girl wiped the wall clean with a halfhearted flick of her hand and considered the terrible thing she had just set in motion. A new barrage of pictures immediately filled her Sight, a new future that followed the fresh path she had created. The Oracle paid them no mind as a slow smile spread over her face. The Voices were going to be furious when they realized that she had misled them, but it was her right. Just by knowing the future, Lena affected it, and the deception had been necessary. The young woman in her visions was, in fact, going to have a dramatic effect on the future of the Three Realms, though not in the way that Lena had led her guardians to believe. Everything, the success or failure of the future, rested squarely on a young girl's shoulders. And it was going to start with the redhead in the sand.

"Good luck, my friends." Her voice was swallowed up by the frozen expanse of the Cair, unheard by her three ethereal guardians. Lena's Voices would have their hands full in the coming months. It would be difficult for them, she knew. Their pride might have been undiminished, but the Fall all those centuries ago had crippled them. They would need to be wary. If the future went as Lena predicted they all would have trials to face before the end finally came. The Oracle suppressed a shudder, the very thought sending a chill down her spine.

The Fall. It was long ago, but the wound was still fresh in Lena's mind and in her visions. The Fall had ruined everything. She shook away her unease and focused   her   Sight.

She didn't like to think about the Fall of the gods.

—Chapter One—

The end of summer was a busy time for the Mayan Hotel. Its doors opened right onto the boardwalk and the camera-toting tourists got a kick out of taking the Skyride straight to the front door. They packed into the Mayan, eager for fun in the Jersey sun and while hotel management was only too happy to accommodate their guests, the three extraordinary girls who lived in room two-eleven were not. Girls who were at that very moment dropping water balloons on the other guests with stunning accuracy.

At eighteen, redheaded Cethy was the oldest. She was an anxious, twitchy creature with thin features and red hair that hung limp to her chin. She was a gangly thing, encroaching on six feet, scrawny and long-limbed. Cethy's squinty blue eyes were in constant motion, darting this way and that, alert to danger even when there was none. Cethy had the tense, exhausted appearance of someone who was under a great deal of strain.

She was lucky. *Really* lucky. Things just fell into Cethy's lap without her trying. She could find anything, whether she looking for it or not. It was a feeling, an unrelenting nagging sensation that prickled at her senses and drove her out of her mind until she gave in and followed wherever it led. So long as she gave in to her compulsions, she would find money, jewelry, wallets, and all sorts of valuable items. That good luck came with a price, however. There was a precarious balance that the Cethy had to keep at all times. Her good luck was usually followed by uncontrollable, mind-numbing *bad* luck. Accidents, injuries, small natural disasters… The more miraculous her good luck, the more ridiculous her bad luck became. Cethy was the luckiest person alive yet she constantly waited for something horrific to happen. Even worse, she waited for someone to finally realize that she was the cause.

In her desperation to appease karma and keep her bad luck minimal, Cethy rarely kept what she found. She held onto just enough money for food and for bills, for bribes to ensure the Mayan's managers did not report the under-aged girls living on the premises, and for 'little emergencies' that usually involved bailing one of the younger girls out of the Island's single cell jail. The rest, and there was a substantial amount left over, Cethy gave to those who truly needed a bit of good fortune. She donated to charities or stuffed collection boxes in an attempt to cover all of her bases. She left no stone unturned in her quest to keep her unnatural misfortune minimal.

The many benefits outweighed the cost but Cethy was convinced that her 'gift' was really an active force bent on her demise. It was impossible for the scrawny teenager to distinguish her good luck from coincidence and by the time she realized that she was on a hot streak, it was too late to stop it. All Cethy could do was ride it out and hope that when karma finally caught up with her, she'd be shown some sort of cosmic mercy. Bizarre perhaps, but Cethy was long used to it. She had been dealing with her luck and the repercussions for as long as she could remember.

Admittedly, that wasn't so long. The overanxious Cethy had woken up in a hospital when she was fifteen with an empty head and an aptitude for coming out on top. Two weeks later she'd holed up in the Mayan and had been there ever since, doing her very best to hide herself away with little success.

"Chill out, Red." A water balloon exploded at Cethy's feet, soaking her socks and Cethy's pale blue eyes flicked upward to the wicked looking sixteen year old that was perched on the ledge of the roof.

The youngest, Missy was a slip of a girl with huge golden-brown eyes. They glinted mischievously while she sought another victim below, a water balloon cradled in her lap. A mass of messy dark curls habitually fell into her face despite the stout clip that struggled to hold them back. Her full mouth seemed permanently quirked in a lazy smile, her skin pale despite the summer sun. Slight and willowy, she barely made it past five feet tall but Missy's diminutive size did nothing to detract from the unmistakable air of trouble that clung to her. She was as outgoing as Cethy was introverted, polar opposites of each other, but the two girls were near inseparable. They took care of each other. Cethy gave Missy a place to stay and Missy kept Cethy from becoming an absolute recluse.

Impulsive and reckless, Missy declined comment on Cethy's peculiarities. The spastic redhead could have been a man-eating monster and Missy still wouldn't have batted an eye. Missy owed Cethy everything. Before Cethy found her, Missy had been alone, dodging the island police and eating whatever she could beg off the vendors or rummage out of the trash. She'd been found by the police when she was twelve, her dark curls sheared short and her golden-brown eyes bright with fever. She had been practically feral, no idea where she was, who she was, or how she had gotten there. Missy would only say, and with startling surety, that no one was going to come looking for her. True to her statement no one ever turned up to claim the child. With no identification and no memories, Missy chose her own name. She decided to stick with what she was called most often.

"Listen here, missy…"

It stuck.

What hadn't stuck was whatever lecture immediately followed. Missy had a very real problem with authority figures. Whatever patronizing speech they threw her way about proper behavior only seemed to deepen her distaste and resentment. The law was hypocritical. Incompetent. Corrupt. It was useless and Missy took the task of holding people accountable for their actions upon herself. Where the legal system stopped... Missy began and the mouthy little scrapper was a force to be reckoned with. The Island police did not appreciate her picking up the slack and she saw her fair share of the inside of a holding cell over the last four years but no amount of punishment was enough to stop her stubborn quest for justice.

Like Cethy, Missy was 'gifted'.

There wasn't a word to explain exactly what the sixteen year old was able to do. She called herself Empathetic, with a capital 'E'. Missy was intuitive, and tremendously perceptive. Her senses absorbed emotion the way a sponge absorbed water and manifested physically. She could feel happiness like a cool breeze on her skin. She could see anger in bright ribbons of color against a person's body. She could even taste and smell how the people around her felt. That in itself was excellent motivation for Missy to avoid people and when she wasn't out playing vigilante she kept her distance from the general population as best she could. The sensation of other peoples' emotions tangled with her own, mingling and converging until Missy could no longer tell what feelings belonged to her and which didn't. It was messy. Her Empathy left Missy a temperamental reflection of those around her, an impossibly moody time bomb that ticked closer to detonation with every interaction. Not even being one on one with a person offered any relief. The Empathy only grew more focused and simple emotion evolved into snippets of tangible thought. Missy was a mind reader and an emotional conduit.

It was enough to drive her mad.

A knot in Missy's stomach moved unpleasantly up into her throat and she let her water balloon slip from her hand to wash over the crowded boardwalk below. Her mind had gone to a dark place, far from the sunny rooftop.

A few short months after she had been found on the beach, Missy had been committed to a mental institution. Her Empathy dragged her into other people's emotions or manifested in ways only she could feel. Missy would answer questions before they were ever asked, unnerving the people that were charged with her wellbeing. She was sent to Westfield Mental Hospital and was forgotten before the ink had dried on her admittance papers.

Missy's fourteen month stay at Westfield taught the little Empath exactly what sort of world she lived in. An endless parade of disinterested doctors tried to cure the little girl of her delusions but her gift did not fade. It only grew stronger and the only thing Missy truly learned was how to hide what she could do. She carefully ignored the mad jumble of moods that constantly barraged her and disregarded the thoughts that didn't belong to her. Missy couldn't stop her Empathy, but she could conceal it if she had to. Her escape back into circulation came with a realization. It wasn't going to be easy for a super powered teenager on her own.

But Missy wasn't alone anymore.

She had Cethy.

And if Missy could live through Westfield, she was pretty certain that she could live through anything.

That included Erin.

Platinum blonde and built like a model, Erin was the last of their little triumvirate. Her position among them was... complicated. Like Cethy and Missy, Erin's past was a fog of amnesia but *unlike* them, Erin wasn't even the slightest bit curious. She had no desire to find out who she was before she was picked up by the NYPD adorned in diamonds, gem stones, and little else. Her only interest was in herself and what she could bully out of her roommates. There was something disturbing about the lovely girl with the gentle blond tresses, and the ghostly gray eyes. Something sinister, even.

She gave Cethy and Missy the creeps.

Erin looked at the crowd below and whipped her water balloon down with far more force than necessary, a dark smile on her pretty face. The light seemed to dim around her, wrapping her in a permanent shadow. That was Erin's 'gift'. The blonde manipulated light. She could draw it to her, illuminating herself like a small star. Or she could repel it. Erin could step into a shadow and be completely consumed by it, vanishing until it suited her to reappear. The seventeen year old beauty queen controlled the contrast between light and darkness down to an abstract level. She could sniff out darkness in people like a scent hound. That meant that Erin didn't just *find* trouble, she was often *in* it as well. Missy suspected Erin was actually responsible for the mayhem that always seemed to drop into her lap, but there was no proof. No proof meant she couldn't throw the blonde monster out of the cozy room that the three of them shared. By nature Missy wasn't all that patient, but in this case she was willing to watch and to wait for Erin to slip up.

Erin and Missy both released another set of water balloons, drenching the passersby and mocking their victims when the soaked strangers started shouting abuse up at them.

"Please can we go inside before we get in trouble?" Cethy was knotting her hands worriedly and Missy sighed. She didn't need to look at the redhead to feel how anxious she was. Cethy was worried about getting in trouble, about Missy sitting on the ledge, about getting too much sun, about the door to the roof locking them out, about the elevator getting stuck back on their way down... Her list of concerns and qualms was too long for the Empath to pay attention to but the dark haired troublemaker climbed down off the ledge.

Erin simply upended the crate of water balloons, not bothering to see them all strike one unfortunate man that had stopped to take a picture of the beach. His furious curses followed the three of them indoors while Erin laughed cruelly and Missy glared. Cethy was too busy hiding in her own hands to notice the hostility between her two roommates as they scrambled out of the elevator and back to room two-eleven.

The tiny second floor suite that the three of them called home was nothing fancy. A set of twin beds was crammed into the space along with one wobbly table and four mismatched folding chairs. In the corner, stuffed between the wall and the poorly made dresser, was a motley collection of junk that Cethy had been stockpiling for months. Car keys, coins, wallets, cameras, credit cards, seashells, bits of string... The list went on and on. Her luck didn't just lead her to cash and cars. She regularly brought home garbage, too. The less useful things had all been haphazardly tossed into the corner and abandoned. There was even a moose head propped upside down against the wall, moth eaten and pathetic looking.

Hundreds of books had been stacked along the walls, all of them tired looking and dog eared. Erin had read every single one of them, most of them repeatedly. Missy often thought that Erin was only tolerable when she was reading. The less she talked the better. Missy's only contribution to the entire room was the picture of the three of them that stood on the nightstand, each of them smiling at something already forgotten. It was as close to a family photo that any of them would get to and Missy treated it like a work of priceless art instead of the digital print out it was.

The door to the room swung open and Cethy, Erin, and Missy all spilled inside, giggling and scrambling to close the door behind them. Cethy struggled to keep her heart from skittering clean out of her chest. Missy dove onto one of the beds, her eyes crinkled with amusement while Erin practically trip into Cethy's junk heap in the corner. "That thing is getting a bit out of hand again," she commented lightly. "Don't you think we should start exporting?" With a slight gesture toward the door, Missy indicated that they needed to start ridding the room of the rubbish that was making the already small space even more cramped.

Cethy frowned at her collection of other people's treasures and useless junk. Missy was probably right. One wrong move and the whole wobbly load would mash them into the carpet. "Sorry." Cethy ducked her head and disappeared into the bathroom, leaving Missy to watch while Erin scowled at the pile and tried to circumvent it without ending up *in* it.

Missy shoved her long, smoky-brown curls out of her face, perpetually amused by the collection of odds and ends that was slowly reaching out across the threadbare carpet. "Seriously, Red, we're going to need an excavation crew and a bulldozer soon. Or spelunking helmets."

Cethy poked her head out the door of the bathroom, a toothbrush hanging from her mouth. Grimacing, she looked over the pile and tried not to flinch. "I'll try. You know I have to wait until I get a compulsion. Curse and all…"

"Don't you mean gift?" Erin fluffed her perfectly smooth ponytail in the mirror, a cruel smile on her glossed lips. The blonde decided to ignore the mountain of garbage that was sneakily trying to assimilate them. "You've got to love a *gift* that helps you find dirty diapers or gets you locked in a padded room."

Cethy's sallow skin turned bright pink with embarrassment and Missy's eyes narrowed, something unpleasant smoldering in their dark depths. Westfield was a dangerous topic to bring up and mocking Cethy in front of Missy was even *more* dangerous. "That thing you keep doing with your mouth, Erin? Stop." The two younger girls did not, seemingly *could* not, get along.

Erin was oily and manipulative, malicious at every turn, and Missy was protective of Cethy and intolerant of the older girl's hostility. Were she able to get into Erin's head maybe Missy would have felt differently but her Empathy always hit a wall where Erin was concerned. It wasn't that the nasty blonde was emotionless, but a tight brace kept whatever Erin was feeling out of Missy's sight. Her power slid across Erin's mind like a sneaker over ice, unable to get traction. There was a fierce control behind Erin's smoky-gray eyes and a challenge that dared Missy to just try and dig deeper. Day by day, Missy picked at the wall in Erin's head. Erin had taken the time to keep her out and Missy wanted to know what was so worth hiding.

Erin examined her nails as though they were the most fascinating things she'd ever seen, purposefully ignoring the curly haired pipsqueak. Missy had been a thorn in Erin's side since Cethy had found her shivering in the sand last winter. If the blonde had her way, she would set Missy out at the curb with the trash, but getting into an altercation with Missy was best avoided. There wasn't much to her, but Missy was vicious when confronted. It wasn't worth it. Erin simply patted her hair with ladylike daintiness and opted to remain silent. A verbal battle was almost as futile as a physical one and would likely result in one or both of them bleeding out the nose.

A nasty smile curled up the corners of Erin's mouth as she watched Missy flop back into the nest of blankets. She was smart enough to never openly stand against Missy but Erin could still hold her own against her roughneck roommate. Unbeknownst to Cethy or Missy, Erin's power had taken a curious turn. Lately she could do more than just sense darkness in people. She created it. With little more than focus and force of will Erin could pull a shadowy film from within herself and force it over someone else. The shadow magnified hostile, hateful feelings, desperation, or any number of dark feelings and Cethy was easier to 'shadow' than most. The redhead's insecurity made her an easy target. Missy's emotions had always been impossible to penetrate. If Erin even tried she only got a headache for her trouble but clever as she was Erin had found a way around that.

A small crease appeared on her forehead while Erin concentrated. Tapping into her power always felt a bit like falling into a well and it required her to focus. The last thing she wanted was to get trapped in that low, dark place where her powers originated. Slowly, she wrapped Cethy tight in a blanket of shadow and waited.

It didn't take long for Missy to notice the drastic shift in her friend's mood. She saw a ripple of dark purple race across Cethy's skin, visible only to her Empathetic sight, a warning of an imminent temper tantrum. "Are you alright?" Missy arched an eyebrow in question and got a frown in response. Cethy glowered, blue eyes uncharacteristically aggressive.

Keep out of my head!

The thought hit Missy hard and she looked away quickly. She hadn't gone into Cethy's emotions intentionally. She'd been pulled in. A dark, heavy sensation settled uncomfortably in her chest and Missy wasn't sure who it belonged to. It might have been Cethy's or perhaps that sense of irritated annoyance and fury was her own? That was the trouble with Empathy. It was impossible to tell what emotions were original and which were simply visiting. The more people she had to interact with, the more feelings and moods overran Missy until she felt nothing at all.

The only thing worse than feeling everything was feeling nothing.

Erin chuckled to herself, a satisfied smirk on her face. It was almost absurd how simple it was to control her super-powered roommates. Missy was inconsequential. She was a mind reader that refused to use her talents to her advantage. Erin couldn't see the point of being attuned to someone's inner most thoughts and feelings if she didn't even bother to bend those thoughts to further her own agenda. Cethy was even worse. Practically afraid of her own shadow, the redhead was helpless to ward off her own luck, let alone Erin's ability. Erin could prey on Cethy and terrorize Missy in the same breath.

It was good fun.

"Now, now. Let's not fight," Erin said innocently. Her voice was sickly sweet and just listening to it made Missy's teeth hurt. "Cethy? How was your day, darling? Did you manage anything useful for a change? If you bring home anymore soggy couch cushions you know I'll make you sleep under the sink. Again."

With a nervous cough, Cethy looked down at the worn carpet. "Uh…" A neon ribbon of panic twisted over Cethy and Missy leaned forward, concerned. That was never a good sign. "I found a Ziploc bag full of cash under the dock off Carteret Avenue. I figure we can hang on to half?"

Erin groaned, dramatically interrupting the redhead. "Half? We're only keeping half? Cethy, why can't we keep the money and just get rid of all this?" She gestured to the junk in the corner and, as though on cue, a coffee pot fell from the top and rolled between the beds.

"If you want money, then go get a job," Missy suggested, her eyes hard on Erin. Cethy stared down at the table, chewing on her fingernails anxiously. Missy could feel her nerves and a small crease appeared between her eyebrows. Something was wrong. She could feel it writhing in her stomach like a live thing. Being an Empath was going to give her an ulcer. "Red… What did you do?"

"What makes you think that I did something?" Cethy asked quietly. She looked up to see both Erin and Missy giving her identical analyzing looks and flinched. "I used my luck," she admitted reluctantly. "But it was an accident, I swear! You know I don't use it on purpose!"

Erin snorted. "Maybe you should start. You're the luckiest person in the world and you live in a dump."

"What did you do?" Missy ignored Erin completely, her golden eyes fixed on her friend. Cethy was easily frightened and Missy could feel the strain as though it were her own. The redhead was one loud noise away from having a coronary. "It can't be that bad," she assured her. "It's not like you helped someone win the lottery or anything."

Her words were greeted by an uncomfortable silence.

"Oh, Red." Missy's tone was tinged with shocked disappointment. "You didn't. The lottery?"

Erin's lip curled with disgust. "Are you out of your mind? Cethy, you're going to get us caught!" Cethy winced away from the dangerous look on Erin's pretty face.

"It was an accident! I was on the mainland and some man asked when my birthday was. I gave him a date without thinking. I didn't know he was looking for lottery numbers."

"You don't have a birthday, Red. None of us do." Missy didn't bother trying to hide her confusion. Her eyes pinched shut and she attempted to not get frustrated. Cethy was the oldest and she provided for the other two but she was unreliable in a pinch. She panicked and Missy had to force herself to have patience. It was a testament to their friendship. Were it anyone else they would have had an cranky Empath to deal with.

Cethy really *was* lucky.

"Thank you, Missy, I'm aware I don't have a birthday. I just made up a date on the spot," Cethy answered hotly. "I didn't realize what I'd done until they announced it over the radio. I gave him winning numbers."

Erin started to pace the cramped room. For the first time Missy was grateful that she couldn't sense her emotions. No doubt they weren't all that warm and fuzzy at the moment. "I hope you're happy," Erin growled. "We're going to be detained by guys in black suits. We're going to be strapped to chairs, poked, sliced, and put under microscopes."

"I've already told you once to stop talking. You aren't helping.." Missy's cool tone cut Erin off before she could get started and she turned to Cethy. "Did you tell him your name?" Cethy shook her head. "Did he follow you back to the Island? Do you think he realized what really happened?"

Cethy frowned. "Not likely. Half the time *I* don't even realize I've done something."

"Then what's the big deal, Erin?" Missy demanded. "Red didn't do it on purpose and there's no harm done. So some stranger won some cash. It's not like he knows that there was anything supernatural going on. You know how people are. They'll do anything they can to explain away what we do." Missy was interrupted by a heavy knock at the door and she sighed, covering her face with a pillow. "Someone else get it. My nerves are jumping through my skin." She paused thoughtfully. "Or maybe those are Cethy's nerves. I can't tell the difference."

Erin eyed the door suspiciously. "I'm not getting it. You go, Cethy. And if they look like Feds tell them I'm not home."

Her tone was distinctly chilly but Cethy didn't blame Erin for being upset. There was no way to explain to the outside world that they could do and exposure was not something any of them were too keen on. They had to stay as inconspicuous as three super powered teenaged girls living unsupervised in a hotel possibly could. Missy might have shrugged off what she'd done, but Cethy had used her luck in a big way and that meant there was some serious *bad* luck heading in their direction.

Whatever it was, she hoped it wouldn't hurt. Cethy hated when it hurt.

The impatient knocking started up again and the redhead twitched. She had ordered takeout while the three of them were still on the roof and it was just more luck, she assumed, that the delivery guy had gotten there so quickly. Yet more proof that she was doomed. Cethy's mood when she opened the door was bleak but instead of dinner, a middle aged man stood on the step. There wasn't a food bag in sight.

From across the room, Missy gasped and clutched at her chest. Her mouth had gone dry with pure terror and sure enough when she found the source of her mood swing, Cethy was caught in the midst of a yellow haze of acute fear. Missy was on her feet and at her friend's side in an instant, a petite, protective presence between Cethy and whatever the danger was. The stranger that loomed in the doorway didn't seem so daunting. He looked tired, haggard, and upon seeing Missy, incredibly confused.

Erin peeked out the door, oblivious to Cethy's panic and Missy's defensive posture. "You aren't Chinese food." She glared, her perfectly glossed lips curling into a sneer. "You've got the wrong room, mister." Erin started to close the door, but Cethy was in the way, eyes petrified.

Something much larger than butterflies began to flap violently in Missy's stomach as Cethy's fear invaded her system. She had to force the redhead's emotion down grinding it away until she could function around it. "Can we help you?" Missy pried Cethy's fingers off the door, her eyes never leaving the stranger. "Or didn't you notice that you're scaring my friend?"

The man chuckled, arms folded lightly across his chest. He filled up the doorframe, dogged and ratty. "Affecting you, is it?" he asked. "Can't you get hold of yourself? Pathetic."

Cethy was frozen to the spot. "That's him," she whispered. Her voice was pinched high with fear, trembling. "That's the man I gave the lottery numbers to."

Ever the drama queen, Erin ignored their audience and grabbed Cethy's shirt collar. She yanked the taller girl down to her own eye level to better yell at her. "You said you weren't followed! I ought to wring your twitchy neck."

"I didn't follow her." Three sets of eyes focused their anger and fear on the man standing on their doorstep. A normal person would have turned around and run with the weight of those eyes on him, but the unwelcome visitor was merely amused. Missy could tell. Light blue and green ribbons danced around him like he was a maypole. There was no aggression, no ill intent. He was just entertained. "May I come in?"

Missy let out a very unlady like snort, ready to tell him to take a hike, but Erin beat her to it. "How stupid do you think we are? We don't just let strangers in our room. That's the fastest way to end up in the obituaries. Shoo."

"A simple 'no' would have sufficed." He glanced at Missy, that air of amusement not dissipating for a second. "She always was snippy. I'm surprised you have the patience for it."

"I'm sorry, do I know you?" Erin sounded anything but sorry. "I thought you were here about a lottery ticket."

"Oh, that." He simply shrugged as though that small detail were unimportant. "I threw the ticket away after it won. I have no need of money. I only wanted proof of who she was and gave me more than enough of that."

Cethy cowered at the man's words. "Proof?" she squeaked. "Oh, Missy, we really are going to be dissected and stuck under microscopes. Get rid of him!" Panicked, she clung to the younger girl's arm, blue eyes pleading.

Missy gently freed herself and shot Cethy a warning look. "What exactly would you like me to do?" Her voice was quiet. "He hasn't done anything wrong. I don't punish people for knocking on doors."

"Look who has finally grown up." His voice was oddly quiet. "It took you long enough."

Missy turned to face him, his words stirring something familiar and unpleasant in her. "Do I know you?" she asked, repeating Erin's earlier words.

The stranger only gave her a tired smile. "You did once. You all did." With a shake of his head he leaned heavily against the door frame. "Are you going to let me in or not?"

For a long moment Missy and the intruder regarded each other. She slid into his emotions, his intentions, and sifted through them carefully. They were like layers, one on top of the other, all merging and bleeding together. His emotions were far more concentrated than Missy was used to. They were uncomfortable to move through but her curiosity was piqued. The stranger's sudden appearance was less than ideal. He knew that Cethy was something more than she appeared and that made him a threat.

"You get five minutes." It was better to find out what he wanted and she stepped away from the door, granting the man entrance. Cethy made a noise to protest and Missy silenced her with a look.

"I hope you know what you're doing," Erin grumbled. She and Missy glared at one another as the stranger stepped into the room. He motioned for the girls to sit at the tiny table by the window and sunk slowly into one of the folding chairs himself. Missy closed the door and took a seat.

"Yeah," she muttered under her breath. "Me, too."

—Chapter Two—

An awkward silence hung over the wobbly table. The girls waited not so patiently for their guest to say something, *anything*, that might indicate why he'd shown up at their door. He seemed perfectly content to sit quietly and stare at each of them in turn. It was as though he was trying to memorize them, to commit each individual girl to memory.

Erin leaned back in her seat, unimpressed. Cethy stared at her hands, folded neatly on the table. She was unable to look up, unwilling to see the disappointment on her roommates' faces. She had unwittingly led this man straight to her friends and if anything happened to them she wouldn't be able to live with herself. Missy just glared at a fixed point on the wall. There were only three other people in the room, but she still struggled with all of the conflicted emotions that permeated the air. Their moods were like pollen in her sinuses, irritating and itchy. Slowly, she let her eyes drift toward the stray that had followed Cethy home.

If she had to guess, Missy would say that the man was only in his early forties though he looked worn out. His eyes were the cool color of jade, deep, green, and intelligent. He had an effortless smile, at least a week's worth of stubble on his jaw, and short, messy brown hair that was beginning to gray above his temples. He slouched over the table, scrutinizing them with an intensity that was making Cethy hyperventilate.

More interesting by far was the internal battle that raged behind his calm smile. He was very unhappy about something, but Missy could still smell his relief as if it were cologne he had put on a bit too enthusiastically. He was pleased, but something was making him nervous. Fearful, even. Missy let a thread of her Empathy slip around him to more closely read his mood. The second they were connected she froze.

"Was there something you wanted?" Erin was the one to finally break the silence, her tone loaded with as much attitude as she could muster.

More amused than intimidated, the man raised an eyebrow. "Indeed. You must forgive me, I wasn't expecting there to be so many of you. We thought you would be alone." He kept his gaze on Cethy.

Cethy tapped nervously at the table. "Who are you?" Her question was a frightened whisper. His green eyes were unsettling, like they were trying to bore through her, and it made her squirm.

"You know who I am. You just don't remember." His voice was gentle. Kind. The stranger abruptly turned his attention to Missy and his expression cooled considerably. "If you are overwhelmed then break the connection."

Missy looked like she was about to be ill. There was something beneath the man's emotion that attacked her nervous system with an energetic delight. It was a hardly contained power that was using the Empathetic thread that connected them to attack her core. Whatever this man was, he was not normal and he was far stronger than her.

Jaw clenched, Missy withdrew her senses from him and the attack on her higher capabilities lessened, though her hands still shook. "You're the guest here. You could at least pretend to be polite and not fry my system just for making sure you don't plan on doing anything shady." Even saying it sounded foolish. If what Missy felt when they were connected was any indication, this man could probably do whatever he wanted and with very little effort.

"Polite?" His emotion was so concentrated that his disbelief scalded her, it hit Missy so hard. "Am I to take that seriously coming from you?"

"Coming from me or not," Missy retorted. "You could stop trying to scare us. Cethy almost had a heart attack because of you. Just because you *can* pull tricks doesn't mean you should. Have a little courtesy for the rest of us."

"Don't talk to me about tricks or courtesy." The anger that accompanied his harsh statement scraped roughly against her skin but Missy didn't so much as flinch. "You're worse than any of us. No control. No consideration for others." He glared until Missy looked away. His emotion slowly backed away from her, leaving her in a blissful cocoon of calm. The Empath stared hard at the table. Missy had no doubt that he had just purposely used her own power against her just to prove he could.

"Now," said the man, "let's all try to control our mouths and our abilities. That goes for you, too, blondie. I know what you're doing and it won't work. I'm immune to your influence. You can't put the darkness in me and you can't trick this one into doing your dirty work for you. Shame on you for trying" He jerked his thumb in Missy's direction, his expression severe. Missy glared at Erin and the blonde shrugged. She certainly didn't look ashamed.

"We are going to have a little chat later, Erin." Missy practically hissed and Erin smiled meanly.

"I look forward to it, dear."

Cethy was slouched low in her chair. Normally Missy and Erin going at it put her into a panic, but she was well beyond panic, now. He *knew.* He knew about their powers. He knew everything. And she had led him straight home. "Stop. Stop fighting each other," Cethy whimpered, stunned and frightened. "He knows. How could he possibly know what we can do?"

The stranger smiled, his eyes losing their chill when they lit on the oldest girl. "Isn't it obvious?"

"He's like us," Missy muttered. She didn't look at him, still reeling from the assault on her Empathy. Erin and Cethy looked at each other uncertainly and Missy sighed. "Trust me, it's in there. He's got the same," she searched her mind for the word she wanted and came up short, "the same *something* that Cethy has inside. The same sense of power. Only his is more concentrated. More disciplined." She didn't add that it had been strong enough to attack her while the man himself sat there smiling calmly at them all.

"What does that even mean?" Erin demanded. "He's like us? Who cares?"

Cethy's dusty blue eyes widened. "I care," she answered immediately. "He found me. He knew what I could do before he even bought the lottery ticket. You heard what he said. Winning the money was just proof." She turned to the stranger, her anxiety a bright beacon in Missy's fleeting vision. "Who are you?"

Erin leaned forward and dropped her disinterested act. "I'd like an answer to that, myself." Missy nodded. It was time for a proper introduction.

"My name is Prometheus. I'm a friend and I promise... I won't hurt you." He cast a dark look at Missy before he added. "So long as you behave."

Erin's expression was unreadable but her mouth was pursed into a dissatisfied frown. "Prometheus? Really? We're supposed to believe that?"

Cethy peeked at Erin through her limp bangs. "You know him?"

With a shake of her head, Erin stood up and walked along the untidy stacks of books that dominated more than their fair share of the floor. When she found what she was looking for she slammed it onto the table in front of Prometheus. It was an encyclopedia on myths. He smiled. "Go ahead and tell them."

"Prometheus was a Titan," Erin explained slowly, clearly believing that her roommates were too daft to understand. "A sort of mega-god to the ancient Greeks.

They're creators. The oldest and most basic of the Divine. It's mythology. It isn't real."

"I assure you, it is." Prometheus placed his hand in the center of the table and the three girls stared, transfixed as a flame appeared in his open palm. He closed his fist and the fire snuffed out. There was silence. Chuckling, Prometheus looked rather pleased with himself. "I was sent to find you, Cethy. To explain a few things." The three girls started at him skeptically.

A guy claiming to be a Greek Titan spontaneously combusting they could believe but they didn't have 'friends'.

"I *am* Prometheus. And I've been looking for you, Cethy, for a long time." He held her gaze and Cethy seemed to forget how to breathe. "It's time you learned the truth about who you are. About *what* you are." They were riveted. None of the girls could have moved if they wanted. "That's what you *want*, isn't it? The truth?"

"The truth?" Missy repeated Prometheus slowly. It was almost too much to hope that the answers she so desperately wanted had just shown up on their doorstep. Things were seldom that easy. "What could you possibly know about us?"

Prometheus regarded the girls solemnly. "Everything. I know exactly who you are. I know your histories. I know your families, your friends. Do you?" He directed his question to Missy while he gestured to Cethy. "Distant cousins, yes, but cousins all the same. And your sister." He pointed to Erin and Missy made a sound of protest. There was no way they were related to each other. "Do you know your enemies, your homes, or the purpose of your gifts? Do you even know your names?"

"Do you?" Erin snapped, her pretty face pinched in a snarl. Families and names were all well and good but

Erin didn't want it. She was perfectly content being an anonymous force of malice. It suited her just fine.

Missy hushed Erin with an abrupt movement of her hand. She was staring at the wall again, but her focus was deep within Prometheus' core. She risked the brunt of his power, an Empathetic thread securely connecting them, but she needed to know. There was no deception. He bore the girls no ill will, and he spoken to them truthfully. After four years of mystery and uncertainty, they would have answers. "Do you really know who we are?" Her tone was tense as she eyed Prometheus, seeking any indication that he was untrustworthy. The second she caught a whiff of dishonesty she would put him out the door herself, but so far... there was nothing. "Can you prove it?"

Prometheus grinned and stood up, eyes lit with some internal delight and, Missy saw, a hint of challenge. "Follow me," he stated, "and find out for yourselves."

—Chapter Three—

The Cowabunga Bar had been abandoned for years. Empty and boarded up, cobwebs clung to the ceiling and the stink of stale beer was stubbornly trapped in the carpet. Chairs and tables were broken or overturned, neglected with time. The high windows were caked with thick layers of dark dust and grime and the bar itself was a refuge for debris and the spiders that scurried brazenly across the filthy surface.

"Cethy, please. Get a grip."

That was the second warning that Missy had issued, and it was one more than anyone else would have gotten. After the evening they'd had so far, Missy was in no mood to be put into a premature panic just because her roommate's emotions were out of control.

Cethy nodded sheepishly, trying to wrestle her fear down as Prometheus brought the girls through the bar's back entrance. To her overactive imagination Prometheus had lured the three of them to the abandoned bar to never be heard from again. She didn't have Missy's emotional discipline and when she was scared there was nothing she could do about it. Catching Missy's eye, she pleaded silently.

There was no doubt what Cethy was asking her to do. Missy had reeled her Empathy in to protect it from Prometheus but Cethy wouldn't relax until she knew for certain that they were safe. The Empath let her ability unfurl and lightly probed at Prometheus with a tentative thread. The last time she'd gotten a shock to her system for her trouble but either the Titan wasn't paying attention or he was allowing the intrusion because Missy gained access without a so much as a jolt. "It's fine," she told Cethy quietly. They weren't in danger and Missy felt the redhead's fear abate somewhat.

Erin was just bored. The little field trip down the boardwalk was a waste of her time. She wouldn't have come at all if Missy hadn't practically dragged her out of the room by the collar of her shirt. Nothing that Prometheus was offering appealed to her and she was impatient. "What are we doing here?" she demanded.

With a heavy *smash* the crates that were propped up against the bar tipped over, and from the other side of the bar rose a forehead wrinkled with time and confusion. An old man slid his elbows onto the bar, leering at them with dizzy eyes. The stink of alcohol on his breath was near lethal and, giggling, he half fell over the filthy counter. "Hello." He slurred the word, stretching it out ridiculously. Missy tried to back away, tried to pull her Empathy back in, but it was too late. She was hit by a dizzy spell that didn't belong to her and the room did an exciting spin beneath her feet.

That was exactly why Missy didn't spend much time with other people.

Cethy grabbed her friend's arm as Missy swayed on her feet and stared reprovingly at the one responsible. Missy tried to shake the neon cloud of inebriation away but it clung to her, turning her stomach with every breath.

He was unpleasant to look at. What hair he had left on his wrinkled, old head was solid white, including the grubby, patchy beard that was sporting bits of dried food and mysterious fragments. Eyes milky with cataracts swept over the girls in a leer. The teeth that remained in his drooling mouth were sparse and lonely, only one or two yellowed remnants remaining. He acknowledged them by shaking a flask in their direction.

"Prometheus," he slurred as he babbled to himself. "Fool. Human-lover. Can't you count? You brought too many girls back."

Prometheus scratched his stubbly chin. "Girls, I'd like to formally introduce you to the King of the gods. Zeus." The old man hiccupped loudly and the Titan sighed. "I'll just get him some coffee." As he walked away Cethy was sure she heard him add, "Again."

Missy staggered over to the least dilapidated table on the floor and eased into a chair thickly coated in dust. Erin and Cethy followed, unspoken questions forming in their minds while Prometheus deposited the old man on a bar stool. He tilted dangerously in the seat until the Titan propped the drunk up against the bar. He sat swinging his legs and singing off key into his flask. Missy chuckled, holding her head. Between the old man's intoxication and Cethy's nerves, she felt like crawling under the table and crying. So much for finally getting her answers. Prometheus had raised her hopes only to shatter them in some dilapidated bar. Her quiet snickers turned into bitter laughter. "This is great! This is just *perfect*." Her head fell into her arms, raising a small cloud of dust. Her shoulders were shaking with humorless giggles.

"Missy!" Cethy hissed, trying to keep her voice down. The curly-haired sixteen year old was too distracted to notice the charged feeling in the air, but Cethy was lucky for a reason. She didn't miss Prometheus slowly backing away, or the dark look on the old drunk's face. "Don't," she insisted, grabbing hold of Missy's arm to try and shake common sense back into the Empath. "Just because he's behaving badly, doesn't mean you have to."

"Badly?" The drooling man finally fell from the stool and shouted at them from the floor. "I am king of the gods! I am the wielder of lightning and ruler of Olympus. If I am behaving badly then it is only right, which means it isn't bad at all. Right?"

"He's a crouton short of a salad," Erin muttered, unable to make sense of the man's drunken logic. "This was a waste of time."

Missy banged her hand against the table and pointed at Erin with a drunk smile. "Blondie's got the right of it." She was so twisted up by her Empathy she was agreeing with Erin.

Prometheus hushed them. "Zeus might not be much anymore, but he is still very proud. Don't insult him."

Missy rolled her eyes, skeptical. "Sure, he's Zeus. And I'm a debutant. He can't even stand up straight." She hiccupped. "I'm not doing so well, either." There was a blinding flash and the table in front of Missy exploded into splinters right under her nose. Missy tipped over in her chair landing on her back. The shock was enough to knock the silly clean out of her. Suddenly her head was clear and she didn't believe her eyes. "Whoa."

The old man was tossing little bolts of lightning into the air and catching them again with an almost bored expression on his face. "Here we go again," Prometheus sighed. "Zeus, no!" He swatted half-heartedly at the man, like he was scolding a puppy that kept repeating the same naughty behavior. The girls were speechless. They stared in amazement at the shuddering strings of electricity that hopped between Zeus's fingers unable to do anything other than gape.

"Anything else you want to say?" the old man ignored Prometheus and unsteadily closed in on Missy, his speech garbled. "Because I have an answer for every comment you make. Every." *CRASH.* "Single." *CRASH.* "One." *CRASH.* At each word another lightning bolt leapt from his hand and punched through the ground at Missy's feet, forcing her to jump back. "Understand?" The old man wound up and Missy had only enough time to throw herself over the decrepit, dusty bar before the lightning struck the wall over her head.

Erin was enthralled. "He really is Zeus."

Zeus gave her a gummy smile. "I am!" he said gleefully. "Not that it matters. No one believes in the gods anymore. No one has time to appreciate us." His excitement dissipated. "It's a real shame, too, since we are the only ones who can save them, now. You." Zeus pointed to where Missy was peeking up over the bar. She ducked, afraid he was still aiming for her, but it was merely a gesture. "Get back to your seat, troublemaker." Cautiously Missy slunk back to the destroyed table, righted her chair, and sat down.

"Prometheus," Zeus plopped into a chair at the table, "you've brought me too many girls. You were only supposed to bring the Norn."

"Norn?" Erin tried to maintain a calm tone to keep the lightning from flying. She looked to her roommates for support but it seemed Cethy was too frightened to speak while Missy could only stare in awe and revulsion at what she could only assume was a Greek god gone to seed.

"Yes, *Norn*. I told Prometheus to bring me the Norn and apparently I got a three for one special. Find one Norn, get two irksome nuisances for free." Zeus put up a small fight when Prometheus took away his flask and placed an oversized coffee mug in his hands. With a sigh, the lightning god took a frustrated sip and grimaced. The girls watched perplexed. This was not, they felt, godly behavior.

"Can I ask a question?" Cethy had at last gotten her voice past her fear.

Zeus sipped on the coffee and pulled another face. "If you must."

Cethy looked nervously at Erin and Missy. Her eyes pled for help, but she received none from her roommates. "What happened to you?" she asked. There was no polite way to ask.

Zeus stared sadly into his coffee and Prometheus made a point to busy himself elsewhere. "Very good question," Zeus slurred. "And its answer is one of the reasons why I had Prometheus seek you out. Well, not all of you." He glanced at Missy and Erin and shot

Prometheus a look that very clearly said, '*I'll deal with you later*'. "You two should not have come. It is foolish of him to think that either of you would be useful to us. Your reputations precede you both. I only wanted her." He pointed to Cethy who shrunk back in fear.

Erin was indignant. "What's the matter with us?"

"Quite a bit, if we are being honest," Zeus said casually. He returned his attention to Cethy and leaned forward eagerly. "What do you know about the gods?"

Missy smiled at Cethy and giggled into her hand. "They wore bed sheets."

Zeus banged his mug on what was left of the table, sloshing coffee everywhere. "This is no joke, little girl."

Cethy paled and hurriedly interceded. "I thought the gods were just stories," she admitted. "A way for a primitive people explained the world around them. I never imagined that they were real."

Prometheus snorted from behind the bar. "A primitive people? You are talking about the fathers of democracy and forward thinking."

"They still wore bed sheets," Missy mumbled, dejected.

"Oh, the gods are real," Zeus whispered. "Long ago we ruled this world. Our own realm simply opened up one day and led us here. How could we stay in Valhalla when we were worshiped by the humans in this world?"

"Valhalla?" Erin interrupted. "That isn't Greek mythology. It's Nordic. I read about it."

"Heaven, Valhalla, Mag Mell. Whatever you chose to call it. They are all different names for the same place," Prometheus gestured dismissively. "All of the cultures are interconnected. Admittedly, we are all a bit cliquey, but that's what happens over centuries. Family loyalties and all that. Still, the Divine Lines exist together."

"They *did* exist together," Zeus corrected. "We *were* worshiped. We *had* temples and shrines built in our honor. We *had* priests and priestesses. Some of the little humans even sacrificed their loveliest young women for us." He winked at the girls and they bit down their disgust. "In return for their loyalty we gave the people the benefits of our gifts and protected them the best we could from their enemies. We were even known to love them." Missy rolled her eyes at Zeus' romantic notion of the past.

"But why were you looking for me?" Cethy asked quietly.

Zeus smiled. "If you remember, those of us on Mount Olympus had very few limitations and a lot of... time on our hands. We tended to get into a bit of trouble."

"Trouble?" The redhead didn't understand. Prometheus looked at her meaningfully and Cethy cleared her throat, blushing. "Oh."

Zeus smiled, palms out in innocence. "What could I do? Women threw themselves at my feet. I could have any mortal woman I wanted, and any goddess, too. Only one goddess was fool enough to risk my anger. Only one ever *rejected* me." His voice was bitter with the memory. "Nemesis." The three girls stirred in their chairs, suddenly captivated.

"She was a powerful goddess who had little interest in the affairs of Olympus. She preferred the company of mortals, though they feared her. Nemesis was beautiful and fiery. Strong. Utterly impossible. Time after time I tried to woo her and time after time she jilted me. I grew so infuriated I made the mistake that would cost all of the gods dearly."

Erin was fascinated. "What did you do?" she wanted to know. "How do you kill a goddess?"

"You don't." Absently, Missy answered Cethy's question.

"How would you know?" Erin scoffed.

Missy looked uneasy. She hadn't even realized that she'd spoken. "I'm not sure," she said truthfully. "Maybe I pulled it out of his mind?" That couldn't have been right, though. There were too many people in the room. It would have been impossible to hear anyone's thoughts. Missy had simply known the answer.

Cethy tugged thoughtfully on a handful of red hair. "What did you do to Nemesis?" Like Erin, she was eager to hear what horrific punishment Zeus had cooked up for the goddess who had spurned him.

Zeus sighed deeply. "Banishment. It had never been done but it seemed so simple. I banished Nemesis through time and space. I did not care where I sent her as long as it was far away from Olympus and—," he stopped himself and coughed to cover up a bit of information he had almost let slip. "I did not know where she wound up, past or future, or if she was even still in Greece. I only knew that her riddance was a good one," he said. "Until the other gods started to vanish."

Erin nodded as if it all made sense. "Of course they did. Prometheus said so, you're all connected. Your entire hierarchy was a pyramid. Knock out a block on the bottom and it all becomes unstable."

"It all fell apart, and not only the Olympians were lost. Without Nemesis, we began to vanish one at a time. Norse, Celtic, and Aztec gods all fell. The Egyptians. The Vedics. All gone. Some of us lost our memories. Some lost their powers entirely. Others fell victim to a partial immortality." Zeus stared into the coffee and hiccupped. "I never used to get drunk," he sighed, lost in his nostalgia. "We were Fallen. Scattered, we simply faded into memory. We became mythology, nothing more than bedtime tales."

"Look, I'm enjoying story time and all, but what does this have to do with us?" Erin snapped. "Why should we care about some goddess who blew you off you thousands of years ago."

"It isn't the past that worries us," Prometheus said. "It's the future. When the gods Fell not everything mythological was ruined. The monsters, the beasts, the nymphs, and other beings of that nature simply evolved to survive without us or went into hiding. Our disappearance has meant little to them or to the world of men. But ancient things are starting to stir. Things that are better left asleep."

"The Moirai," Zeus hissed. His distaste was obvious. "Even in the height of our power it was difficult to contain. Only the Norns can handle the Moirai."

"Explain," Missy demanded. "What are Norns? What are the Moirai? And what does any of this have to do with Cethy?"

"The Moirai? They're better known as the three Fates," supplied Prometheus. "They were goddesses. In fact, they were Nemesis's older sisters, but they were nothing like her. The Moirai were low level magicians with three unimportant gifts between them. A weaver, a gambler, and the bearer of the Abhorred Shears, a horrible little tool that cuts anything. The three grew tired of being mocked for their less than impressive powers and so they gave up their place in the Pantheon for a higher status. They traded their very essences for the ability to control the destinies of all living things. That included the gods who had so mercilessly mocked them."

Erin looked thoughtful while Cethy and Missy sat with politely confused expressions. "That follows mythology. The three Fates controlled the mortal coil. One to do the actual weaving; one to decide the path a life would take, and the last to cut the thread, signifying death."

"There was a condition for the Moirais' new position, however," Zeus said. "There's always a price, a consequence to deal with when you fight your own destiny."

"Indeed," Prometheus sighed. "The Moirai were able to control the fate of the entire world, but their own fates were in the hands of the guardians. The Norns. The Moirai were prisoners. They would never be free again. Even as their power grew, they could not escape from the enchantment that the Norns put on them. Over time, the Fates began to... to reflect their handlers. The personalities of the Norns could be seen in the Moirais' work, in the very weave of the Life's Tapestry." He looked up to see three sets of eyes glued to him. Erin's, tempest gray, hostile and insolent. Cethy's dusty blue, intelligent and cautious. Missy's, golden, rebellious and fierce.

Zeus sighed. "Now after all these centuries the Moirai have resurfaced and now they are unfettered by their guardians. Their reappearance will draw the gods back..." He shuddered at the thought. "We never should have left Valhalla."

"Draw them back?" Cethy started tugging anxiously on her hair again.

"Can't the Norns just enchant them again or however it works?" Missy asked, fascinated despite herself.

Prometheus lifted an eyebrow. "Were it that simple, it would already be done, but thank you for your input." He sounded anything but thankful. "The previous Norns have been... retired, so to speak. They're old and they're damaged by the Fall. They'd never survive the enchantment a second time. Suitable replacements have to be found.

"That's why we came for you, Cethy."

Erin snorted. "You think that Cethy is your new Norn? Ha," she said derisively. "You'll fail before you begin."

"Stuff it, Erin," Missy snapped. "Of course they were looking for Red. She a walking rabbit's foot. If anyone could do what needs doing it's her."

"Too bad I won't do it," Cethy said, stunning them all into silence.

"No?" Prometheus was genuinely surprised. "Why not? I thought you would *want* to save the world."

Cethy ignored the shocked looks from the men at the table and the / very obvious *lack* of surprise from her roommates. "It's too dangerous. My luck is not exactly at my disposal. It comes and it goes as it pleases. Maybe I *will* be able to help, but at what cost? You can't just expect me to go get myself killed for you."

"It *is* a difficult job," Zeus quietly agreed. "But the consequences of failure are dire."

"If the old Norns aren't willing to take responsibility then why should I?" Cethy looked ready to faint. "Don't drag me into a fight you aren't willing to get into yourself."

"You are approaching this too simply. The Fates are only the beginning," Prometheus said. "With the rise of the Fates comes the rise of the gods once more. We *are* going to return to power, Cethy. Slowly, but surely the gods are going to Rise."

Missy made a face. "Are you telling me that there are going to be mythological gods springing up around the world? Does anyone else think that is a *terrible* idea?"

Prometheus nodded, agreeing with Missy wholeheartedly. "Those who remember the old ways will want to be the ones to influence the Fates this time around. They will start looking for the Moirai and if they find them... I told you, the three Fates take on the traits of their guardians."

"Get to a point." Erin was well beyond done with this conversation.

"The point is whoever controls the Moirai controls fate itself. The fate of the world and everything in it," Zeus growled. "On their own the Fates are not good or evil. They are simply a nuisance. In the hands of, say Ares or Sekhmet, they are a terrible weapon." He paused to let that sink in. "Think about it. The Moirai cannot be trusted enough to be left to their own devices, nor can they be left to just anyone. They reflect the personalities of those who control them, therefore three very *specific* people are needed. There are forces at work that would see the Moirai controlled by evil. Evil guardians will usher in Ragnarok."

"The end of the world," Erin clarified the strange word for the benefit of the other two girls.

"For the Moirai to affect the world positively, their guardians must be forces for good. Perhaps gods of compassion, love, or benevolence. Any of those will do." Zeus said. "Perhaps the goddess of luck and fortune?"

"Cethy's a goddess?" Erin's face was twisted with incredulity. "Are you kidding?"

"Insolence," Zeus muttered. He gave up on his coffee and went back to juggling the miniature lightning bolts in his hand.

Missy slammed her fist onto the wrecked table. This was not the direction their conversation was supposed to take. Prometheus had promised to give them information about their pasts. Instead a drunken hobo was feeding them make believe. Not that she didn't believe him. If anyone was a goddess, it was Cethy. Beautiful, powerful, tortured... it fit. No, it just stood to figure that Missy's one friend in the world had been chosen to take on a quest that would probably get her killed. She wasn't sure what was so *lucky* about that.

"What about us?" she snapped at Prometheus. The heightened emotions in the room were making her quiver. Her eyes hurt from the glare of the bright colors that bounced off of the gods and her roommates. "What about me and Erin? You told me earlier that Cethy was my cousin. Who am I then? And Erin? Who is she? Aphrodite?"

Zeus's eyes narrowed at Erin as he looked her over. "You are no Aphrodite," he said. "She is painful to even *look* at so intense is her beauty."

Missy sighed and slumped over in her chair. "You don't even listen," she said tensely. "I just want to know *who I am*. They found me wandering around the beach alone." Missy's voice cracked. "No one ever came looking for me. No one."

Prometheus turned away uneasily. Guilty brown spots erupted all over him. Zeus was unfazed by Missy's outburst. "Why would anyone look for you? I told you, we were all pleased when you disappeared," he said.

"Nemesis."

—Chapter Four—

Cethy's face was frozen in horror. Erin gawked at Missy as though some sort of proof would be scrawled across her forehead. Missy ignored them both and blinked at Zeus, unimpressed. "Do you think you're being funny?"

"You wanted to know." Zeus's words might have slurred together but his eyes were fiercely focused on her. "The Fall changed you, but not enough to fool me. Who you are...who you *were*... it still burns in your eyes, Nemesis. You're still retribution in the flesh, of the flesh."

Cethy's eyes had gotten almost comically large. "Do you know what they called Nemesis?" she asked, voice hushed. "A woe among mortals. Missy, you're the goddess of vengeance!"

"No," Missy snapped. "I'm not." She rounded on Zeus, dark eyes flashing dangerously. "You said you didn't know where or when Nemesis was. What makes you think it's me?"

"I would never forget you, Nemesis," Zeus said almost reverently. "Never. You've haunted me since the day you disappeared. Your age might be different, your memories gone, but the divinity in you is unchanged. I would know that anywhere. Denial won't change who you are."

Missy was seething. "How can you put that on me?" she demanded. "How can you blame me for the destruction of the gods? So what if I use my power to punish people who deserve it? Anyone with my gift would do the same. I'm not Nemesis! I am not the reason you... you *Fell*!"

"Partly true." Zeus conceded. "It isn't your fault the gods Fell. It was my own rushed judgment. It was my anger, my jealousy, that doomed us. But you are still a part of my pantheon, like it or not. You all are." Zeus looked at Cethy. "Tyche," he said fondly, "goddess of fortune. And you…" Zeus shot an annoyed look at Erin. "You're our very own goddess of conflict. Eris. I was sort of hoping you'd just stay lost."

The girls were silent as they looked at each other out of the sides of their eyes.

Goddesses…

They were goddesses?

It wasn't possible.

Cethy was the first to nod hesitantly. "What else can it be?" she asked the other two quietly. "It explains everything. Our powers, our memory loss, everything."

"No," Missy whispered. "No. I'm not accepting this."

Cethy pointed to Zeus. "Who else throws lightning?"

For the first time ever, Erin sided with Missy. "Come on, Cethy. It's more likely we were exposed to radiation or bitten by a nuclear bug. And even if it's true," Erin hissed, glaring at the two men, "do you really think that we are going to fall back in line? I have to warn you, I don't do subservient very well."

"And I'm pretty sure that people aren't just going to let you take over once you get your Fates under control," Missy pointed out.

"The gods must *never* return to power here," Prometheus said severely. He looked around the table, careful to look each teenager in the eye. "This world is not meant for us. We should never have tried to rule it in the first place. When we Rise it will only be to bind the Moirai. Then we must all leave the Mortal Realm."

Erin laughed. "You expect us to believe that you are going to gain power just so you can give it up? That's even more ridiculous than Cethy being a luck goddess."

"I don't care what you believe," Zeus flailed and waved his coffee mug overhead. "Once the gods Rise, we will force you back into Valhalla, kicking and screaming if need be." He slammed the mug onto the table and the handle snapped off in his hand. Missy stared at the broken pieces on the table and felt like she was looking at her own shattered life. Her head fell into her hands. She couldn't handle much more of this.

"Oh, you'll have a fight on your hands, make no mistake about that," Erin spat meanly. She glared at Cethy. "If you help them, I will make you suffer. You know I'm more than capable of that." Missy was on her feet and at her friend's defense in an instant but Erin did nothing. She simply rose to her feet. "See you soon, sweetie." She stormed out of the bar. They all heard the door slam behind her and Cethy flinched. The two remaining girls were alone with the older Olympians in uncomfortable silence.

"Eris wasn't meant to be a part of this." Prometheus said calmly. Erin's fit hadn't surprised him at all. "Can you imagine the influence that she would have on the Fates?" He shuddered at the thought. "No. She can't be allowed near the Moirai."

"Which brings us to you, Nemesis." Zeus looked Missy over with both loathing and regret. "It's time for you to go, as well. You have no place in this circle."

Missy hesitated. She didn't mind leaving, but she *did* mind leaving Cethy. "She's no longer your concern," Prometheus said quietly, correctly interpreting her pause.

"Cethy's my friend. I'll always be concerned." Missy looked at her friend… her cousin, and left the decision up to her. Cethy looked shaky and miserable, but no more than usual and she gestured Missy toward the door with the barest hint of a smile. Missy nodded. "I'll see you at home," she said quietly. She turned and slowly followed Erin out into the street, her face worried. The door closed behind her with a click that sounded all too final for the sixteen year old.

Cethy stayed in her seat even though all she wanted to do was chase after Missy and hide them both under their beds until all the crazy went away. "Are you telling the truth?" she demanded, looking from god to Titan. "Are we really... I mean, Missy? She's really Nemesis? And is Erin..." Cethy grasped for the name.

"Eris," Zeus provided. "Yes. I still can't believe they were with you. Before the Fall, they tended to keep to themselves. Especially Nemesis. She's never played well with others." He sounded so bitter that Cethy suddenly felt bad for the ancient king that had lost everything.

"Swear." Cethy demanded. She was having an information overload, her synapses all firing at once. "Swear that it's true."

"I swear to me," Zeus said with a toothless smile.

Prometheus stared at the door that Erin and Missy vanished through. "It's the truth," he said. "Look at the life you've led. Your powers, *their* powers, are obvious. You're a goddess of Olympus. Congratulations." He didn't say it with much enthusiasm.

"And you think that I'm a Norn?" Cethy asked. "I mean, I'm lucky and all, but I have no *real* powers. Not like Missy and Erin. They're the ones with the muscle."

Zeus snorted. "What does their muscle matter? There are dozens of gods with just as much power if not more. We want *you*. We have been watching *you*. *You* need to be a Norn."

"But why?" Cethy whined. "Why do you need me?"

"It was foretold, Tyche. We have access to an oracle that named you as the first in this quest. You are the goddess of fortune. Luck in the flesh. You succeed in your every endeavor. You cannot fail," Prometheus said gently. "You see how that might be attractive in a situation like this?"

Zeus hiccupped. "With you on our side, the Norns will succeed and the Moirai will be controlled by good once more. With you on our side, we can all go home."

"And if I choose not to?" Cethy asked.

Prometheus and Zeus looked at each other. "We would find another god, of course, and hope that they were appropriate for our cause. Maybe they would have the power needed to save the world, but this quest is... it is not likely that one would succeed without your particular skills." Prometheus spoke very carefully, purposely leaving out words like 'dangerous' and 'failure'. "Our best opportunity to succeed is if luck is on our side. If *you* are on our side. With you we will win the Fates. Without you," he shrugged, "we will still try. Whether or not you agree, the quest will still happen. It must."

"You said there'd be others. What if the people who get there first don't have good intentions?" Cethy asked.

A low growl erupted from Zeus's chest and the lightning ran up the length of his arms, popping angrily. "Charonte," he snarled. "Evil guardians. If they reach the Moirai before the Norns..." he cracked his knuckles against the table, leaving little scorch marks. "The Fates would reflect that evil. Monsters down to their core, the Charonte are." He hiccupped and looked around furtively before pulling *another* flask out of his vest.

Prometheus ignored Zeus' determination to get drunk. He sat back in his seat, considering Cethy carefully. "The Moirai have always been the only individuals with the power to tamper with the gods," he told her, his jade eyes heavy. "Given the wrong kind of guidance they would turn men and nature against themselves. They would see the mortal world end." He paused. "They would weave the destruction of Valhalla, Cethy. All that would remain would be the underworlds. If the Moirai fall to the Charonte, there will be nothing left. Nothing. No one. Only Erebus. Only the underworld."

Cethy swallowed loudly. The future that Prometheus described was not one that sounded particularly attractive. "Well, where're these other two goddesses who are supposed to help me?" she questioned.

"Each Norn comes from a different Divine Line. Most likely it will be as it was the last time. A Greek, a Celtic, and a Nordic god." Prometheus ticked each off on his fingers.

Greek…Celtic…Nordic… they were all real… Cethy rubbed her head, totally overwhelmed. "Who, then?" she asked, a bit dazed.

"That *is* the question, isn't it," said Zeus.

Prometheus glared at the sloppy old man. "What Zeus means is we haven't gotten that far yet. The first step was finding you."

"Great," Cethy snapped. "I'm glad to see you guys are on top of this potential Armageddon." She fell silent as the two men watched her. "Is there time to think?" she asked finally. "This is a lot of information to process."

Prometheus hesitated. "Time is a luxury for you now, Cethy. I can only give you until noon tomorrow. I'll send someone to you at the hotel to make sure that you are put on the right path and kept safe. And Cethy," he said meaningfully, "make sure that Nemesis is gone before he arrives."

"Why?" Cethy frowned, a crease appearing between her brows.

The Titan stood and stretched. "Never mind why. Just do as we say and you should stay safe. Zeus, it's time to go. We've been here too long already."

Zeus turned red. "Don't you tell me what to do!" the ruined god yelled. "I was a *King*." A flash of lightning lit the bar and Zeus was gone.

Prometheus shook his head, as though Zeus were a toddler throwing a tantrum instead of an unstable god throwing bolts of electricity. "Until tomorrow, Tyche," he said, using Cethy's true name. With a pop, Prometheus vanished as well, and Cethy was left alone with only her growing sense of panic and the weight of the world on her shoulders.

—Chapter Five—

Missy sat on the curb outside the hotel and waited. It felt like ages before she spotted Cethy finally walking doggedly through the parking lot. The redhead stumbled right past Missy, too involved in her own thoughts to pay any mind to her surroundings or the girl dancing around her with anxious concern. Without a word, Cethy blew past Missy and headed up to the second floor.

"Yeah, real nice. Way to make me feel important, Red," Missy huffed, chasing after her friend... cousin... whatever. "Well, what happened? I thought you would be right behind me!" Missy trailed Cethy straight into the room. "I was worried about you."

"Sorry." Cethy moved like she was in a trance. Her mind was heavy with everything she had learned in the last hour. "It took a while to walk back. There are police all over the boardwalk. Looks like something caught fire down on the pier."

Missy shrugged and pushed a handful of curls out of her face. "Forget about that! Are you alright?" Cethy was vaguely aware of those sharp, golden eyes looking her over for any sign of physical or emotional damage, but Cethy ignored her. Silently, she went over to the shoddy dresser and began to pull out clothes. Cethy shoved them unfolded into her book bag, her face blank. Missy watched it all in disbelief. "No way, Red. You don't buy into this stuff, do you? You can't!"

Cethy nodded, spaced out in a daze. "It makes perfect sense, Missy. Everything we are, they explained. They answered every question, filled in every blank. We're Greek goddesses, Missy."

She'll understand. I have to go.

The thought wriggled into her head and Missy's eyes widened. "You can't be serious!" Missy blew right past concerned and landed somewhere in the vicinity of hysteria. This was all her fault. She had wanted answers, had demanded them, and now she had them. She just hadn't expected that to get them she'd have to trade in her best friend. "It isn't true. It doesn't have to be true!"

"He was throwing lightning, Missy," Cethy said heavily. "I believe him."

Missy yanked Cethy's book bag away from her and clutched it to her chest. "That doesn't mean we have to listen. We don't have to be goddesses, Red. We don't have to be who they're looking for."

"We aren't. They only want me. I leave noon tomorrow."

Missy chucked Cethy's bag across the room and out of reach. "And then what?" she asked. "You go running into a fight that isn't yours to begin with?"

"What are you so worked up for?" Cethy asked, still too shocked to feel any sort of emotion. "I'll come back."

Missy pulled at the roots of her hair in frustration. "People don't come back from these sorts of things, Red. You mess with the gods, you get involved in that sort of life, and that's it. You'll get hurt, or lost, or enchanted. You've read Greek mythology. It's all quests and monsters and punishments. People die."

"What's gotten into you?" Cethy spat. "You should be thrilled. You finally know who you are. Your past is all tied up in a neat little package, for you. If you're worried about money, I'll leave you funds."

Cethy wasn't cruel by nature, but she couldn't have hurt Missy worse if she tried. "Right." Missy went over and picked up Cethy's bag. After she wiped an invisible piece of dust from it she handed it back, her face smoothed into an emotionless mask. "Have a good trip," she said, her voice void of intonation.

Cethy sighed, and struggled to articulate an apology. Missy was just worried about her. She knew that. "I'm sorry, Missy, but we know who we are, now. There are responsibilities that go with it."

"You're eighteen. You shouldn't have responsibilities." Missy knew she was being stubborn, but Cethy running off into danger was a decidedly bad idea. Cethy was afraid of her own shadow, her 'luck' got her into major trouble even when she was being careful, and without Missy, there was no one to keep her safe.

For a long time the two girls sat on their beds staring silently at the carpet. "You're really going?" Missy finally asked.

Cethy nodded. "I have to. You didn't hear him, Missy. If I don't help, everything we know, everything we love, will be gone." Cethy attempted a smile." Drama, drama, drama."

Missy studied Cethy's face. She could smell Cethy's fear, but her sincerity and resolve were painted on her face. "You're sure this is what you're meant for?" she asked. "This is what you want to do? You want to fight mythological beasts and wear togas? You want to face certain danger and possible death to find the Fates and spend the rest of eternity babysitting them?"

"I'm not sure of anything," Cethy admitted. "But this is what I need to do. Even if this is just some really complex practical joke, I can't take the chance. I'd rather face the myths and the togas than do nothing and let the world end."

"The world…" Missy rubbed her eyes and held her head. "Either you go or the world ends? Are those really our only options?" There was no answer. Missy hadn't really expected one. With a sigh she turned off the light and climbed under her covers. "Alright," she said. "We had better get to sleep. We have a big day tomorrow."

"What do you mean, 'we'?" Cethy asked. "I told you, Prometheus said only me."

Missy laughed. "Prometheus can kiss my divinity. Do you really think I'm going to let you go off and have adventures without me? Someone needs to look after you."

"You aren't allowed near the Fates," Cethy insisted. "They were pretty adamant about that."

"That's fine with me," Missy murmured. "You deal with the Fates and I'll deal with you. Someone needs to make sure that you survive this." She yawned. "I don't care how lucky you are, you'll need me."

"I don't think it's a good idea. He said you had to be out of here before the guide showed up tomorrow."

Missy was silent in the darkness. After a while she asked, "Red, do you want me to go with you?"

"Yes, please."

That was that. Missy wrapped herself in her blankets and tried to soak up what was possibly her last night indoors. She had no idea what was in store, but she had a feeling that down comforters and indoor plumbing would not be included on their quest.

"Missy?"

"Yeah?" Missy had started to fall asleep.

Cethy had only just noticed that the room was too quiet. Too empty. "Where's Erin?"

Missy turned uncomfortably. "Gone."

"Well, when is she coming back? I don't want to leave with things bad between us."

"Erin isn't coming back."

"Why?" Cethy demanded. Missy didn't answer and Cethy sat up, groping for the light. "Missy, where's Erin?"

"Don't know."

The light clicked on. Cethy stood over Missy, her hands on her hips. "You don't know? Missy, you have thirty seconds to explain yourself."

"Like it's my fault." A wave of worry washed over Cethy and Missy raised her hands in surrender. "Alright, fine. You know that my Empathy has never worked on Erin. She had a wall in her head, like a pane of glass that kept all of her emotions protected from me." Missy could sense Cethy's doubt and anger but the redhead nodded. "It finally cracked. I think she was just too upset after talking to Zeus and Prometheus because... I mean I wasn't even trying. We were just walking back to the hotel and suddenly I felt everything. It was," she took a steadying breath. "It was terrible, Red. Her mind was... it was all twisted up. I've never experienced anything like that before."

Cethy pursed her lips. "What happened?"

Missy bit her lower lip, nervous. "All that anger. It hurt. It was too intense. I tried to pull away, but..." Missy hung her head. "I knew she was hiding something from me, but I had no idea. I had to do it, Cethy. I... encouraged her to leave."

"You mean you threw her out." Cethy knew Missy well enough to make the translation. "For what?"

"For...?" Missy made a face. "What do you mean for what? Didn't you hear what Prometheus said when he was here? Erin causes hostility. She has spent the last three months using her creepy powers to influence your feelings! I'm an Empath, Cethy. Your feelings are my feelings! She's been deliberately hurting us, Cethy! If I hadn't..." she snapped her mouth shut quickly, but not quick enough.

"If you hadn't..." Cethy prompted. Her eyes widened suddenly as she put two and two together. "You're the reason the police were everywhere? And the firefighters? Missy, what did you do?"

Missy looked up at Cethy innocently. "There might have been a small fire."

"You set Erin on fire?" Cethy exploded.

"No!" Missy exclaimed. She scratched her head and mumbled under her breath. "It was the Frog Bog." Cethy threw her hands up while Missy sputtered. "But it wasn't on purpose! I've never been a firebug in my life. I remember being getting angry and then... poof. I don't think I could do it again if I tried."

"And what happened to Erin?" Cethy asked coolly.

Missy's hid under her blankets. Her muffled answer was not encouraging. "She bolted. Erin is gone."

—Chapter Six—

The weather the next morning matched the moods of the two girls in the hotel room. Dark and cold. Cethy had spent the night seething, and the morning ignoring Missy's attempts to explain herself. Logically, Cethy knew it was better that Erin was gone. She'd heard Prometheus just as plainly as Missy had. Erin had manipulated them, interfered with their emotions, but Missy's literal hot-headedness had robbed Cethy of closure and she was not yet ready to forgive.

Frustrated that her words had fallen on Cethy's deaf ears over and over, Missy had finally stalked outside to sit on the curb and relocate her patience. Her mind went over the previous night. She still wasn't sure how the fire had started. Erin's feelings had been violent and painful, and Missy had been furious. That's when the fire started. One of the games on the pier just erupted in flames. It had scared her as much as it had scared Erin.

Missy groaned, her head in her hands. Nothing made sense anymore. Her entire world had flipped upside down with little more than a knock at the door. The answers she had wanted so badly now begged more questions. One stood out in particular. "What now?" She was so involved in her own thoughts Missy didn't notice that she was no longer alone.

Two young men stood on the boardwalk, their eyes glued to the dejected deity on the curb. One sported a long leather coat despite the late August heat. His blonde hair curled slightly in the light rain. Cold and hostile, his icy blue eyes watched as Missy fumed and snarled to herself. The other boy was taller and heavier with dark hair and even darker eyes. He wore a sweatshirt from Ithaca College and smiled broadly when Missy sighed and wandered back up to the room. He turned to his companion, nudging him repeatedly until he was shoved away. "Look who's back on the radar," he said brightly. "I've missed her."

"What's she doing here? Prometheus didn't say anything about *her*," said the blonde unhappily. "Who's next? Pegasus?"

The first man laughed, a bright, cheerful sound that matched his sunny disposition. "Not likely. Pegasus couldn't fly his way out of a wet paper bag, I doubt he found his way to Jersey."

Still frowning, the blonde sniffed delicately at the air. The scent of divinity was strong enough to make him wrinkle his nose. "Let's get this over with." Silently, the two young men wandered over to the door Missy had vanished behind and listened. Inside two girls spoke together heatedly.

"I know you aren't happy with me but we have to be ready to leave by noon so stop dumping my bag out." Missy began to gather her belongings for the fourth time.

"You aren't coming, Missy. Zeus said that the Fates reflect their watchers and the last thing the world needs is fate acting like some two year old throwing temper tantrums. *Lunatic.*"

"Really? You're calling *me* a lunatic?" Missy shot back. "Do you want to take a look around this room and maybe reevaluate who is and who isn't insane?"

Cethy snarled. "You're going to turn on me, now? I guess it was only a matter of time, right? Are you going to set me on fire, too?"

"Oh, ha ha." Missy snarked. "Don't tempt me."

There was a knock at the door and both girls fell silent. The clock on the night table between the twin beds told them that it was not yet noon.

Cethy started to the door. "Wait," Missy whispered. Her throat itched with anger. It had appeared suddenly and there was a darkness to it that didn't belong to Cethy. Whoever was on the other side of the door was livid. "Don't open it." Missy tried to cough the anger from her chest, but it was stuck. "Red, *no!*"

Cethy ignored her warning and tore the door open.

Thud.

Cethy was knocked back into the room, hands clutched to her face. The redhead collapsed as blood pumped out between her fingers to stain the carpet. Missy was dumbfounded. She stared at the intruder, her golden eyes wide with fear. Standing in the doorway was what she could only describe as a monster. It was almost a man with deeply tanned skin and broad shoulders, but a hideous dog head was perched on its shoulders. The beast held a terrible curved sword in his hand and it was leveled at her.

"Move."

The dogman was shoved aside and Erin entered the room, smiling sweetly. "Honey, I'm home."

"You have to be kidding…"

Missy wanted nothing more than to stomp on Erin until there was nothing left but pretty, blonde paste. She had to consciously hold herself back and stay focused on the problem at hand. Namely, the dogman with the blade. Missy lunged for Cethy, flattening them both against the carpet as the growling monster took a swing at them. Missy hooked her hands under Cethy's arms and dragged her unconscious friend into the bathroom, away from Erin and her new pet. Ridiculously, Missy did up the little chain that served as a lock knowing full well that it had no chance of holding against the creature who had laid Cethy out flat with one well placed fist.

"Wake up, Red. Wake up!" Missy shook Cethy urgently, heedless of her friend's broken nose. "Come on, this is not the time for a power nap!"

Cethy opened one eye then another. They were spinning in different directions. "Someone hit me," she muttered, completely disoriented. "Someone hit me. Why are we in the bathroom?"

"Erin's home," Missy hissed. She threw open the bathroom window. "And she brought a new friend with her. Come on," she pointed to the window, "get out."

"You get out," Cethy whimpered disconnectedly. "I don't want to."

"We're only on the second floor." Missy was aware that a twenty foot drop wasn't going to be a good time. Her only goal was to get them away from Erin. "Besides, the alternative isn't so great. Now, get out! I can't save myself until I save you. Now out. Out. *Out!*"

Stumbling, Cethy climbed onto the toilet and wiggled out the window. She had the top half of her body outside when a crash rocked the bathroom door clean off its hinges. Erin smiled and slid in past the dogman just as the rest of Cethy disappeared over the sill.

"So," Missy tried to keep her voice level, "I see that you've raised the standards for the guys you bring home. Well done." The dogman stood behind Erin and growled menacingly. There was no way out. Missy didn't dare turn her back on Erin to escape through the window, and the door was barricaded by a monster. Missy eyed the dogman's bulging muscles and the sword that glinted in the fluorescent lighting. She was a scrapper for sure, but even she drew the line at mutant jackals with scimitars.

"What are you doing here, Erin?" Missy asked, eyes searching for a way out. "This isn't a good time."

Erin laughed. It was chilling and Missy felt her fingers go numb with cold. Damn her powers. They manifested in the most inconvenient ways. She shook her hands out while Erin laughed in her face.

"Honestly, Missy, what are you going to do about it? You can't fight Anubis here, and all of your luck just went out the window."

"Very clever," Missy snapped eyeing Erin's pet. At least now she knew the name of the monster that was about to chop her into little pieces. Anubis. That sounded familiar but Missy couldn't be bothered trying to remember why. She had a great many *other* things on her mind. "Obviously you are the goddess of witty conversation, Erin." Missy tried to jump back toward the window but the dogman was too fast. The monster pounced and grabbed her around the waist before she had even managed to turn. Missy was bodily slammed into the tile floor and held there, teeth snapping inches from her face. Missy kicked and squirmed, but it was like being pinned beneath a boulder. It was useless.

Erin smiled slightly, her gray eyes malicious. "Don't be an idiot, Missy. Helping Cethy is a death sentence and you know it. Luck goddess or not, she's a tragedy." Missy glared as Erin continued. "You could come with me. Vengeance and Strife. Imagine what we could do together."

"Don't be a cliché, Erin."

"Don't be a martyr, Missy." Erin smirked when Missy made no move to speak other than curse off the god crushing her face into the grimy floor. "Fine. Have it your way. See to it she suffers a slow death, Anubis."

Hairy fingers wrapped around her throat with almost deliberate slowness, allowing Missy time to realize exactly what was about to happen as she was dragged up off the floor. Her feet dangled inches over the tile while she dangled in Anubis' grasp. All in all, she did not think it was the worst way to die. Other than the fire in her lungs and the pounding in her skull, Missy was fine. The lack of oxygen left her disconnected from the brutal bruises welling up under the dogman's hands. She was even delirious. She could have sworn that there was a giant bird outside the window.

"Hey! Put. Her. Down."

Well that was just perfect.

The bird could talk.

The dogman stood and threw Missy against the wall so violently the drywall cracked where her head struck. She slid into the tub and smacked her forehead on the faucet with a resounding peel like a bell. Missy tried to pull herself out of the bathtub but her muscles refused to lift her. The room pitched with every movement she attempted and finally Missy stopped trying and lay limply in the tub. The bird came back to the window and a cherub-like face appeared. It wasn't a bird at all.

"You're in trouble now," Missy mumbled. "There's an angel in the bathroom." She closed her eyes to stop the room from spinning, but awareness slipped away from her. Everything went blissfully dark.

"This isn't your business!" Erin yelled at the young man as he climbed in the window and perched on the toilet's tank. "I am Eris. Tremble at my power!"

The winged man folded his white and tawny wings comfortably and yawned. "I wouldn't be yelling that if I were you. A *real* god might decide to teach you a thing or two."

Erin scoffed. "I'm the goddess of strife and conflict. Who's more powerful than me?"

Stone faced, his ice-blue eyes were electric with power. "I am."

"Exactly who are you?" Erin asked. "Besides a gene splicing experiment gone tragically wrong?"

He grinned like a Cheshire cat, a warning in his eyes. "Cupid."

The dogman let out a yelp and backed quickly away. The young love god reached over his shoulder and a white quiver appeared on his back. He held the arrow like a knife, poised to attack. "Why don't you run along before I make you redefine the phrase, 'dog lover'?"

Anubis didn't hesitate. He fled, his tail between his legs. With her backup gone Erin quelled under the furious blue gaze of the Greek love god that stood between her and Missy. "This isn't over," Erin growled through clenched teeth. She turned on her heel and ran after her monster.

Cupid sighed. "I didn't think that it would be." He returned his arrow to the quiver and it vanished. He stood there, still and silent while Missy laid unconscious in the tub, face impossible to read. "Nemesis…" The word fell past his lips, an emotionless whisper, but she didn't stir. Blood dripped down the length of her face from the open gash above her eye. He was tempted to save himself the trouble and just leave her there. No one would blame him for it. Nemesis had lost the right to expect help from him a long time ago.

Still…

Cupid fished Missy out of the tub and propped her damaged head against his shoulder. The look in his clear eyes was utterly undefined as he made his way to the window. Erin's words still hung in the air and he agreed. "Things are rarely over."

—*Chapter Seven*—

Cethy woke up disoriented and more than a little sore. She rolled over and pushed away the remnants of a nightmare. Monsters and pain plagued her mind as she pulled her comforter up under her ear. The clock's red numbers were bright in the darkness that had fallen outside the window. Nine PM? Why did she feel like she was late for something? And since when was her alarm clock shaped like a football?

"Morning, babe." An over cheery male voice broke the silence and Cethy sat up with a jerk. "Or... night, I guess. Hey, Cue, you owe me twenty bucks. Mine woke up first."

The events of the last several hours flooded Cethy's mind. Images of Prometheus and Zeus and her argument with Missy returned to her with painful accuracy. After that, she could remember nothing, not even the identity of her grinning host and where she was. The homey hotel room with the ever growing pile of rubbish in the corner was gone. Instead, Cethy was tucked into a bed in a room so small that the dual beds, desks, and closets all touched. Clothes and feathers were all over the floor along with half empty food containers, books, sports equipment, and empty drink cans.

"Take it slow, honey. You took one spectacular dive." A tall, heavyset boy watched her from where he sat at a cluttered desk. He was dark with short hair and eyes that looked almost black. He leaned back in his chair while he played a video game on the tiny television by the door. Every few minutes he would glance at Cethy as if to make sure she was still there.

"What happened?" Cethy asked. She gingerly touched her swollen nose. "Who are you?"

"Name's Dionysus." He turned off his video game and twisted around to talk to Cethy, a charming smile on his face. "Party god, at your service. As for what happened, you decided to take a header out of a second story window and your friend went toe to toe with some very cranky myth units." He gestured to the other bed where Missy was curled up in the blankets and another boy sat vigilant. "She faced Anubis *and* Eris before Cue pulled her out of there."

Cethy closed her eyes and opened them again, convinced that she was seeing things.

The young man who sat at Missy's bedside was a worried looking blonde in his late teens. He sat perfectly straight, a frown on his handsome face. He changed the ice pack on Missy's head and glanced at Cethy, offering a nod in acknowledgement. He had bright blue eyes, a defined jaw, broad shoulders, and, Cethy was sure she was mistaken, wings that hung down over the back of his chair in a smooth cascade of white and tawny feathers.

Cethy's jaw dropped. "Impressive, isn't he?" Dionysus whispered. "Just don't stare. Cue doesn't like the attention."

Cethy had woken up in Wonderland. "I don't understand. Where am I? Who are you people?"

"You're in Ithaca." The angel pointed to the college paraphernalia hanging on the walls. He put some ice into a towel, and handed it to Cethy. "Put that on your nose." He waited for her to obey before he continued. "You may call me Cue. Prometheus asked me to keep an eye on you until you get your feet under you."

"Prometheus sent *us,*" Dionysus corrected.

Cupid made a face that plainly said he didn't care. "We were supposed to get you straight to business, but... we had to detour." He looked down at Missy, a strange combination of distaste and worry on his face. "D," the other boy waved incase Cethy forgot who he was, "and I live here. We needed to wait until you were ready to travel and here was as good a place as any to wait while you recovered."

Dionysus grinned. "Sorry about the mess," he said with a wink. "I'm not used to entertaining *real* goddesses."

Cupid turned back to Missy. The look on his face changed from concern to irritation and back again as he brushed a stray curl away from her face. "I'm surprised this one was fighting with you instead of against you. She always has to be unpredictable. Even if it gets her into trouble."

Cethy tried to get up but Dionysus, and her spinning head, stopped her. "Is she alright?"

Cupid did not take his eyes from Missy. "She just hit her head," he said tightly. He gestured to where crude stitches had been sewn over Missy's left eye. "She thought that she could fight an Egyptian god. Stupid. Everyone knows that they're incredibly fierce warriors." He cleared his throat. "She could have gotten herself killed. Idiot."

"This is why I like having Nemesis around," Dionysus said happily. He nudged Cethy in the side. "She always keeps things interesting." Cupid shot Dionysus a dark look and the fun-hearted boy had to turn away to hide his smile. "Is she going to be a problem for you, bro?" Dionysus asked, laughter in his voice.

Cupid's jaw was locked in annoyance. "Of course not," he said. "Because she isn't coming. I was only told to take Tyche. Nemesis is adverse and you know it."

Cethy stiffened. "What do you mean, adverse?"

Cupid's expression was one of acute irritation. "Adverse. Undesirable. Not wanted," he said. "Evil."

"You don't know anything about her." Cethy defended her friend.

Cupid fixed Cethy with an icy glare. "Don't imagine for one moment that you know Nemesis, kid."

"Missy's my best friend," Cethy snapped. "She saved me."

"No, *I* saved you," Cupid corrected. "*She* got her head beat in." Cethy's eyes narrowed as Cupid continued. "Weren't you already told that she can't be a part of this?" he asked. "You didn't really think that the goddess of *vengeance* would be a Norn, did you? I won't let her anywhere near the Fates."

"She doesn't want to be anywhere near them." Cethy felt herself growing angry. "She just wants to come with me."

"It doesn't matter what she wants," Cupid said coldly.

Dionysus cleared his throat, effectively silencing their argument. "Don't take it personal, babe. The big guys are just worried that Nemesis could have a bad influence on the Fates. She doesn't have such a hot track record as far as good and evil goes."

"Whatever you believe we're different people now," Cethy stared at her feet but weakly defended her friend.

Dionysus smiled. "I don't know about that. I think we're still the gods we were thousands of years ago, just modernized. I still enjoy a drink now and again." *BURP.* "You still have esteem issues, I bet. Eris is still scary, and your friend Nemesis probably likes to punish people. I mean *really* likes it. She can't help it" He stood and scratched himself. "And she's still a fox."

"Enough," Cupid snapped. He glared at Cethy over his shoulder. "Let me guess. She has authority issues and has her own version of 'justice'." Cethy's silence was all the answer he needed. "You just don't know any better," he said. "You don't realize what is at stake. We can't risk Nemesis corrupting the Fates. She stays behind."

"So I just leave her here with the frat boy?" Cethy demanded, pointing to Dionysus. "Absolutely not."

Dionysus pouted and Cupid shrugged. "I can take her back to the hotel if you want, but she won't be safe there. Eris might come back and I won't be there to save her a second time. She is better off here with Dionysus... where he can keep an eye on her." Cethy opened her mouth to protest but Cupid cut her off. "She isn't your problem anymore. The only thing you are to concern yourself with is finding the Fates and building the enchantment to hold them."

"Either Missy leaves with me, or I leave with her. Either way is fine with us." Cethy threatened. It would have been more meaningful if her voice hadn't broken, but she made her point.

With a groan, Missy began to stir. She sat up, delicately holding her head, and looked around the room. Slowly her eyes took in the posters, the messy floor, and finally the three people who were watched her intently.

"Welcome to the party, beautiful." Dionysus winked at her.

"It's just Missy, thanks." Missy grimaced when her fingers found the stitches on her forehead. "Who're your new friends, Red?" Missy's eyes paused on Cupid and the wings that flowed down his back, and then moved on. "Where's Erin?"

"Gone," Cupid answered, clearly annoyed.

Missy stood up, a little wobbly on her feet and Cupid watched her carefully, as if she might spring at him any moment. Missy was surprised by the barely masked animosity that she read off of the winged stranger. It was a bitter fragrance that left an even worse taste in her mouth. Whoever the angel was, he was no fan of hers. "Problem?" The angel's hands were the deep vibrant red that indicated strong feeling and restraint. Anger buzzed around Missy like a swarm of mosquitoes. "Who are you?"

For a moment Missy thought that he wasn't going to answer her. He just glared from his seat, his blue eyes cold and unforgiving. "Apparently I'm no one worth remembering," he said finally.

"Missy, please. Not now." For the first time since Missy met her, Cethy's voice was solid and authoritative. "We aren't getting anywhere like this. Just tell Cue what side you are on, so we can get on with it. Prometheus made this sound like a time sensitive issue."

"This *is* time sensitive," Cupid snapped. "But I won't talk with her here." He pointed at Missy. "She doesn't belong."

"What's your damage?" Missy growled. "I don't even know you."

Cupid's wings snapped open and nearly filled the dorm room. "I'm Cupid."

Missy smirked. "If you're Cupid, where's your diaper?"

"I have ruined greater gods than you," Cupid hissed.

"I would love to see you try." Missy's eyes flashed, taking up the challenge that Cupid's body language was issuing.

Fight.

Dionysus and Cethy pulled their friends apart before their verbal argument took a physical turn. Cethy sat on Missy to keep her away from the older boy while Dionysus was doing his best to grab something other than feathers. "What it comes down to," Cethy held onto the back of Missy's shirt, "is that she comes with me, whether you like it or not. She doesn't go, I don't go. Do you want to be the one to tell Zeus that you lost him his good luck charm?"

Cupid was silent. Dionysus laughed quietly and started playing his videogame again. "I think she's got you there, bro," he said. He winked at Cethy and Missy from behind Cupid's back.

It was obvious that Cupid was weighing his choices. He could go back to Prometheus and admit that he lost Cethy and all of the good luck that went with her or he could suffer the presence of the very goddess that had caused the Fall. Finally he gave a brisk nod, his shoulders stiff and his face like stone. "Try getting in my way, Nemesis," he said to Missy, his voice filled with loathing. "Just try it. You'll wish you had stayed banished."

—*Chapter Eight*—

The dorm room was not nearly big enough for four people. Missy kept getting tangled in Cupid's wings while Cethy tripped repeatedly over Dionysus' discarded cans and dirty laundry. Tensions were high by the time the four of them finally agreed on a course of action.

Missy would be allowed to tag along and keep Cethy safe but, Cupid warned, she would be on probation. Until he could trust her the angel would watch Missy like a hawk. Cethy had to stick her elbow sharply into Missy's ribs before she grudgingly agreed. "Don't worry," Cethy whispered. "When he gets to know you he'll back off." Missy only glowered as the four of them settled in.

With a flick of his wings Cupid indicated for everyone to listen up. "The thing to remember is that there isn't much time," he said. "You're in for the fight of your life and every moment wasted other elements of evil are preparing to take the Moirai." Missy rolled her eyes at his melodramatics and Dionysus hid his smile. "You already know that you need to find the Fates, Cethy, but your presence among them won't mean anything if you can't control them. You need certain materials, certain items to maintain your hold."

Dionysus nodded and crushed a can against his forehead. "Moirais' Circle." *BURP.*

Cupid glared at his roommate, clearly trying to keep his itching hands from smacking Dionysus upside the head. Missy couldn't help but giggle into her hand at the frat boy's easy attitude. It suited his status as the god of revelry. "Yes, D, thank you. The enchantment is called the Moirais' Circle. There are ten pieces necessary to build the Circle and keep the Fates under your control. If you skip any of the ten trials, you won't have all the pieces. Without them, you might as well not even bother."

"What are we looking for?" Cethy wanted to know. Her eyes were steady for a change, focused. Missy couldn't help but be proud. Cethy could do this. She was going to save the world. It seemed *right* somehow that it was Cethy.

"They're objects none too easy to get your hands on. The Circle is made up of things that are important to the gods. Some were lost in the Fall. Others are fiercely guarded. The Divine aren't always good at sharing, even if it's for their own good. And we have to move *quickly.* If Eris is out there working against you, we can be sure that time is already running out."

"Why don't you tell us what exactly we have to find?" Missy asked, "so that we don't have to guess."

"Why?" Cupid's response was immediate and unkind. "So you can run off and get to them first? You won't be happy until you destroy everything, will you?" Missy started to form an angry reply, but Dionysus' hand clapped over her mouth.

"We aren't going to get anywhere if you two can't stop bickering," Cethy sounded tired. "There's no getting around it. You two are working together so the sooner you play nice, the better. Cue, Missy is coming with us. And Missy," She indicated Dionysus to take his hand from over Missy's mouth, "Cue is our guide. Without him we have a quest and no way to go about it. So both of you...Shut up."

Missy glared and Cupid just crossed his arms.

Cethy smiled weakly. "I think that is as close to a truce as we're going to get."

The god of revelry laughed and popped open a new can. "I wouldn't worry. They'll kiss and make up soon enough. Ain't that right, bro?"

Cupid leveled a glare at Dionysus. "The Circle is made up of godly artifacts and objects of myth," he continued as if there had been no interruption. "Most are hidden or preserved here in the Mortal Realm.

Thor's hammer, Hermes's sandals, Excalibur, Athena's shield, Heimdall's horn, and venom from the Midgard Serpent. They're hidden right here in this world. There are a few things we need from Valhalla and Erebus. Spring water, a Lethe rock, and the Borabu, a horn that can raise an army of the elements."

"That's only nine." Cethy counted them up on her fingers. "Hammer, shoes, sword, shield, horn, venom… Water, rock, whatever a Borabu is…"

Cupid's scowled and Missy mirrored his action automatically connecting to his stress. "Number ten is tricky. We'll worry about it later. First things first, we go to Tir na n-Og." He said it with a smile that told the girls that this would be anything but fun. "The Land of Eternal Youth. Can either of you remember Valhalla?" Missy and Cethy both shook their heads. "It's a lot like the Mortal Realm, broken into countries and tiny kingdoms. Tir na n-Og is a Celtic part of Valhalla. Very pretty place. They have the first thing on our list."

"Which is?" Missy prompted.

Cupid smiled. "Water. From a very special fountain."

Cethy's eyebrows shot up as comprehension dawned on her. "The Fountain of Youth?" she asked, her eyes wide. "That's real?"

"Why wouldn't it be?" Dionysus asked with a yawn. "The best part is with every task you complete, every step you take toward the end of the quest, you'll get stronger."

"So will the other gods," Cupid pointed out. "So one falls, we all fall. So one rises, we all rise."

"How poetic," Missy muttered.

Cupid glared at her. "Your quest will give you an edge, Cethy, but it still won't be easy. Like I said, there are ten trials, each one harder than the last. I'll do my best to help you through them."

"Me, too!" Missy chirped. "But where are the other two who are supposed to be helping her?"

Dionysus nodded. "Prometheus is working on it." BURP. "Once he finds Cethy's little friends, we'll make sure that they find her. Until then you and Cue will be filling in. Right, buddy?"

Cupid closed his eyes for a moment in search of reprieve from his childish roommate and the girls. Finally his blue eyes slid open, frustrated but controlled. "Prometheus wanted me to remind you that there is a difference between being immortal and invincible. You might not die, but you *can* get hurt so don't you forget it. Don't take any unnecessary risks," he warned. "Especially against the Charonte. Don't face them unless you have to. Without the other two Norns you won't be able to stop them. The Charonte are to be avoided at all costs."

"God bless you?" Missy didn't recognize the strange new word and she looked to Dionysus for conformation. "What's a Charonte?"

"You," Cupid mumbled.

"Play nice," Dionysus warned. "A Charonte is the evil equivalent of a Norn. Norns, good. Charonte, bad. Very, very, bad." *BURP.*

"What about that dogman?" Cethy asked. "Is he a Charonte?"

Cupid laughed but the sound was void of humor. "No. That was Anubis, an underworlder. He isn't smart enough to be anything but a nuisance," Cupid said, not bothering to hide his distaste.

Missy frowned. "So he's just going to keep coming after us?"

Dionysus nodded. "Him and others. The Charonte and even the Moirai themselves will throw every possible distraction and obstacle at you. You'll have to be on your guard at all times."

Cethy laughed nervously. "So, what you are saying is that we are in a race against the clock to collect everything for this... Moirais' Circle and find the Fates, while simultaneously dodging whatever monsters come our way? Well, that sounds easy enough." She looked at Missy. Her friend. Her cousin. "Are you still sure that you want to come, Missy?"

"And miss all the fun?" Missy faked insult. "Never."

Cupid made an exasperated sound. "This isn't a game."

"Then you aren't playing right." Missy and Dionysus high fived, snickering good naturedly while her Empathy felt out Cupid's extreme annoyance.

"I suggest," Cupid grated out through a clenched jaw, "that we get some sleep. You girls can stay in here. D and I will sleep in the lounge." Dionysus started to protest but quelled under Cupid's glare. "And don't stay up all night. This is not a sleepover. We have a lot to do tomorrow, and if you slow me down I'll leave you behind." His words were directed at Missy, but she was all smiles. Instead of snapping back at him she climbed back into the bed she had woken up in and fluffed up a pillow. "Out of curiosity, Cue," she asked, pulling a feather from the pillow. "Did you stuff this yourself?" Cupid shoved a laughing Dionysus out into the hall before he slammed the door shut behind him.

"Oh, Missy," Cethy said. "Was that necessary?"

"No." The mouthy Empath settled herself more comfortably, curled around the pillow with the blankets snug around her. "But it was extremely funny."

—*Chapter Nine*—

Cethy had expected some sort of brilliant display of power, but the journey to Tir na n-Og the next morning was little more than Dionysus flicking his hands at them in a tired, hung over gesture. Cethy felt like the walls of the dorm room simply fell away to reveal a rocky shore and a forest. Missy, however, fell to her knees, panting and swearing up a storm. "I think I left my respiratory system back in New York," she gasped. "That *hurts*." Cethy had not felt a thing and said so.

"It depends on what you're used to." Cupid absently looked around. "I guess you don't remember, but that's how you used to travel, Cethy. You just think of where you want to be and space just sort of *bends* for you." He glared at Missy. "Nemesis was never able to bend. She just didn't have the talent for it."

"Look who's talking," Missy growled. "If you had any talent, why did D just do all of the work?"

Cupid's cheeks flushed red. "Do you see these?" His wings opened, and Cethy had to force herself not to touch them. Missy's eyes were locked on the white and tawny feathers in awe, momentarily silent. "Those who were not granted wings with which to travel were given the ability to bend space. I can fly. Cethy can bend. What can you do, Nemesis, besides get on my nerves?"

"Missy," she corrected. "My name is Missy, featherbrain. Try and remember that."

Cupid sneered. Unlike the girls, Cupid still remembered everything from the time when the Olympians thrived. He never forgot the life he'd enjoyed before Nemesis scorned Zeus and it was all stripped away. He had kept his memories and powers, but Cupid had lost everything that mattered in the Fall and he knew exactly who to blame. Now he had Nemesis trailing along after him and it was like his loss was being rubbed in his face. What was worse, she didn't even remember. Missy's blissful ignorance only added insult to his injury. "You don't belong here, Nemesis," Cupid said as Missy climbed back up to her feet. "*You* remember *that*."

"So what's the plan?" Cethy pulled Missy away and looked around at where they had appeared. Everything was more vivid in the Divine Realms. The colors, the smells, the sensations… It was midday, the sun bright over the three deities. They stood close to a cliff that dropped off over an ocean. Rocks jutted out from the pounding surf. Cethy could see a rocky beach to the East. To the South and West was a forest that stretched for as far as she could see. The trees were monstrous, reaching heights she had not thought possible.

"The plan?" Cupid shrugged. "The plan is completely up to you. I am just a guide."

Missy glared. "Yeah? So guide her."

"Do you want to learn how to fly, little girl?" Cupid threatened. He looked rather pointedly at the cliffs beside them. "Accidents do happen."

Cethy felt her irritation rankle. "The two of you are supposed to be helping me, not fighting each other!" she snapped. "And a suggestion or two would be appreciated, Cue. It's not like I can go door to door and ask if people if I can take a dunk in their enchanted pond."

Cupid looked at her critically and Missy came to Cethy's defense. "We don't even have a decent handle on our powers, Cue. Cethy has yet to intentionally use her luck with any desirable results. Sorry, Red, but it's true." Missy apologized when she saw her friend's face fall. "And my powers aren't good for much, either."

"For all that mouth, you have no confidence," Cupid told Missy sharply. He rounded on Cethy next. "And what are you so afraid of? You're the goddess of Luck! You were chosen to be a Norn for a reason. I'll do what I can to help you, but this isn't *my* quest, Cethy. It's yours." He glanced over the girls' shoulders and sighed. "Whatever your plan is, figure it out fast. Here comes the welcoming committee."

Slowly, Cethy and Missy turned around. "Oh." Missy's voice was a startled whisper. Emerging from the trees was a group of the largest women either of them had ever seen. Dressed in pale blue, they strode out purposefully with bows drawn and arrows trained on the Norn and her entourage. Cethy gulped loudly. Every one of them was tall with bulging muscles and thick necks. Their hair was pulled back into heavy braids and Cethy could not help but notice that each of the women who approached was disfigured. Horrible scars covered their hands and arms, faces, legs, and torsos. None of them were untouched.

"Cue, who are they? What do we do?" Cethy panicked.

"Oh, don't whine." Cupid watched as the women came closer. "They're just Amazons. Think big, mean, and stupid. If you weren't such a shrimp you would fit right in, Nemesis."

Missy paid Cupid's unkind words no mind. She frowned as the archers drew closer. Most of the women drew their bows with mutilated hands. Someone had cleanly removed several fingers from each hand, and left behind gnarled remains in their stead. Missy dragged Cupid and Cethy as far away from the giant women as the cliff allowed, but the Amazons quickly closed the distance, arrows nocked and ready to fly. They towered above the two young goddesses. Even Cupid had to crane his neck back to look into their faces.

Missy had never been a coward, but all bravery left her when she caught the first whiff of homicidal power that emanated from the women. A murderous bloodlust spilled from them like a signature scent. Whoever they were, they were seasoned killers and Missy felt their pleasure at the prospect of another possible battle.

"Trespassers die here." It was the smallest of the Amazons who spoke. "Do you wish to die?"

"No. No, we aren't trespassing," Cethy squeaked. "We're just lost."

"Ignorance is not an excuse." The Amazon's scarred fingers twitched on the bowstring.

Missy's mind raced. Saying the wrong thing here would cut their mission tragically short and she wasn't much in the habit of failing... "We're warriors." The words tumbled out before she could stop them.

The silent tension on the cliff lasted but a moment before the Amazons roared with laughter. "You? Warriors?" the spokeswoman for the group commented, tears of mirth in her eyes. "You are flimsy like the women on the mainland. Warriors... Ha!"

Cethy looked down at herself. At nearly six feet tall, she had never considered herself flimsy and Missy was the most athletic girl that she knew. They just lacked the post-steroid look that these archers had perfected.

The Amazon wiped her eye with the back of her disfigured hand. "Warriors," she said, still amused by the joke. "You are underdeveloped, you carry no weapons, and you travel with..." she paused. "Why does your slave have wings?"

Missy and Cethy looked at each other, confused but Cupid caught on quickly. "You think I'm a *slave*? Why don't you go *sit* on your arrows you giant, cow-faced..."

Missy grimaced. She had just figured out how Cupid was going to help and he wasn't going to like it. She drove her elbow into the love god's stomach and knocked the air from his lungs. She hesitated, unsure, and then grabbed his ear and shook it. "Silence. You speak only when you're spoken to." Cethy and Cupid were stunned. So were the Amazons.

The lead Amazon was the first to lower her bow and her women slowly followed suit. "I am Hippolyta," she said. There was no amiability in her voice, but the wary deference of one leader addressing another. "I am queen of these Androktone."

"Androktone?" Cethy asked. "I don't understand."

Hippolyta grinned darkly. "Male killers." Cupid made a choked sound in the back of his throat, but Missy stomped on his foot. "We will take your offering, now." The queen's ruined hands reached toward Cupid and Missy suddenly snarled. She grabbed the angel's white quiver without thinking and pulled him away from the giant woman, putting herself between them defiantly. An unexplainable, white-hot fury welled up inside her as she faced the queen.

"Don't try that again," Missy warned, her voice uncharacteristically low and deadly serious. Missy knew better than to think that she could stop Hippolyta, but her anger blocked out rational thought.

Hippolyta raised her bow and the entire troop of Amazons did the same. "You dare bring a man here without offering him as payment? You are a fool."

Missy felt how eager the queen was for battle. Splashes of hopeful blue were wrapped around the scarred fingers that held back the arrow that pointed to Missy's heart. "He belongs to me," Missy said. She moved closer to the queen until the arrow's razor tip pushed against her sweatshirt. She could feel it pricking her skin, but she did not look away from Hippolyta's heated gaze. Missy's voice was iron, solid and unquestionable. "You will not take him."

"Perhaps you *are* a small warrior." Hippolyta paused and regarded Missy cooly. "You have guts, I'll give you that. Perhaps I will spill them for you."

Cethy could not help but gasp, earning matching looks of annoyance from the Amazons and a look of annoyance from her guide and cousin. Cethy tried to focus her luck and use it in her favor. Instead, one of the albatrosses circling the cliffs chose that moment to empty its bowels onto her shoulder. The Amazons all roared with laughter their eagerness for battle forgotten in their delight. Hippolyta lowered her arrow. "Very well. You may live for now. If nothing else, you will amuse us. Androktone, let us lead our guests to Niamh."

Embarrassed and feeling useless Cethy tried to wipe the wet mess off her shirt. "Who is Niamh?" she asked. "Is she an Amazon, too?"

The giant women smirked. "Niamh is not human. She is the faerie queen who rules here," Hippolyta said. "I may rule the Amazons, but *she* rules Tir na n-Og."

Cupid cleared his throat violently and jerked Missy back by the hood of her sweatshirt.

"Excuse us, just one moment," Missy said. "It's so hard to find good help these days." There was a murmur of consent from the Amazons as Missy and Cethy turned to Cupid.

"Are you trying to get us killed?" he demanded.

"I could ask you the same thing," Missy hissed back. "I just got them to put their weapons down and you start choking me? They're going to think I didn't train you properly." She grinned cheekily at him, her eyes dancing. Cupid was stuck in the role of servant until further notice and Missy couldn't think of anyone who deserved it more.

The love god practically shook her. "It figures that you are enjoying this. Don't you realize the danger? They are taking us to Niamh! The keeper of the Fountain!"

Cethy looked hopeful. "Good. Then we can just ask her for some water. It will save us from having to look for it."

Cupid made a strangled noise of frustration. "You don't get how these quests are supposed to work, do you? These are *trials*. Of strength, of fortitude, of spirit, of character. You have to do the work. *All* of the work. You can't just ask everyone to accommodate you and hope they give over what we need. Besides, Niamh will kill anyone who gets near that spring. She's practically a god herself and extremely irritable."

"Irritable, huh?" Missy said. "Imagine that. I can't believe that anyone involved in this would be *irritable*."

"Don't play with me right now, Curly," Cupid said, hyperventilating. Missy made a face at the nickname but Cupid was already ranting again and paid her no mind. "Niamh has been around for as long as the gods. What if she recognizes us? We have to stay away from her."

"Do not make us wait," Hippolyta's voice held off whatever else Cupid might have said. The girls turned to her. Once again dozens of arrows were trained on the Norn and her companions.

Missy turned back to Cupid and Cethy. "If we are going to die," she whispered harshly, "it will be as close to the end of our goal as possible. We don't have a choice." She followed Hippolyta into the trees, dragging Cethy and Cupid behind her.

—Chapter Ten—

The girls and Cupid found themselves in the middle of an Amazon convoy as they trudged through the forest. Missy was on full alert, her senses tingling. Dozens of armed archers surrounded them and so much as a toe out of line promised a quick and painful end to the tentative truce between them. There was no hostility in the air now. Only curiosity and interest. It colored their captors with rich color, and Missy found herself smiling despite the seriousness of the situation. Cupid had been wrong. The Amazons weren't stupid at all. They were fascinated by the strange people who had appeared in their land. They were eager to learn from them, and to teach, too.

She eased behind Cupid and felt a twinge of guilt that belonged solely to her. Missy's Empathy showed her that the god's hands were still obscured by that dark red cloud of strong emotion. She could taste his embarrassment and his unease. The vision lasted only a moment, but her stomach plummeted. She hadn't done herself any favors bullying him. In fact, she'd behaved exactly like he thought she would.

"I'm sorry," Missy crept close and whispered over his shoulder. "There was nothing else I could do."

"There's always a choice," Cupid muttered.

"Would you have preferred being turned into a pincushion? That was the other *choice*." Cupid ignored her and just walked on, his blue eyes stubbornly trained ahead. "I was trying to help."

Cupid chuckled darkly. "You only help yourself," he growled softly, still refusing to look at her. "And let's make one thing perfectly clear, *Nemesis*," there was an edge to his voice that Missy couldn't help but flinch away from. "I am not *yours*. The next time you make any claims on me, I'll kill you."

Missy was left speechless for a minute, her golden eyes stunned by the depths of his anger. "So much for make love, not war," she hissed in his ear. "Next time Hippolyta can *have* you."

Cupid said nothing. He just picked up his pace and put distance between them.

"It was a good plan," Cethy told Missy when her dejected friend fell back into step beside her. "We wouldn't have gotten past the Amazons any other way."

Missy's confusion gave way to frustration. "I know it was a good plan. It was the *only* plan we had. Maybe next time you could step up, Red. This is your quest, not mine." Missy dropped back in line, putting a few Amazons between herself and her cousin. She let out a frustrated sigh. Cethy had stood there. Just... stood there. How was anyone supposed to follow when Cethy refused to lead?

Missy eyed her cousin shrewdly. Unless Cethy took on the responsibility Prometheus had given her, the quest was going to fail and fail miserably.

Missy couldn't do everything.

Cethy stared at her feet and doggedly kept the pace that the Androktone had set. "That's your best friend, huh?" Cupid said stoically from in front of her. "Nice."

Cethy didn't want to hear it. "She didn't mean it. She was just upset. You don't need to be an Empath to know that her heart is in the right place. Why can't you give her a break?"

"A break," he repeated. There was no warmth in his bright blue eyes and his expression was typically stoic, his frown was so tense his lips seemed to disappear. "You think Nemesis deserves a break?"

"I think that *Missy* deserves a break, yes."

He growled a bit in the back of his throat before he whipped around and walked backwards, facing her with enough arrogance and disapproval that even Cethy could see it in every strong angle of his face. "I find it so convenient that you two can't remember anything. You'd think that a thousand years of worship and ruling would have stuck in those empty, little heads of yours. I had thought that she at least would remember, but no." Cupid's voice was cold. "Perhaps it's better that she forgot." He seemed to speak more to himself than to Cethy before he snapped his attention back to her. "And in the future try to think a little faster on your feet. She's right. This is *your* quest, not hers."

Missy hung back by Hippolyta. She had pushed her annoyance away and was focused on the convoy's progress. Normally she was a fair hand at remembering routes and directions but in no time she was completely lost. Every tree and rock looked the same. There were no trails to walk on and the Amazons changed directions often to throw their imprisoned guests off of the true path to their home.

They walked for miles. Cethy was limping and Missy had discarded her sweatshirt by the time the group left the trees and stepped into a clearing filled with flowers and faerie lights. It was massive, green, and perfectly kept. Chickens, pigs, and cows ranged freely under the watchful eyes of children that were near as big as Cupid. Laughter and delighted shrieks drifted on the wind along with the sounds of arrows thudding into their targets and swords clashing enthusiastically. Missy looked up and spotted tree houses tucked into the giant oaks that surrounded the meadow carefully camouflaged in the leaves. Smoke drifted lazily from small fires and Missy froze in her tracks when they reached the main camp.

Women were everywhere. Metal working, sparing, fletching, running. There were massive piles of weapons. Swords, spears, daggers, arrows, staffs and so many more that Missy couldn't begin to know the names or purposes of. The few men that were there were chained and harvesting food from the gardens along the tree lines. They watched Cupid walk freely through camp, truly green with envy to Missy's eyes.

Cethy stared. She finally understood why Hippolyta had called her and Missy flimsy. The lookouts that had come to meet them were the smallest of their tribe. These new women were no shorter than eight feet tall and every inch of them bulged with muscle. They moved with a grace and speed that seemed impossible for women so large.

"So you're the island's new warriors, are you?" An amused voice caught their attention. On the knoll in the center of the meadow was a skillfully carved oaken throne where a regal woman watched them with interest. The faerie wasn't at all what Missy expected. She wasn't some tiny blinking light, but a full grown woman, tapping her nails against the armrests with blatant irritation. She was stunning, far too pretty to be human or even a god. She had long blonde hair that was plaited past her slender hips, and her emerald eyes were narrowed at the three intruding deities. Most remarkable were the shining, gossamer wings that hung over the back of her throne. They quivered in annoyance.

"And that makes you Niamh?" Missy asked as she was shoved in front of the faerie. "You're the guardian of the Fountain of Youth?"

Niamh inspected them from her seat. Her eyes traveled slowly over the dirty young people and her eyebrow hopped up daintily. "What manner of creature are you that you feel you can interrogate me?"

Cethy could only imagine what this inhuman beauty was thinking. Here were two unremarkable girls in their simple mortal clothing, ripped jeans, ponytails, and scuffed sneakers. Cethy's face was still horribly swollen from her confrontation with Anubis and Missy's bangs kept spilling into her face. How could Niamh take Cethy and Missy seriously when she played the role of goddess so much better than they did? The redhead promptly stared hard at her feet. Missy glanced at Cupid for some sort of direction but he was carefully not looking at her. Cethy was too busy trembling to answer.

"No manners at all, I'm afraid." Missy smirked and faced the faerie with wide golden eyes. "We've no intention to intrude on you for long. We were just hoping for a favor."

"You've come for the Fountain?" Niamh's face was expressionless.

"We have come to ask for your help," Cethy clarified. Cupid made a strained noise, a clear indication that the girls should not mention the Circle. He didn't dare to speak. There were still too many armed Androktone around for comfort. "We know that you are the protector of this place, so please, we only need enough water to fill a jar."

"I know why you're here," Niamh snapped. She glanced at Hippolyta, her green eyes annoyed. "I thought I told you to dispose of them the second they arrived on the cliffs."

Hippolyta shrugged, a smile on her scarred face. "They're funny," she said simply.

Niamh frowned. "I know better. Questing warriors and their slave? Did you think I wouldn't recognize Cupid when I saw him? And Nemesis, this used to be your home. I know you."

Missy blinked, startled. "Home?" Confusion knotted up her face. "Here?"

"I am a guardian of the spring and have been for an eternity." Niamh ignored Missy's bewilderment. "This island's history is *my* history. Nothing happens here without my knowing and experience tells me that those who come here are either fools or they are desperate. Which are you?" Niamh focused on Cethy as she rose elegantly from her throne. "Are you fools? Or are you desperate?"

"Both, I guess," Cethy muttered. "Believe me, we wouldn't be here if it wasn't for the direst of reasons."

Niamh regarded the small group evenly, her eyes and voice harsh. "Would it come as a surprise to you if I said that you are not the first to arrive here today for a dip in our spring?"

Cupid twitched.

"I didn't think so." Niamh motioned for them to follow her. "A young woman was here only hours ago. Blonde. Loud. Unpleasant. She thought she would help herself to a drink. I wish I could say she was apprehended but there was little I could do once she had tasted the water."

Cupid's silence finally faltered and he swore loudly in anger. The Amazons recoiled and raised their bows but Hippolyta motioned for them to hold their arrows. "She drank it? You're sure she actually drank the water?" Cupid demanded.

"Unfortunately, yes." Niamh was irritated at being questioned by her own prisoners. "As you know it is forbidden to drink from the Fountain. The injured may bathe in it and its water is used in ceremony, but to drink from the Fountain of Youth is to live forever cursed."

Missy didn't understand. "That's got nothing to do with us. We're already immortal." She looked at Cupid. "Aren't we?"

Cupid was livid. "I've already told you. There's a difference between *immortal* and *invincible*," he spat. "Whoever drank from the Fountain can't even be hurt now, save by a weapon stronger than the spring. There are few such weapons in existence. And I'll give you a guess as to who was here guzzling enchanted water."

Missy had no idea but Cethy caught on faster. Blonde, loud, and unpleasant? She only knew one person that fit that bill. "Erin was here? How did she even know about this place?"

"I grow weary of this," Niamh said with a delicate yawn. "Kill them." She nodded at Hippolyta and the Amazons were on Cupid in an instant, restraining his arms and his wings.

"Let him go!" Missy dove headfirst into the scuffle and was just as quickly plucked out by an Amazon with thick brunette braids and a no-nonsense face. The colossal woman held Missy by one leg while Missy's lashed out violently with the other, snarling and hissing like a rabid beast. Niamh was grim. The faerie was a fair, if unyielding, ruler and she allowed no harm to come to her people or her island. This demonstration was an unhappy but necessary one.

Cupid struggled vainly against his assailants while Cethy sputtered wordlessly, frozen in fear. "Red, do something!" Missy shouted as her captor spun her overhead like a lasso.

Niamh glanced at Cethy as the Amazons finally subdued Cupid. "Yes, Tyche. Why don't you *do* something?" The faerie sneered. "Lebitta?" Niamh gestured to the fierce woman whirling Missy through the air and the Amazon nodded with an ardent smile. She held Missy like a toothpick and threatened to snap the girl's back over her knee. Missy let out a shriek of frustration and pain.

"You'd better make sure you kill me here and now, pixie, or I'm coming for you. That's a *promise!*" Missy's voice was thick with agony, her eyes dark with dislike. If anyone would follow through with a promise of vengeance, it was the dark-haired goddess. That was her specialty, after all.

"Please, stop! Please! We came to you for help!" Cethy wailed. The Amazons all had their arrows trained on her. A few had even unsheathed swords. "Someone is out there trying to end the world! You don't understand!"

Niamh watched Cethy intently, something distinctly puckish in her expression. "Is that how you plan to save us? Whining and whimpering? I'm sorry, Tyche, but I am afraid that we are not interested in helping you. Your battle does not concern those on Tir na n-og. We are above it and you are clearly not up to the challenge."

"None are above this war!" Cupid growled. "Valhalla will suffer along with the Mortal Realm. That includes Tir na n-Og!"

Niamh whirled on the god, his face ground into the dirt. He got a very good view of her dainty green slippers before she pressed her foot against his cheek. "So angry, Love god. So out of balance. Who do you fight for?"

Cupid's eyes narrowed with his displeasure. "I fight for my world, Niamh."

"I. Asked. *Who*." Niamh's voice cut through the chaos and Cupid flushed red. Niamh smirked and stepped back.

Missy's captor dumped her on the ground and dragged her toward the far end of the field by her foot. It was almost cartoon-ish the way Missy dug her fingers into the ground, looking for enough traction to halt her bumpy progress. Cethy was receiving similar treatment, tears pouring down from her blue eyes. The wide maw of a prison pit was only feet from them and Missy saw no hint of the bottom. The Amazons dragged them towards it, glee on their battle scarred faces.

"Wait!" Missy yelled. "If you don't want to help us, then help yourselves. If we fail, the goddess of discord will have no one standing between her and the Fates. She will corrupt them. Don't let her win!"

Niamh laughed. "The Fates have been sleeping for millennia. I suppose next you'll tell us that the Midgard Serpent is about to awaken and swallow the world. You waste my time."

"Do you really think that we would come here for anything less than the Moirai's Circle?" Missy ignored the threatening Amazons, and Cupid's order to be silent.

"You're building the Circle?" Niamh's laugh was tinkling and cold. "Do the gods think to control the Fates again? Your kind are not meant to return to power. The mortals would never accept that sort of rule again."

"We aren't looking for power," Cethy said. "We just want to save our home. If the Fates are corrupted…"

"I know what would happen if the Fates are corrupted," Niamh snapped. She glared at Missy.

Missy didn't miss the meaningful look as Lebitta released her leg and hauled her upright at the pit's edge. "Why does everyone keep assuming that I'm evil?" she demanded, shoving the giant woman away from her. At least, she tried to. The Amazon didn't budge and Missy very nearly knocked herself backward into the hole.

"I've already said. I know you," Niamh snorted.

"Why would we need to steal from your Fountain if we had already sent someone?" Missy questioned in a hope to appeal to the faerie queen's logic. "You said yourself that you saw someone drinking from the spring. She's a blonde chick with gray eyes. Most likely she had a giant dog…thing with her."

"We didn't know that Eris would come here!" Cupid yelled from under the pile of Amazons. "Or we would have warned you. If you don't listen, she'll keep stealing from the gods. We will all be in very real danger!"

Niamh laughed again and it made Missy shudder. "And you three think you'll stop her?"

"We're meant to try!" Cethy yelled as she and Missy were forced back toward the edge of the pit. "You are making a mistake! Don't do this!"

"Enough!" Hippolyta stepped forward and shoved Cethy hard. Missy lunged for her but was too late. Her hands closed on empty air. Cethy disappeared over the lip of the pit.

Missy fell to her knees at the edge of the crater and stared down into the seemingly endless hole. "No. Red..." There was no answer, not even a scream. There was only the silent darkness. Fury gripped Missy, uncontrollable and acute. She stood and faced the surrounding Amazons and they all took a rather large step back.

Missy's eyes were pure, molten gold. Smoke curled up from her fingertips as small flickering flames mixed in with her hair. Fear flitted across the faces of the gathered Amazons. They were only mortals and an angry goddess would make short work of them if that was what she intended. Even one as out of practice as Nemesis.

"You will regret your decision when you are woven clean out of existence." Missy's voice had turned low and eerily musical. "We can stop them. Tyche is Prometheus's chosen, a Norn. She is meant to create the Circle, and I'm here to protect her."

"You aren't doing a very good job," Hippolyta said. Fire erupted at the queen's feet, forcing her back and singeing her leather boots.

"All we need is a jar of water," Cupid said. His eyes were narrowed at the goddess that had burst out of Missy. "If Eris succeeds, you're as dead as the rest of us. At least help us fight her."

"You're warriors aren't you?" Missy yelled. "Act like it!"

Hippolyta drew in a breath. "You dare question us?" she hissed. "You're a prisoner."

"*You* are the prisoners." Missy growled as more fire consumed her body. From the top of her head to the soles of her sneakers she was alight with the fire that had sprung from nothing but her raw anger. The Amazons were again forced back from the heat that rolled off of the furious sixteen year old. "You're trapped by your own narrow minds and short sightedness. We're not stealing from your spring. We're asking you to *give*. Share. Without everyone's cooperation, there is no chance for any of us."

"*There* you are, Nemesis," Niamh said. A smile appeared on her lovely face. "It took you long enough." Missy growled, golden fire licking from between her lips. "Very well. We shall strike a deal, you and I. I will give you water from the spring, but I do not waste water, or time, lightly."

Missy frowned. "What's the catch, faerie?" She looked Niamh over dismissively, her golden eyes scorching.

Niamh motioned to Hippolyta. "You will rejoin the tribe, Nemesis, and you will learn how to be a warrior once again. If this is a quest you insist on taking part in, then I will see to it that you are prepared. *I* would rather see a job done right than just done quickly." She looked loftily at Cupid. "As a goddess you would not be expected to revere me as ruler of the island, but you can offer your protection over the Amazons. It would give me less to worry about."

Missy couldn't help but try to edge away from the pit, her anger was fading and so was the fire that licked at her skin. Only a few flames remained tangled in her curls and wrapped around her arms. "I can't even protect myself against you. Do you really think I can save you from your enemies?"

Niamh laughed. "You gods may have become weak and useless but your arrival here heralds the rise of your kind once more. If Tyche can gain control of the Fates, you will fulfill your pledge to us at that time."

"What if we fail?" Missy asked.

Hippolyta scowled. "If you fail, it will not matter. As you said, we will no longer exist."

Missy looked at Cupid. He was a mess of curly blond hair and feathers held in the dirt by a force of massive, battle hungry women. She looked behind her. Somewhere in that hole was her best friend. "And Cethy?" she demanded. "Cue? You'll let them go?"

Hippolyta grimaced. "If we must, we will let the god go free. But he cannot return to Tir na n-Og. He doesn't belong here," she said. "Your companion will stay right where she is. Consider it insurance."

Missy practically snarled. "Let him go. Now." Hippolyta motioned to two of her Amazons. They hesitated only a moment before they stepped forward and grabbed Missy's flaming arms. As their hands closed around her biceps, the fire extinguished with a hiss of smoke.

"Take her to the armory," Hippolyta ordered. "And see her properly clothed for training and fitted for weapons."

The two Amazons began to lead Missy away. The flames in her hair and eyes were gone. Once again she was just a frightened sixteen year old girl. "Cue?" Cupid pressed his lips together and did nothing more than stare as Missy was hauled off into the forest. Slowly, the Amazons released him, one at a time. He stood and shook out his wings.

"You are to leave here, Cupid," Niamh said. "You should never have come here in the first place. You are adverse. Undesirable. Not wanted." She smiled knowingly as Cupid's eyes widened with surprise.

He had said those very words to Cethy about Missy before they had left for Tir na n-Og.

"How?" he asked.

"The spring does more than just heal and grant immortality," Niamh interrupted. "It can also grant clarity. Sometimes it shows the future, or the past, or the present. I have seen them all."

"You knew that we were coming," Cupid said, angry that he had let himself forget the prophetic powers of the water.

"I've known for weeks, Cupid. I just had to sit back and wait. I knew the lot of you would come blundering through here sooner or later. It took more than I thought it would to push Nemesis out of the girl. She keeps her divinity locked away."

Cupid made a face. "She warmed right up to it, though. She fell back into Nemesis, easy enough." He busied himself with settling his feathers. "So?" Cupid said with nonchalance. "What have you Seen? What does the future hold?"

"You know better than to ask," Niamh said. "My very purpose in this place is to keep the future hidden. However, I will suggest that you try to treat Nemesis with a little more kindness lest you regret your harsh words." Cupid snorted. "And now, you must leave this place. You may return in one month's time to collect your charges."

Cupid was indignant. "A month? There isn't time enough for that! Eris already has water from the Fountain. We can't waste a month!"

Hippolyta bristled. "It is not a waste. If your quest is truly for the Moirais' Circle your goddess will need to fight. We will all benefit from her training."

"She isn't even a Norn. She's just a mercenary and an unwelcome one at that. Cethy forced me to bring her," Cupid growled. "And she is not *my* goddess."

Niamh shook her head, amused and annoyed in the same breath. "In one month the girls will be returned to you along with water from the spring. So long as Nemesis upholds her part of the bargain," she added. The faerie hesitated. "She has changed. There is still chaos in her blood, but she handles it differently than she used to. That is very interesting." Niamh pulled herself from her thoughts. "It is time for you to leave, Cupid."

Cupid hesitated only a moment. "Don't hurt her. *Them.* Don't hurt *them*." He spread his wings and rose into the air to put distance between him and the island before he said anything else he didn't mean to.

Niamh watched him until he vanished from sight. "See that your warriors make sure Cupid does not come back before the month is up," she said to Hippolyta. "He is just foolish enough to attempt an early release. " Niamh returned to Hippolyta and her throne and sat with a sigh. "Did you notice what Nemesis did when we threatened the others?"

Hippolyta nodded. "It was very unlike her." The Amazon queen was not overly intelligent and did not wish to delve into the philosophy of Nemesis. She was a warrior. She knew only training and killing and could recognize the scent of war in the air. She had only one month to turn her new sovereign into a goddess worthy of the title. She and Niamh stood together and watched the sky. "I don't need magical water or fancy gadgets to know that trouble is close. We both know what the future holds," Hippolyta said. "I intend to be on the winning side."

"So what are you going to do?" Niamh asked.

Hippolyta was grim. "I plan to teach Nemesis how to win."

—Chapter Eleven—

Erin was having a really bad day.

Dejectedly, she swiped at the tears that fell unbidden down her cheeks and dripped off the end of her nose. Try as she might, Erin couldn't stop crying. Her brief visit to Tir na n-Og had been a nightmare and it was all Anubis' fault. He had led the way, urging her to follow his instruction. All she had to do was collect a little water. Have a little drink…

From the first sip, Erin knew it was a mistake. It felt like shards of broken glass were tipping down her throat. Her stomach was being shredded and her mouth turned to pure fire. In an attempt to cool her burning body Erin cupped the water in her hands and drank more. The pain only grew worse the more she drank. Her limbs were leaden and her head was in a vice. She had never before felt so overwhelmingly weak. What was worse, those giant, mad women with the arrows had appeared and nearly turned her into a pincushion.

Erin ran her hand over the spot on her chest that had been pierced by one of the Amazon's arrows. Smooth skin met her fingertips and she couldn't help but smile through her tears. There wasn't even a scratch.

Just as Anubis had promised, the Fountain made Erin invulnerable to injury. No matter the wound, no matter the extent of the damage, her body healed within seconds. Anubis had made her 'bend' around the world all day and try out her new gift. She had been shot, trampled, beaten, and stabbed. She was exhausted.

She was also completely unharmed.

When Erin finally appeared outside of the hotel Anubis was still waiting for her and the Egyptian god growled at her approach. "Don't make me muzzle you."

Erin stumbled through the door to the room she had shared with Missy and Cethy at the Mayan. Anubis was on her heels, sulking at the reprimand but carefully watchful of the blonde discord goddess. Everything was exactly as Erin had left it the day before. The beds were unmade. Two book bags were left abandoned on the floor, their contents all over the carpet. The bathroom door hung off its hinges, and the window was open. A picture of the three girls was crumpled on the worn carpet, its frame smashed.

Home sweet home.

Erin was heedless of the mess. She fell onto the closest bed, hardly able to keep her eyes open. It seemed like so much longer than only two days ago that she had argued with Missy on the boardwalk. "You didn't tell me it was going to hurt," Erin moaned to Anubis and the underworld god growled and bared his teeth. Erin rolled over and clutched her pillow as unwelcome memories plagued her. She'd run from Missy. There hadn't been a choice. The second that Missy had gotten into her head Erin knew she would no longer be welcome and that small glimpse of the vengeance goddess was more than enough. She'd run. She ran from the fire and from the girl that had caused it, but Erin had nowhere to run *to*. She lurked on the boardwalk for hours contemplating what kind of future a chaos-causing goddess could possibly have when an indistinct figure had beckoned to her from the shadows. It was a messenger. A terrible, impossible monster. Anubis. It seemed that Prometheus wasn't the only one recruiting the Divine. Anubis had sensed Olympian power and for days had kept a close eye on the three girls. Apparently, Erin was just the goddess he was looking for.

Erin dozed, sweating through her clothes. Anubis had promised to make her invincible. He was going to make sure that Missy and Cethy never stood in her way again. Next time, Erin would be strong enough to face them without having to run. All she had to do was take water from the Fountain of Youth. Just enough to fill a small jar and maybe take a little sip. Even the smallest mouthful of water would be enough. After she drank from the pool Erin would be impervious to harm.

Not just immortal but invincible.

Invincible? She shuddered. She did not feel invincible. She felt worse than ever. Erin was hurt, confused, and she was alone. The pain was excruciating and she whimpered into her pillow. In her mind's eye she saw the three smiling girls in the picture on the floor. The fire in her throat and the nails in her gut dulled as her anger grew. Pain or no pain, she was going to keep her promise to Cethy. Erin was going to stop the timid, gangly redhead and the curly-haired mouthpiece from finding the Fates. The Norn and her champion would suffer.

Erin would see to it.

—Chapter Twelve—

A strange stillness fell over Los Angeles. People seemed to stop everything they were doing as their eyes grew heavy and their bodies slowed down. The entire city was frozen in time, a still life image. Only one person continued his trek up the sidewalk unaffected and it took a while for the twenty year old in the long jacket to realize what had happened. Startled, he ducked into an alley between two brick buildings, alert for danger. He wasn't certain what was going on but he didn't need anyone to notice that he hadn't frozen with the rest of them.

"Hello, Love." The young man started, and turned to face the woman that had appeared at his side, a dazzling smile on her face. Her blue eyes were massive as she looked up at him, the picture of innocence and ladylike daintiness.

"What're you doing out of the underworld, Hel?" His tone was chilly. If the Norse goddess of the Crossroads was loose in California it was going to be a bad day for the west coast. Hel was *not* one of the good ones. "You thought you'd just pop up and work on your tan?"

"Don't be silly." Hel's voice was silky. "I just missed you, Love. I thought that we could catch up."

"You're dreaming," the young man shook his head. "Whatever you're looking for, you'd better go find it somewhere else."

The girl giggled and gently brushed her fingers along his strong jawline affectionately. "Poor, abused heart. You don't even believe in what you're selling anymore, do you?"

"Why are you here, Hel?"

"I'm being bad."

There was no scream. Everything happened so quickly there wasn't even time to struggle. There was only a startled gasp and a sickening thud when the body hit the ground. A cloaked figure stepped out of the shadows and looked grimly down at the now lifeless man lying in the dank alleyway off of Santa Monica Boulevard.

That had been too easy.

"You were supposed to distract him, not throw yourself at him." The cloaked figure lowered her hood to reveal a woman in her late twenties with blood red eyes and a mean expression. A strange pair of scissors, damp with blood, was clenched in her fist.

"He was pretty," Hel said, crouching down to examine the body. "I do love killing the attractive ones. The Void is almost bearable if I can have a few pretty toys to keep me company." Hel was practically a queen in the under realm, and the dead were her willing servants. Like most vapid girls, she preferred to surround herself with things that were aesthetically pleasing. That's what the souls of the dead were to her. Things. Tools to be used. She frowned down at the lifeless body at her feet, her head tipped to the side. "Why such a clean kill, Bave? We could have tortured him a bit first."

"This is about efficiency, Hel, not fun. We can have fun once we secure the Moirai." Bave was no stranger to death herself. In her heyday the Celtic war goddess was a force to be feared. She ravaged the fields of battle, reaping countless souls. There were none who didn't know her name and it was spoken in fear and respect. Those days were gone but time had not diminished the warrior maiden at all. She was as bloodthirsty as ever. Bave cast the body sprawled at her feet a dismissive glance. "He wouldn't have liked being mortal. Were he alive, he would thank us for killing him." She poked him with the toe of her blood red pump.

Hel shrugged. "I know. It's just pathetic. He survived all this time with his facilities and powers intact only to lose both in a dark alley like some mortal getting mugged. We might have given him a proper death." Bave snickered and Hel patted the corpse's cheek before she straightened up. "A pity it had to come to this but he would have ruined everything. He was always such a goodie-goodie and far too clever for his own good. Looks *and* brains…"

Bave nodded. "He would have found a way to alert the other gods, Hel, and no one can find out what we're doing. Our plan relies on the rest of the Pantheons remaining ignorant for as long as possible."

With a malicious grin, Hel leaned against the alley wall. "Soon," she whispered, gleeful. "Soon they'll be scared. I want them paranoid. I want them all chasing ghosts and rumors and finding nothing. The longer the rest of the Divine stay in the dark, the better. His power should prove useful in that. Imagine the distractions we can cause with it."

Bave stared down into the now lifeless, shocked, blue eyes, proud of her handy work. Already bored by it, Hel ignored the body altogether. Instead, she took a glass vial from Bave's hand. It swirled with red and gold gases, blinking and sparkling even in the dim light of the alley. "This is all we need," Hel whispered. "With this, the Fates are as good as ours."

Bave grinned. "Your plan had better work or it will be *our* powers taken away. We don't have a plan B. If we fail there'll be no place to go and no way to reclaim the Fates from those idiot Norns."

"This *will* work," Hel said through bared teeth. The very thought of the Norns made her furious. How dare some group of self-righteous, lower level goddesses think that they were worthy of the power that went with guarding the Moirai.

Bave watched Hel close her fist over the tiny crystal vial. "You'd better know what you are doing. We can't afford to make a mistake and trust the wrong people."

"Are you referring to the pouka?" Hel asked with a bright, maniacal giggle. It was a childish sound that didn't suit the cold, hateful look in her eyes. "Do the little shape-shifters make you nervous, Bave?"

Bave scowled. "I hate those nasty, little rats. Pouka are miserable tricksters, Hel. It's not in them to remain loyal forever. Eventually they'll realize that helping us only hurts them. They'll turn."

Hel agreed. "But for now they serve their purpose, dear friend." She was already working on the next part of her plot and, indeed, it didn't involve the irksome, morphing pouka. The brilliance of her plan was in the fact that absolutely no one would see it coming. The two of them had to keep it that way for as long as possible. Hel smiled ruthlessly down at the body in front of her. *He* certainly hadn't been expecting it.

That's what had made it so easy.

"For now the pouka won't betray us." Hel gave the crystal vial a good shake, swirling the reds and golds together into a blurry mess. "We've got what every pouka wants. As long as we can give them immortality and Divine power they will do whatever we want."

Bave shrugged and looked deep into the glassy blue eyes of her victim. This was the cost of war. This was what she lived for. "Hello, what's this?" Her eyes were drawn to the leather cord around the young man's neck. "Pretty." Her voice was darkly gleeful. She cut the cord with her shears and dangled the pendant, a shiny white arrowhead, in front of her eyes. "Ow!" Hel glanced at her so she quickly added, "It shocked me."

"Don't steal from the body, darling. It's tacky." Hel glanced up at the sun that had kept moving despite the frozen city. "We should go. There's a long night ahead of us." The two young women vanished from the alley in a swirl of cloaks and curls. The city sprang back into motion, none the wiser to the life that had been taken.

The two girls reappeared in a thick, dense forest. The Arctic Circle was the perfect hiding place for two goddesses with nowhere else to go. Hel deposited herself on a rotten log and warmed her hands in what was left of the fire they had built earlier. She caught Bave looking at her and leaned back, melting into the shadows with a dark glower.

Before the Fall Hel had been part of both Valhalla and Erebus. Heaven and Hell. The left half of her body had been that of the light. With her long brown hair, blue eye, and tanned skin, she was strikingly beautiful. However, the right side of her body had been a reflection of Erebus, the under realm. Dead, blue, flesh fell rotting from her body and her eye was bloodshot, yellow, and blind. Her hair had fallen in grey, thin clumps. Simultaneously beautiful and hideous, Hel was the balance that stood in the Crossroads of the under realm and assigned souls their final resting place.

Then those cursed Olympians had ruined everything.

Bave shook her head. The trouble that the Fall had caused her young friend was enough to make one sick. Thick brown curls fell past Hel's shoulders, glossy and smooth. Two deep blue eyes set in her perfectly tan, unblemished face followed the dancing flames. Hel's fearsome looks had been replaced by downright loveliness. Since the Fall Hel's balance had tipped. The darkness dwelled only inside her now. Her duel-mindedness was warped and replaced by a feral desire to make mankind as corrupt and violent as she was. Beautiful on the outside, terrible on the inside.

Bave stood outside the ring of firelight and watched. She was tall and sickly thin with vicious beady eyes that never appeared to blink. They were a deep red, unnatural and battle hungry. Her hair was black and short, slicked back from her face and Bave seemed to always wear a perpetual smirk, her teeth filed to frightening points and her hooked nose appeared more like a beak than anything.

"It won't be much longer now, Bave. We're almost ready for the next phase in our plan." The two goddesses had hidden in the underworld for thousands of years, powers and memories intact, but recently the undeniable pull of power called them to the Mortal Realm. A power that could only be one thing.

The Moirai.

Thankfully, they were not alone. Hel had smuggled a spy out of the under realm with them. The monster was a god himself, a warrior before the Fall. Now he was little more than a mindless animal to be manipulated by the Crossroad goddess.

"Anubis!" Hel grinned and opened her arms expectantly. Moments later another set of eyes appeared at the fire.

Bave laughed meanly at the massive dogman, her sharpened teeth menacing in the fire light. "I see you've taught your pet to heel. Shall I give him a cookie?"

Anubis snarled at the Celt's tone and bared his teeth. The god's slavered canines put Bave's to shame. "I have news." The dark god's voice was like gravel, rough and gritty. "I've found your third."

Both girls perked up. That's what they had been waiting for. Since they had not been able to move freely about the Earth themselves lest they run into another god and their plans be discovered, Anubis had been their eyes and their ears in the Mortal Realm. He tracked the gods and reported where and when their victims were alone. He watched and waited for the perfect moment to strike. He was also on the scent of a very special goddess.

The one that would make their circle complete.

"Tell me, dear friend, did she drink from the Fountain?" Hel asked eagerly. Her fingers combed gently through the fur on Anubis' head. "Did she survive?"

Anubis growled with the pleasure of a job well done. He'd gone through several less than savory gods and goddesses to find one that would suit Hel's criteria. Cold. Malicious. Hated. Powerful. Many had not survived the Amazons that guarded the spring and the few that did had been driven mad by the water they'd stolen. His newest fought to survive. She was strong. She was bound to be the lucky chosen that would complete Hel's Charonte. "She yet lives. She sleeps." While he was pleased by the attention, the close proximity to Hel was unsettling. Anubis' tongue hung out of his mouth in a nervous smile. Harmless as she looked, Hel was not cuddly or kind and sure enough as Anubis prepared to leave the fire he let out an earsplitting yowl and dropped to his knees. Hel was still smiling, her eyes narrow slits of anger as her nails bit deeply into the fur at his throat.

"You're leaving something out, are you not?" Hel grinned and dug her nails in further. "Something important?"

Anubis turned his large eyes to Bave in hopes for sympathy but the cruel goddess was unmoved by his quaking and pitiful yelps. "Fool," she spat. "You dare withhold information? Hel is the goddess of the Crossroads. There are no secrets from her." Bave's red gaze settled on Hel. "What do you see?"

Expression thoughtfully reposed, Hel pursed her lips. "Not what I expected. Anubis did find a potential candidate... But it is one who recently parted ways with two goddesses. They were taken by a winged man."

Bave swore and grabbed Anubis by the scruff of his neck, dragging him from Hel's grasp to snarl in his face. "Cupid? You are sure?"

Anubis was too busy whimpering like a scolded puppy to answer. "Yes. Cupid was there. Do you know what that means?" Hel glared into the fire, smiling darkly.

"It means that goodie-goodie is *still* finding ways to ruining our plans." Bave released Anubis and the god raced into the woods, yelping and howling in fear.

"No. It means that one of those Olympians was a Norn. A Norn who knows and trusts Cupid." Hel grinned as her friend caught on. "Already the Fates are working in our favor. This is meant to be, Bave. We are meant to dominate the Fates and this world." Her dark blue eyes grew distant, her smile all the more sinister. "Poor little Norn. You have no idea what you're in for."

—Chapter Thirteen—

The pain grew worse but there was nothing Erin could do save toss about in a fevered sleep. She rolled over and clutched her pillow, sobbing, her blonde hair matted to her face in sweaty hanks as she dreamed of fire.

Bave appeared silently in the mangled room and smirked. The Norn had clearly put up a fight. The bathroom door was in pieces on the floor. Two book bags were abandoned, their contents spilt out. There was even a relatively fresh bloodstain on the threadbare carpet. Bave loved a good battle and the events replayed in the war goddess's mind clear as if she had been there herself. It had been a rather one sided fight... Disappointed, Bave's tiny red eyes fell on the picture that lay forgotten in its broken frame and she made a face. Her sharpened teeth flashed in the lamplight as she snarled at the images. "Hel, come look." She plucked the picture of Missy, Cethy, and Erin from beneath the shards of broken glass. "How sad is this? They thought they were friends."

Hel giggled childishly. "How could they believe this would last?" She looked at the picture and sneered. The three girls each smiled brilliantly, their faces happy, eyes dancing. "They're enemies."

Erin groaned in her sleep and buried her face in the pillow, drawing the attention of the two malignant goddesses.

Hel snickered as she took in Erin's sleeping form. "She's not very imposing, is she?"

"No, not very," Bave agreed. "But she might be useful. We need someone to get us coffee in the mornings and walk Anubis. Hey!" She stripped the blanket off of the bed with one yank. "Wakey, wakey!" Erin sat up with a groggy expletive and blinked tiredly at the two women who had appeared in her room.

"Go 'way." Erin fell back against her pillow and Hel and Bave exchanged a look.

Hel caught Erin's ankle with biting fingers. Much like Bave did with the sheet, Hel yanked Erin from the bed, dropping the younger girl on her rear between the two of them. It wasn't very nice but, then again, neither was Hel.

"She reeks of Olympus," Bave words dripped with disdain.

"But a strife goddess might prove useful." Hel regarded Erin like she was a stinkbug or some other malodorous creature. "They're not exactly our favorite of the Divine Lines but we need to look at the bigger picture. At this point I think her genealogy can be overlooked."

"And I suppose she does make us a full set," Bave conceded.

"Excuse me, who are you?" Erin was fully awake now and practically peeing her pants. She was sandwiched between the two strange goddesses as they discussed her the way one might talk about a broodmare. She was surprised they didn't check her teeth. Erin held her pillow like a baseball bat. It was a poor attempt to threaten the intruders. "Get out!"

With a giggle, Hel's eyes flashed dangerously. "What are you going to do? Challenge me to a pillow fight?"

Bave tore the pillow away from Erin's hands and whacked her in the face with it, knocking her back down to the floor. "Delightful." Tossing the pillow aside, Bave lounged on one of the squeaky hotel beds. "So, you're the new Charonte. Lucky us." Her tone was light, as if the topic was as unremarkable as the weather, but Erin's interest piqued. Anubis had mentioned the Charonte. Evil, powerful, and bent on total domination... They sounded like her sort of people.

"Me?" she said, her fear abating a bit. "I'm a Charonte?"

Bave's filed teeth were menacing in the fluorescent lighting as she smiled at Erin. "Let me give you the skinny, honey. Once upon a time, you were one of the most feared goddesses the Greeks ever had the misfortune of worshiping. You were cunning, cruel, and very powerful."

"I like it," Erin rasped. The pain in her chest made her voice sound weak and wheezy. "Power is good."

Bave ignored the interruption. "You should be able to magnify hostile, unharmonious feelings and, most importantly, you can summon."

"Summon?" Erin looked between the other two goddesses, sweaty and exhausted. "You mean I can call things to me? I've never done that before."

Rolling her eyes, Hel sat beside Bave and adjusted her skirts around her. "It will take practice. There aren't a lot of gods that can manage that particular gift and you've been out of commission a long time. The Greeks were the worst affected by the Fall. That's courtesy of your little friend here." The underworlder flicked the picture, her dark nail leaving a mark over Missy's grinning face.

Erin wished that she could concentrate on what Hel was saying. She saw the goddess' mouth move, heard some sort of pitched whine that must have been her voice, but the words had stopped making sense. Erin was wholly focused on the burning, stabbing pain in her throat and stomach. The pain that was only getting worse. "I'mma nap." She fell back onto the bed in a miserable heap of overheated limbs and blonde hair.

"She's as unglued as the rest of them," Bave said derisively. "We don't have time for this."

"I suppose we'll have to make time," Hel lifted an eyebrow. "Eris, did you drink from the spring? Is that when you became ill?" She spoke slowly and loudly as if Erin did not have the sense to understand plain English.

Erin nodded, miserably. "Anubis told me that it would make me invincible."

Bave sighed. "Her essence has likely been poisoned. That faerie witch is constantly hexing the water. And people call *us* monsters." She looked over Erin and sized her up. "She's lasted longer than any of the others. What do you think, Hel? Would a pixie do it or might she need something a bit bigger?"

"A nymph would be better," Hel said, distracted. She had returned her attention to the photograph of the three smiling girls. She looked up, her dark blue eyes aggressive. "But we'd better make it a wood nymph. You feed off a water nymph and you're hungry again an hour later."

The two goddesses grabbed Erin by the shoulders. "Come along, dear. Time to hunt."

"Dun wanna," Erin moaned. She could hardly stand. She wanted nothing more than to crawl back into bed and continue to sleep off her pain.

Bave was far too impatient to try and coax Erin to do as she said. It wasn't in her nature to beg for anything. "I think that you do." Bave grabbed Erin by the throat and bent out of the hotel room. Hel clapped her hands in delight and followed.

Everything was finally falling into place.

It took only a few hours for Hel and Bave to return Erin to health. All they needed was a single, frightened wood nymph and a highly disturbing procedure that Bave had called *Harvesting*. With the help of a nasty little tool that Erin thought looked like pair of rusty scissors, the war goddess separated the nymph from her immortality. The shears opened more than just flesh and muscle. They cut into the very essence of the immortal. As Bave slowly worked them free a shimmering gas clung to blades. Hel caught the nymph's essence in a small glass bottle and all Erin had to do was inhale.

The instant that Erin breathed in the glittering power she had felt infinitely better. With new, healthy, uncorrupted immortality in her body, Erin felt stronger than she ever had. It was intoxicating and she sneered down at her unwilling donor. The nymph, newly made mortal, was left stranded and crying on the forest floor while the Charonte bent, vanished into thin air, and reappeared in the Arctic Circle.

"You're truly one of us, now," Hel purred. She ran her hands through Erin's thick platinum blonde waves. She didn't think much of Olympians as a rule but at least, Hel reasoned, Erin was pretty. Hel only surrounded herself with pretty things. Pretty things that she could manipulate and mold as she pleased. "It will be different for you now," she whispered. "You drank from the spring, same as us. You will never suffer a permanent injury again. You are indestructible, Eris. There is no longer necessary to do things like eat or sleep. You are beyond mortal needs, now."

Erin frowned as Hel tangled her fingers in her hair. "But eating and sleeping are two of my favorite things."

With a cold laugh Hel gripped those silky blonde locks and yanked the younger girl's head back. Erin shrieked angrily but Hel was not going to be displaced. "I suggest you make fighting and killing your two favorite things," the warped goddess said simply while Bave chortled. "That's what it'll take to win the Moirai."

She released Erin and the blonde scrambled away, dolefully rubbing her scalp. "How much killing are we talking about here?" She had never killed a person in her life… At least, not that she could remember.

"As much as we need to," Bave said with an eager grin. "As much as we *want*."

Erin ignored the growing sense of unease that was settled in her stomach. "Doesn't that draw an awful lot of attention?"

"I think that you will find we are fairly efficient," Bave said, curtly. She glanced at Hel, beady eyes full of malice. "Shall we let Eris in on our plan?"

By the fireside, under the stars of the Arctic Circle, Erin sat back and listened with wide eyes as Hel described the end of the world.

—Chapter Fourteen—

Tir na n-Og was alive with cheers and the sound of metal striking metal. Almost the entire Amazon tribe had stopped their daily work and their own arms practice to sit on the training yard fence and watch the spectacular fight that was underway. Two young girls circled one another, swords raised and eyes wary. They had been locked in combat for almost two full days, neither one willing to yield. They merely waited, harassing one another and keeping a keen eye for the moment their opponent made the fatal mistake that would end the fight.

The smallest seemed at a disadvantage. Compared to the other girl she was a twig that was just waiting to be snapped in two. Missy felt the effects of forty solid hours of combat in every inch of her body. The sweat that had poured into her eyes long since dried on her skin. Dehydration left her feeling shaky, but she knew the penalty if she gave up. Someone had to win before the match was over. There was no tapping out.

No surrender.

For three weeks, Missy's life had revolved around training and fighting. There was nothing but pushups, pull ups, curl ups, chin ups, and running up hill. Every day she reported to the training yard for sword practice, target practice, small weapons practice, and barehanded combat. Missy was no longer recognizable as the same girl who had arrived on the island. Very quickly her small body became taunt and muscular, able to endure for long periods of time in hard conditions. The goddess that she had completely forgotten struggled to the surface with all the skills and instincts that Missy had lost with the Fall. Almost overnight she found the strength to shoot with the Amazons' long bows. She relearned how to move quietly and quickly. She was taught strategy and tactics. Missy rapidly proved to the Amazons that she was a fierce opponent when fighting barehanded and, though they still bested her, it was not without genuine effort on their part.

It was with swords that Missy was truly a master. After three weeks of physically jogging her memory, Missy had not only recalled how to wield a blade, but wondered how she could have ever forgotten in the first place. She felt natural with a sword in her hand. It was a part of her as surely as her other limbs and with that blade in her grasp Missy was a force. As it was, she was locked in battle with the queen's youngest daughter, Antianara, and needed every ounce of skill and then some not to get herself lopped in half.

Missy and Antianara were the same age, but physically a more uneven match could not have been found. Antianara was a solid eight feet tall and bulging with muscle. She was a wild blonde, scarred from the rough life she had among the warriors. Her blue eyes were narrowed in anger at Missy, and her breathing was heavy. Missy grinned. Antianara was exhausted.

Missy wasn't faring so well herself. Barely able to remain standing, she wanted nothing more than to fall face first into the dirt of the training yard and go to sleep. The only reason she did not succumb to the demands of her body was that she refused to accept the humiliation or the punishment that accompanied surrender.

It was a lesson that Missy learned her first day in the camp when Hippolyta had handed her a sword and shoved her into the training yard with a woman almost twice her size. Missy had abandoned the fight before it had even begun and the queen had issued her the standard punishment for a first time offender. It was in that moment Missy learned the secret of the Amazon's mutilated hands. With a flick of her sword, Hippolyta cleanly severed the pinky finger off of Missy's right hand.

The cruel punishment came with a warning. To back down from a fight was to repent with a pound of flesh, but the next time Missy surrendered she would not be the one who lost the weight. The punishment would be passed onto Cethy. That and that alone was enough to push Missy through the rest of that day until she was able to crawl onto her sleeping pallet and nurse her ruined hand. It was for Cethy that she endured the past three weeks, and once she had gotten over her fear, she found that she truly enjoyed the Amazon's way of life. To be part of the tribe was to have what Missy lacked all of her life.

Family.

From the moment that Missy was accepted into Hippolyta's tribe a strange sense of belonging had stolen over her. There was a familiarity about the training routine and the constant practicing. The blisters, cramps, bruises, and soreness quickly became second nature and were easily ignored. And, even though she paid for it in blood and sweat, she had the respect of the tribe. At long last she had found a place that felt natural.

Missy was once again an Amazon.

Her vision swam and Missy narrowly avoided a direct downward swing at her shoulder. Sloppy. She could not afford to lose focus now. Antianara screamed some oath at her, but Missy ignored it. It drove the Androktone crazy when she did not engage in their customary exchange of insults. It unnerved them to see those golden eyes so intent on their defeat and that impish grin cemented on her face. Antianara charged again and jabbed for Missy's throat. Missy parried the blow and glared at the princess.

They weren't supposed to be bent on murder. The fight had merely begun as an exercise to see who the better combatant was but after almost two days the tension between them was palpable. They were each straining not to lose control, and struggling not to collapse. This had escalated into more than just a test of skill.

"It was only a matter of time," a spectator said from her place on the fence.

Her companion nodded. "My money is on Anara. She's a dirty cheat."

A third Amazon shook her head. "Nemesis will handle her own. You'll see. She'll put Anara in her place."

It was common knowledge in the Amazon camp that Missy and Antianara had been butting heads from day one. Hippolyta had allowed the other Amazons to initiate Missy by beating her raw and Antianara had been the most energetic of her assailants. Missy had been forced to wait for the day when she could thank the princess properly. She had had to combat and win against every other Amazon in the camp before she was allowed to so much as draw her sword against Antianara. This battle was about pride and respect and neither girl was willing to give in so much as an inch.

On the other side of the island, Cethy watched everything from the bank of the enchanted spring, her dusty blue eyes wide with horror. The sight of her young cousin wielding a blade and taking abuse from the giant Androktone had her hiding behind her fingers.

Niamh stuck her hand into the water and caused a ripple. The images distorted and Cethy looked up with damp eyes. "You look, but you do not See."

Unbeknownst to Missy, Cethy had been out of the prison pit for some time. As Hippolyta had taken Missy under her wing, Niamh had turned Cethy into her own apprentice. Under the fairy's careful direction Cethy was learning to feel for the future and to descry.

"It is important to remember to keep your mind clear of all outside distractions," Niamh prompted. "In time, scrying will become second nature but for now you have to concentrate on what and when you want to See. Don't let your thoughts or the noise around you keep you from Seeing. Don't let your own fear stop your mind from traveling further than the other side of the island."

Cethy tried to concentrate. She had been at it for weeks and she was still unable to See beyond the isle or the present. Her preoccupation with the safety of her young friend meant that she had only been able to watch as Missy was pummeled time and again by the giant women. The time was broken up by an occasional victory for Missy, usually followed by a brutal loss. Niamh had been patient with Cethy, but the faerie queen expected progress.

"Try again," Niamh said. "Focus on the future. The spring will help for now but you won't always have enchanted water. You must be prepared to scry in fire, puddle water, dirt, or in the air itself. You need to be stronger than the Sight itself to control it."

Cethy shifted and set her focus on the now still surface of the water. The future. She steadied her breathing as Niamh had taught her and projected her wants onto the surface of the spring. A darkness welled up from the depths. Slowly, though the water remained as still as glass, images rose to meet the waiting goddess and faerie.

At first Cethy thought that what she saw was just Missy in the training yard yet again, but the scene was too different. The noise was deafening. Pained screams and the twang of loosed arrows filled the air as Missy ran uphill through a field, a short, gleaming, sword in hand. She reached the peak and let out a wordless war cry to rally those behind her. The girl was covered in war paint and dressed for battle in strips of the same blue fabric that the Amazons so favored. An unfamiliar, silver tattoo wrapped around Missy's left arm from elbow to finger tips. It almost glowed, its thin tworling design adding to her wild appearance.

Tongues of orange flame blended with her dark curls and her face was an unfamiliar, ferocious mask.

A deep earth-shaking howl shook the ground.

Missy was locked in combat with a man that appeared to be made completely of water as a wolf the size of a bus loped over the hill, snarling, salivating, and snapping up anyone in its way.

"Fenris," Cethy heard Niamh mutter, astonished by the giant animal. The massive wolf was a monster most foul and his appearance could only mean the end of the world. The faerie watched on over Cethy's shoulder, startled. The vision continued, too strong to stop.

The sword in Missy's hand flashed a warning. She dispensed of her opponent cleanly and screamed with the rage of battle and raised her arms to attack the unnatural beast before it did any more harm. She had not gone more than two steps when her face twisted with confusion and surprise. Missy dropped her sword and grabbed her stomach as her surprise gave way to pain. Her whole body pitched forward into the muddy battle-churned earth. Cethy saw two identical shafts sticking out of Missy's back. A pair of black arrowheads protruded out of the sixteen year old's stomach. The mammoth wolf clearly preferred to make its own kill and stepped over Missy's seizing body. He sauntered off to wreak havoc elsewhere. Cethy could do nothing but watch as her friend died on the hilltop.

Over the chaos of battle, Cethy heard the sound of wing beats. Cupid landed at Missy's side, covered in war paint and holding a bow. She only had time to see the quiver of black arrows on his back before the image vanished back into the depths of the water leaving Cethy hip deep in the spring, loudly keening her friend's future.

Niamh watched somberly from the bank. "That was very good." The faerie queen was dour. "Unexpected, but still. You did very well, Tyche."

"I have to warn her!"

Niamh grabbed Cethy's shoulders as the frightened goddess tried to run past her. She was unnaturally strong for one so slight and Cethy was drawn up short. "No, Tyche. Seeing the future may be a useful tool, but there is nothing glorious about it. There is nothing wonderful or fantastic about what we See. That is why it is secret."

"Secret?" Cethy did not understand. "But I have to warn Missy. I can't just let her die!"

"You do not have a choice." Cethy backed away, horrified at Niamh's calm. "She can never know what you have seen. Neither can Cupid." Niamh shook her head sadly. "People, especially gods, cannot handle knowing too much about the future. That is the true reason why I guard this spring. It is not just to keep people from drinking or healing themselves. It is to stop them from learning too much. People cannot be trusted with this sort of knowledge."

"But why not?" Cethy cried. "Why can't I tell her?"

Niamh was gentle. "Because you do not know what that knowledge will do. It might prevent Nemesis's murder, but it might also be what leads to it. You do not know, so you must keep what you saw guarded. To know the future is to affect it. I know that it seems cruel, but you must listen."

"Is there a way to change it?" Cethy whispered. Nausea turned her stomach at the mere thought of what she had Seen. She would never escape that horrible vision. Even now she saw Missy's eyes glassing over as she drew her last shuddering, painful breath. "I can't just let her die. She's all the family I've got."

"The future has always been fluid. It changes with every decision we make." Niamh motioned for Cethy to return to the bank. "What you saw could be only a warning. Maybe it is Nemesis' destiny to die on that hill. It may be but one of the endless futures that lie ahead. Perhaps just by being vigilant you can stop this. What is yet to be can always be changed. Nothing is written in stone. Remember that."

Cethy felt like she couldn't breathe. Niamh gently cupped her hands in the spring and tipped the water over her unwilling apprentice. Slowly Cethy's tension melted away, though the terror of what she saw kept her heart pounding. "I want you to keep practicing," Niamh said. "You need to learn to bring the image to you instead of chancing upon it by accident. Challenge it to the surface. Command it. Do not let it command you. Look and learn."

Niamh pointed to the water. After a heartbeat's pause another image came to the surface. A woman with short brown curls and golden eyes knelt in a temple, a candle lit on the altar in front of her. Tears fell silently down her cheeks as she whispered her prayers. The look of serious determination on her face was startling and familiar.

"Missy?" Cethy leaned over the image in the water. "How? What future is this? Look at her. She's old."

"This is not the future, Tyche." Niamh's wings fluttered in agitation. "It is the past. Nemesis was an adult when she was banished from the Pantheon. Now, hush." The two women watched as the vision continued.

Nemesis pulled a delicate, leather cord free from around her neck and carefully set it and its shining white pendant on the altar. A floorboard creaked in the silent shrine and Nemesis tensed, eyes narrowed. Fire erupted from her palms as she spun to face the darkness. "Show yourself."

"Shhh," a man's voice whispered through the gloom. His tone was gentle, kind. "It's only me." A hand from the shadows indicated the necklace that Nemesis had so tenderly placed on the altar. "That was a gift."

"You should not have come," Nemesis snarled and kept the fire lit in her hands. "It is not safe."

"I know what happened." The phantom sounded out of breath. "All of Olympus is talking. Did you think that you could threaten the king of the gods and walk away scot-free, Nemesis? You have put yourself in danger."

Nemesis snorted derisively. "Don't you mean I've put *you* in danger?"

For a moment there was silence. "Must you throw your words around like daggers? You've endangered us with no thought at all. You've turned Olympus into a circus. And for what? Your pride?"

Nemesis was livid but her voice was steady as she pointed to the shrine's open door. "Get out."

"You think to send me away from my own temple?" the shadow demanded. "Don't do that, Curly. Don't punish me too. Not when I haven't done anything." He pleaded, his words so full of love and sincerity that Nemesis had to look away.

"I am warning you. Idiot Zeus will be looking for me and I don't have time to worry about you. Go. Leave." Nemesis's voice was void of emotion. Cethy could recognize how desperately she was trying to control herself.

"Let me help. I can distract him. I can send him after someone else. You aren't alone–"

Fire flew from Nemesis's hands and for a moment the church was lit as brightly as if it were day. "I said to leave me alone. I don't want your help and I don't want *you*. Get out!"

There was a long silence, only Nemesis' heavy breathing disturbing the angry shroud that hung over the altar. "I hope your arrogance will sustain you, Nemesis. That is all you have. That is what you truly fight for."

Nemesis was alone again before the altar, her face the perfectly controlled mask that Cethy had never seen on her emotional and animated friend. "I fight for you," she whispered. "Always."

The image vanished, dissipating into the pond water.

Cethy stared at the faerie, bewildered. "I don't understand."

Niamh was still looking into the water, her expression somber. "You will."

Chapter Fifteen

The match raged on.

Antianara rushed Missy in an attempt to stampede her, sword slashing the air. Missy blocked and parried the blow and quickly retreated. The goddess was fast on her feet, but Antianara's powerful strikes made her sword vibrate. Each attack numbed her hands and jarred her arms. Missy fought through the pain and refused to drop her sword, but she would be unable to take the abuse for much longer.

It had been two days. *Two* days and Antianara still hadn't presented Missy with a target. She had to find a way to force her into it, to get the Amazon to make a mistake. Maybe if Missy could get her angry enough, she'd be able to deal a blow that would stun her and at long last end the match but there were few taunts that could ruffle any member of the Androktone. It was their practice to sling insults at each other to harden their hearts and hone their minds for real battle. Even within the tribe, however, there were lines not to be crossed. Pushing Antianara's buttons could prove dangerous for the petite swordswoman and an angry Amazon in the bloodlust was nothing short of deadly.

Then again, heatstroke wasn't such a great option either.

"Anara!" If there was one thing Missy was exceptional at, it was throwing people into a red-hot rage. Her words were barbed, her tone acidic and the smirk she shot the Amazon princess was designed to infuriate. "Look at your sloppy stance, your weak grip on your sword. You count on your position and your bulk to win fights. You're nothing more than a careless cow."

With a furious shriek, Antianara raised her sword and began to rain down blow after blow over the smaller girl. Missy might have become faster and more agile than a normal human, but she was still nothing compared to the Amazons. She was barely able to get her sword up in time to hinder the path of the wild Amazon's blade.

"Don't take your frustrations out on me," Missy growled, doing her best to keep her body away from the bite of Antianara's weapon. "It isn't my fault you haven't been able to win. If you were as good as you thought this fight would be long over." Each jarring block sent pain shooting through her fingers and into her palms.

Unbeknownst to the rest of the tribe, Missy had engaged herself in two separate battles. Not only was she dodging Antianara's sword, she was also making a conscious effort to keep the Amazon's emotions separate from her own. Rage swarmed Missy like angry bees, stinging her when she wasn't careful. The last thing she needed was for her plan to backfire and lose her own temper. "You're slow. You're clumsy, and," Missy parried and laughed. "You're weak."

Antianara froze. With a furious scream she plunged her sword into the dirt, practically frothing at the mouth. "What did you say to me?" For a moment Missy thought that her opportunity had finally come. The princess looked as if she were going to abandon her sword altogether and lunge at Missy, her only weapon her outstretched fingers that clutched for Missy's neck.

"I said," Missy reiterated and raised her sword. "You. Are. Weak."

The last thing Missy expected was for her opponent to smile. "That's what I thought you said." Antianara jerked up the point of her sword, sending sand and dirt into Missy's eyes. There was a furious outcry from the sidelines as Missy fell back blinded. Antianara let out a victory roar and rushed the smaller girl, ready to kill.

Frantically, Missy thrust her sword up to ward off the strike she knew was coming. She felt the bite of cold steal slide down her sword and rake across her left forearm. A sticky, warm sensation erupted along with the searing pain as blood dripped down her fingers, making them slip on her sword. She quickly switched to her mutilated right hand and cursed her decision to taunt her stronger opponent. Missy was only thankful that she was just as good with her sword right-handed. Now she sensed more than just anger from Antianara. Murderous rage, the Amazon bloodlust, was directed at her. For the first time in two days, Missy felt the uncomfortable grip of fear. She back-peddled, putting distance between them, and tried to pry open her burning eyes.

"You can play Divine sovereign and you can pretend to be one of us all you want," Antianara goaded, "but you are nothing more than a mosquito to be swatted. I refuse to be under the thumb of a weakling like you. The Androktone pay homage to none." Missy swung her sword in the direction of the voice but struck nothing.

The whistle of her opponent's sword cut through the air behind her. There was no time to react. The last three weeks had awaken centuries of training in Missy but she still was not quick enough to lift her sword and block the deathblow Antianara was wielding while blind and injured.

Thousands of years of instinct took over. Missy dropped her sword and foolishly held up her hands to protect herself from the sharp blade as it flew down to cleave her in two. An explosion shook the yard, scattering Amazons and knocking them off of their feet. When the smoke cleared Antianara stood over Missy. She clung to her sword hilt but the blade was gone. Melted metal glistened on the ground around the two confused girls. Antianara threw down her ruined sword.

"You are a cheat!" she spit. "You used a godspell!"

Missy's heart pounded but not in fear. Power swelled within her, exhilarating and absolute, just as it had the day she arrived on the island. Nemesis was awake. "I am not the one who shamed myself," she said scathingly. "You've not only lost the fight, you have lost the respect of your tribe. I could demand a pound of flesh for your desperate cheating, but I will show you the mercy you refused to show me. Now, get out of my sight," Nemesis ordered. Antianara glared at the goddess she had provoked to the surface and at the angry faces of the rest of the Androktone.

Furious, the princess snarled. "Remember this day, goddess. You will regret what you have done. I will have vengeance." Antianara turned and stomped out of the training yard.

Nemesis smiled blindly and let Antianara leave. "And here I thought vengeance was my job." The fire in her was threatening to grow out of control. Missy could feel an insatiable power rising in her, and knew that it was Nemesis demanding to be set free. She could feel the flames in her hair running along her arms, dancing down her back, and taking over her fingers. She had never before realized how much power was there, just waiting to be tapped. All she had to do was dive into that inviting, pulsing, fire and she would be untouchable. She was Nemesis, the goddess of vengeance and retribution. She was justice. She was revenge.

"Goddess!" Hippolyta's voice sounded very far away. "Get control."

Lip curled, Nemesis glared blindly at Hippolyta. *Insignificant speck. How dare a human try to rein me in.* It would be easy to punish the Amazon for her arrogance. Too easy.

Something in the girl shuddered. It was too much power, too fast. Missy couldn't help but think of the way that everyone always reacted when they first met her. They despised her, distrusted her. Nemesis had been hated and reviled. The flames flickered and the power vied for her attention but Missy blanched and pushed it away. She didn't want to be that goddess again. She didn't want to be so despised. That wasn't who she was anymore. The fire made one last attempt to seduce her, but Missy's willpower crushed it back down. She was *not* Nemesis.

Hippolyta watched, a proud smile on her scarred face. With the threat to her safety gone, the goddess disappeared and left behind little more than an angry, hurt child. The Amazon queen approached slowly, the tip of her sword dragging in the dirt. "Very good, little warrior," she said solemnly. "I am glad to see that your active powers are gaining in strength. Perhaps you should try exercising some control?"

Missy accepted the canteen that Hippolyta pressed into her hands. After taking a sip, she dumped the rest into her eyes to wash away the dirt. The training yard came back into slow focus and Missy ducked her head, embarrassed. Amazons hung on the fence with awe on their faces. For a moment they had seen the goddess emerge that would one day be their patron. She was their future and she was fierce.

"There is no weapon more savage than the fire within," Hippolyta said. "Sadly Antianara still confuses the fire with an inferno. You must forgive her. As my daughter, she thinks she is entitled to be careless and stupid and when she's not throwing her weight around, she's throwing tantrums."

Missy scowled. Shutting down Nemesis had left her feeling weak and insubstantial. A moment ago she was sure that she could have taken on the entire Pantheon even dehydrated and blind. Now, she just felt... human. There was no strength in her mortal state, only the symptoms of her awful powers. She could feel Hippolyta's concern and admiration colored the nearby Amazons a rosy pink. The vision quickly ended, but inside Missy ached for just one more taste of that power. It stirred inside, more than willing to rush to the surface but Missy squelched it.

Hippolyta saw the look on Missy's face and could not imagine the struggle that the girl faced. "You will find balance," she whispered. The other Amazons were already leaving, back to their work and own training. "You will find someplace between who you were and who you are. Until then," the queen raised her sword and dropped back into a defensive stance, "back to practice." Missy groaned but grabbed her sword up from among the twisted, melted metal on the ground.

She and Hippolyta had barely begun their bout when a warning trumpet sounded. The Amazons immediately ran for their weapons, pointing into the sky. Following their gaze, Missy looked above the trees. Circling over the island was a blue-eyed angel with curling blonde hair.

"Oh, Cue, no." While Missy loved being among the Amazon, she had cut a single chit into her gauntlet every night since her arrival on Tir na n-Og. It kept track of the days that remained until she and Cethy could leave the island. Her marks were still far too few for Cupid's return but there he was, winging through the blue without a care in the world.

Missy ignored Hippolyta's order to stay put and ran off through the trees. The grace and speed she had been so envious of three weeks ago had been reawakened in her and she moved with all the speed she could muster to watch Cupid land.

Niamh stood beside her thrown, a frown on her face and Cethy at her side. A rush of relief washed over Missy at the sight of her friend. Cethy looked no worse for wear. In fact, Cethy seemed wonderful. She looked like the goddesses that were painted on the ancient Greek kraters, somehow taller, older, and wiser. She was even dressed like a goddess in the same green gossamer gown as Niamh. She was swathed in a haze of hostility, though. Missy's Empathy picked up on it from across the meadow as Cethy glared at winged god circling lower and lower.

The Androktone emerged from the trees with weapons in hand, arrows pointed at Cupid as his feet touched the ground in front of Niamh. She was incredulous, a small, furious spasm making her right eye tick. "You dare return?" she demanded coldly. "We free you and you make us regret our kindness."

"I don't break my word lightly," Cupid said shortly. "I've come to reclaim my goddesses. Wasting our time is no longer an option."

Niamh was furious. "Wasting your time? You impertinent child…"

"The Charonte are on the move," Cupid interrupted. "We are in very real danger of failing before we even begin. It is time to leave."

"Have they started the Circle?" Cethy asked. She had paled at Cupid's announcement, her fingers nervously twirling her short red locks. "Did they get something other than the water, I mean? Are we falling behind?" Cupid ignored Cethy and stared over her shoulder, wide eyed and open mouthed.

Missy approached the knoll slowly. She had not realized how she must have appeared after three weeks with the tribe and two solid days of combat. Toned and hard, she was covered in dirt, sweat, and blood, and dressed in the Amazon battle gear. Strips of pale blue leather covered only what needed to be covered, billowing around her legs in a serviceable skirt that ended at her knees. Her wild curls were pushed back with a blue scarf. Missy's wrists were protected by leather gauntlets, and the left one dangled off her wrist by a single strap and was bloodied after Antianara's attack. Daggers peeked out from where they were hidden in the folds of cloth on her hips, the small of her back, and in her bootstraps. She still clutched her sword in her hand and the tribe had even marked her with two permanent dark blue lines under her right eye to signify her position of power among them.

"I knew you would become one of them," Cupid sounded in awe but his lip curled as he looked over her. "Just another mindless killing machine." He turned to Cethy and Niamh in their matching robes and his eyes narrowed. "It's a good thing I didn't leave you here for the full month or you would have been completely integrated into this place." He turned and walked away, ignoring the armed Androktone who fell in step around him. "Get dressed, the both of you. We have real work to do."

Missy watched him go, a peculiar look on her face. Her vision flashed before her eyes, but nothing was there. The murky red cloud that had followed Cupid since their meeting was gone. No emotion came from him at all. Her senses were tingling, but it was her own confusion and fear that plagued her. Missy could no longer read Cupid. It wasn't like when she failed to read Erin. With Erin, Missy's Empathy had hit a wall, bounced off of a barrier that had kept her out for months. With Cupid, there was just a distinguishable lack of feeling. He was not hiding his feelings. He simply didn't have any.

"What are you waiting for?" Cupid had stopped only a few paces away and was glaring at Missy with obvious fury. Still Missy felt nothing. "Get out of those ridiculous clothes and try to remember what century it is." He left her standing there with Hippolyta, Niamh, and Cethy, all four of them scowling at his back.

—Chapter Sixteen—

Cethy was lacing up her shoes when Missy came tearing through Niamh's tree house in the throes of a temper tantrum. She was red faced and scowling and spouting off at the mouth and Cethy couldn't help but flinch. She'd gotten used to the quiet tranquility of Niamh and the Fountain. Exposure to Missy's explosive emotions again was nerve-racking.

"I hate him!" Missy shrieked. "I actually hate him! Did you see the way he looked at me? Like I was dirt! I wish I could get him in the training yard for two minutes. Just two minutes! That would shut him up."

Cethy smiled nervously and took control of the fuming girl. "It doesn't matter if you hate him or not. We need him to lead us to the next item in the Circle. Niamh was explaining to me what we're going to need and believe me, if we don't have a guide, we don't have a chance. Oh, Missy, this is right through the muscle!" An ugly gash stretched the length of Missy's left forearm, the worst of her remnants from her match with Antianara.

"Can't I pinch him or something?" Missy ignored her wound, too worked up to care. As ordered she was scrubbed and back in her T-shirt and jeans, but Missy still bore the Amazon ink on her face and the pale blue scarf to keep her curls back. Cethy could see the faint outline of two flat daggers strapped to Missy's back and a sword was sheathed in a plain scabbard attached to her belt. She may have changed back into her street clothes, but Missy was taking the Amazons with her.

She was taking a fair few new scars as well. Cethy shook her head while she wrapped Missy's arm with clean strips of gauzy fabric but declined comment on the multitude of bruises and half-healed injuries that riddled her cousin's pale body. "Cue is a jerk," Cethy said quietly. "And pinching him probably won't make things better between you two. There. How's that feel?"

Missy practiced using her arm and grimaced. "It feels like an elephant tried to cut my arm off."

A shadow fell over the pair and they both looked up to see Cupid standing in the doorway. His eyes were cold as he surveyed them. And lingered a moment on Missy's bandaged arm before he turned to Cethy. "What's the word on our water situation?"

Cethy regarded him frostily. Niamh had warned her not to treat him any differently because of her vision, but it was impossible to ignore what she had seen. Every time she saw Cupid, she saw Missy skewered by the very same arrows that hung off his back. She grit her teeth and answered Cupid in a dark tone. "Niamh wants Missy to go down to the spring before we leave."

"What are we just standing here for then?" Cupid gestured sharply toward the door but Cethy lightly put her hand on Missy's shoulder to keep her still.

"She didn't ask for you. What Niamh has to say is for Missy alone."

"I don't think so," Cupid snapped, glaring at Missy. "You see, Nemesis isn't trustworthy enough to do anything that concerns this quest alone. I'm not going to let her put you, myself, or this mission in danger, Cethy. It's for your own good."

Missy shook with anger, her hands balled into fists. "I can promise you that I'm not a danger to Cethy or the mission," Missy said, pointedly leaving him out.

Cupid silently took in the wild goddess. Her fierce expression. The daggers. The tribal marks under eye. Her hand gripped the sword on her hip and he growled, her threat perfectly understood. "You don't have a choice. You go with me, or you go home. Now, move. The sooner this is over, the sooner I can wash my hands of you."

"Excuse me, what is your problem?" Missy couldn't feel so much as a blip of annoyance from Cupid, but Cethy's distrust and fear came in loud and clear. Something was wrong with him and it was putting Missy on edge. "I haven't done anything to you and yet you seem to think you're completely justified in being as nasty and as miserable as possible."

With a derisive snort Cupid glared right back at the tiny goddess. "You were expecting hugs? Or high fives? Am I hurting your delicate feelings?" He took a step closer, his anger obvious despite the emotional black hole around him. Missy's golden eyes scrutinized him carefully, searching for any indication that her ability still worked on him but there was nothing. "What are you looking for, Nemesis?" His words hissed out in a hateful whisper.

Missy sighed and shoved her bangs back. "You're a love god, aren't you?," she demanded. Cethy had a biting grip on her shoulders to hold her back but there was no curbing Missy's tongue. "So where's the love, Cue?"

His expression might have been funny if Missy weren't fairly certain that he was about to throw her out the tree house window. Cupid seemed beyond words and for a long time the pair of them just glared daggers at one another. Finally, Cethy dragged the small goddess away. "Come on, Missy. Niamh is waiting." They left Cupid standing in the room and only Missy looked back. She expected to see him seething.

She didn't expect to see him watching her with a lost look in his icy eyes.

—Chapter Seventeen—

Indeed, Niamh was not amused when Cupid appeared on the knoll at Missy's side. "I asked for Nemesis to come alone." It was plain from her voice that she did not care for being disobeyed.

"Nemesis can't be trusted to do anything alone," Cupid retorted deftly.

Niamh's irritation was obvious but she held a hand out to guide Missy along beside her. "Come, Nemesis. We have much to talk about." The two deities followed the faerie through the meadow and into the woods. Niamh changed directions constantly to throw Cupid and Missy off course and while they walked, Niamh spoke to distract them further.

"The Fountain has many tempting qualities, Nemesis. It heals. It regenerates. It can show the past, present, and future. It can grant invincibility but that, as you know, comes with a price." The three entered the spring's clearing and Missy almost felt letdown. There was nothing significant about the pool in front of her. The water gurgled pleasantly and the surface reflected the trees above it. It was just a pond. Niamh sat by the water's edge, motioning for Missy to join her.

"Today you are going to leave this place to undertake a dangerous and difficult journey. You and Tyche have both grown close to the hearts of Tir na n-Og and we are not going to let you go off into battle without first offering all of the help we can."

"First, the water you were promised." Niamh reached into the stream and pulled out a jar filled with the crystal clear water. Missy moved to accept it, but Cupid slapped her hands out of the way. He took the jar from Niamh himself. Niamh glared angrily at the god. "If you want your goddesses to gain any power from this quest you have to at least let her touch it."

"I'll have Cethy touch it." Cupid argued, unwilling to bend even a little.

"It was not a request." Niamh's voice was dangerous. Missy wasn't sure what damage a fairy could do a god, but she imagined that Niamh was more than capable of dealing with the pompous bully.

Cupid scowled as Missy accepted the jar of water from him and she promptly dropped it into the grass. "Ow!" She shook out her hands, blushing furiously. They tingled painfully as though she had jammed a fork into an electrical outlet. "It shocked me!"

"And so the Rise begins," Niamh said, toneless. "May history not repeat itself."

Cupid picked the jar out of the grass. It was deceptively unimportant looking, just a jar of water, but he reverently tucked the jar into the black quiver that was slung over his back. Missy frowned. She could have sworn that Cupid's quiver and arrows had been white when he had left the island.

"Second, I have a small gift for Tyche, our goddess of luck and fortune." Niamh removed a silver chain from around her slim neck. A tiny amulet dangled from her finers, catching the light and sparkling. "This is a drop of water from the Fountain, frozen. It will never melt and will only grow cold to warn of danger. All Tyche need do is hold it to her eye to See." Missy accepted the necklace and carefully tucked it into her pocket. "If you would be so kind to remind her that the future is not yet written in stone. All things can be changed.

"Now for you, Nemesis," Niamh's smile was tense. Missy caught the fetid stench of distrust mixed with the soft sensation of hope and she sighed down at her feet. "In time you will have our trust, little goddess." The faerie put a hand on Missy's face and tipped her chin up so that she could look her more fully in the face. "In time you will prove yourself. I have seen it." She patted Missy's cheek while the girl beamed. "As for your gift from the Isle, Hippolyta wanted to send you off with all manner of loud, bloody weapons but I thought we could do better than that. Any idiot can kill, but it takes a great deal more to heal. I offer you a vial of the Fountain's water for your journey, so long as you understand that it comes with a condition attached."

Missy perked up. Condition or not, water from the pool meant that she could heal herself or her friends if they were injured. On such a dangerous journey, injury was more than likely. Anything that could help her and Cethy on their way would be appreciated. "What's the condition?"

Niamh pressed her lips together and raised an eyebrow at Cupid. He still hovered behind Missy, his focus eerily intent. "You have what you came for, love god, now stand back. This is for Nemesis and Nemesis alone." She stared him down, emerald eyes glittering until Cupid begrudgingly moved to the other side of the clearing, glaring daggers as he went. "Good, god."

Niamh waited for him to get out of ear shot. The faerie queen was wrapped in a sense of urgency and she faced Missy, her expression stern. "It is very important that you listen to what I am about to say. A drop of this water can heal any injury or illness. It's powerful enough to even pull a soul back from Erebus itself," Niamh whispered. "But the condition, Nemesis, is that you can never use the water on the Divine. That means Tyche, Cupid, or any other deity you come across. No matter the wound, even if it is fatal, you are forbidden to use it to heal a god. That includes yourself."

Missy's face crunched up in confusion. She wasn't so good with the roundabout way the gods spoke. Cethy was better with their riddles and lofty grammar. Missy was the muscle, not the brain. "So what good is it if I can't even use it?"

"Do you think the gods are the only ones you're going to meet on this quest of yours? There are more beings in the Three Realms than just self-serving deities." Her wings fluttered in annoyance. "Or didn't you notice I'm a faerie?"

Missy smirked. "It'd be hard *not* to notice," she answered. She received a yank on one of her curls and Niamh held up a scolding finger.

"There is not time for your sense of humor. Do you accept the condition as I have explained it to you?

There was no need to ask again. Missy held her hand out. Condition or no condition she wasn't about to turn away anything that would help Cethy along on her quest. "I'll take it," Missy said assuredly. "And thank you."

Niamh nodded solemnly and handed her a small stone beaker stoppered with a black cork. It looked so incredibly *un*remarkable but inside the slate vial was something that was so much more than just plain water. "Remember," Niamh warned, "it's not meant to be used on a god."

Missy carefully tucked it into her front pocket. "Out of curiosity what would happen?" she asked. "If I used the water to heal myself or I used it to heal Cethy or whoever, what would happen?"

Niamh leveled a severe look at the small goddess. "I will tell you this only once so listen well. If you choose to heal a god, of course the power of the spring will work. The wound will be healed and the victim will recover fully but the cost to you will be staggering. Every Divine injury you heal will be at *your* expense. *You* will suffer their pain, their wounds, and ultimately their fate. You will bear it all."

"Wait." Missy struggled to make sense of it. "Are you saying that if a god gets hurt and I try to fix them, I get hurt instead? What if I just use the water on myself?"

"I strongly suggest that you don't," Niamh cautioned. "You are the bearer, Nemesis. The healer cannot be healed. You would lose your immortality, your powers. Touch that water and you will cease to be an Olympian goddess. From this point on those are the rules. Are you certain that you still accept?"

Missy dragged in a determined breath. So she couldn't use any Fountain water on herself or her buddies. That would be easy enough. It was sure to come in handy anyway. "I'm certain."

With a nod, Niamh patted Missy's head. "Just one more thing," the guardian whispered. "You may tell no one. It may not seem like it now but this is going to be a difficult secret for you to keep. Your companions will want to know why you do not help the dying or the dead. They will not understand why you watch others suffer and do nothing to ease the pain around you. They will call you cruel and hateful, but you must not tell them about the water's conditions. If you do the enchantment will spoil and all you will have is a beaker filled with saltwater. Do you understand?"

Missy had to wonder if Niamh had chosen her ridiculous rules and stipulations specifically to drive her crazy. To have the power to help and be unable to use it was frustrating. To not be able to explain herself was even worse. "I understand," she said, "but I hope you understand, too. If it comes down to my power, my life, or Cethy's…" she squared off her shoulders and lifted her chin. "I may not be a Norn but I promised to protect her. That's why I'm here."

She thought Niamh was going to say something biting or insulting as she was wont to do, but the faerie was quiet. "Long ago, I knew Nemesis." She seemed unable to look at the sixteen year old, her eyes glued to the surface of the Fountain. "I never cared for her much. She was cruel and cold. She claimed to act for the greater good but there was a hatred in her that was nearly impossible to curb. She would have hated you, that is for certain."

With a snort Missy played with the blue scarf that restrained her cascade of curls. "Aren't she and I the same?"

Niamh smiled kindly. "No. No, you are not." She finally tore her attention from the enchanted spring and nudged Missy back toward Cupid. "Go on. It's time to make your goodbyes to Tir na n-Og. Your quest is about to truly begin."

—Chapter Eighteen—

Cethy dangled the tiny chip of ice and from her fingers and watched it shine in the candlelight. Even when the amulet was not against her eye Cethy could see movement in its frosty depths. Colors swirled and skidded at its core, constant and ever-changing. A sudden blaze of blue and a flash of black made Cethy's heart jump up into her throat. She had no doubt what scene was playing within the ice. She Saw it replay every time she closed her eyes. Each time Missy's body jerked as the arrows hit home with stomach churning thuds, her golden eyes glossed over and dimmed as death took her.

With a panicked yelp Cethy slammed the amulet down onto the table. Everyone stopped what they were doing to stare at her, their faces a mix of annoyance and pity. Hippolyta sat at the head of the table and shook her head before she went back to her maps and lists. The heads of the tribe had been called to the meeting table to discuss their next move. Cupid had mentioned the Charonte and the Androktone weren't taking any chances.

They were in war council.

"What did Niamh mean, Cethy?" Missy stood behind the redhead's chair, finely tuned to Cethy's stress and trying in vain to soothe it. Out of boredom Missy absently threw her daggers into the air and caught them again before they hit the ground. That was doing very little to relax the luck goddess. "'The future is not yet written in stone. All things can be changed.' That's heavy."

Cethy looked away from her and buried her head in her arms. "She's just reminding me of something that I have to fix."

"Let me know if I can help." Missy offered brightly. She caught a dagger smoothly behind her back and another under her leg. "I don't mind."

"And I don't want to talk about it," Cethy muttered.

"Good, because isn't really time to talk anyway." Cupid tripped over his own wings as he tried to sit down. He'd spent the last several hours getting underfoot, barking at his two charges, and generally being moody but so far nothing he said had convinced Cethy and Missy to split before the war council had reached a decision. He'd only succeeded in annoying everyone. "We shouldn't be sitting around. The Charonte have already joined together and you are still two members down, Cet– Will you knock that off? You are going to put someone's eye out."

Missy caught both daggers and quickly sheathed them back inside her sleeves. "Aren't you and I filling in for the missing Norns, Cue? That's what Dionysus said. We're the place holders until the other two Norns *'reveal themselves'*." She wiggled her fingers in an attempt to look mystic but quickly broke into a grin. "Are we really getting our inside information from an Oracle? That's so cool."

"Yes, it's fascinating," Cupid grumbled. "But we're not going to be as useful as the actual Norns would be. Remember, there are rules to this quest. If Cethy is going to gain the Moirai and hold them, we have to follow the rules."

"Why don't you tell us what the rules are," Cethy said coldly, eyeing Cupid with twitchy hostility, "instead of just complaining that we've broken them?"

Cupid crossed his arms. "The Norns are responsible for weaving the enchantment that binds the Fates. Yes, the ten items for the Circle are important, but who gathers them is just as significant. The bond between the Norns is powerful enough to contain Fate itself. It is outside of destiny, outside of the Moirais' reach. It cannot be tampered with or broken... or substituted. If the right three are not found, the enchantment will not be strong enough to hold the Fates in check."

Missy whistled. "How do you know that you and I *aren't* Cethy's other Norns?"

"Because the Norns can't all be from the same Divine Line. We," Cupid gestured between himself and the girls, "Are all of the Greek Pantheon. The last time this Circle was built there was a Greek, a Celtic, and a Nordic god. It will likely be the same this time. Until the rightful Norns are found, Cethy is at a very real disadvantage. She won't gain nearly the amount of power she should until the proper two come out of hiding and take their rightful place at her side."

Cethy rolled her eyes. "We're always at a disadvantage. I'm used to it by now. What's the big deal?"

Hippolyta slammed her fist down on the table where she sat with other members of the Androktone war council. "The big deal is that we have discovered who the Charonte are, and your mission just became that much harder. You have three very nasty goddesses working against you. Hel and Bave will stop at nothing to secure the Fates and thanks to your friend Eris, they have an unlimited supply of information about you."

Missy quickly took a seat. "What's Erin got to do with it?"

The Amazons all looked to Cupid. "She's one of them. Eris is a Charonte."

Missy sighed and rested her forehead against the table. "Of course she is. And who are Hel and Bave?"

"Hel is a Norse underworld goddess. Bave is one of the Celtic battle goddesses." Hippolyta turned to Cupid, anger in her eyes. "Loki has something to do with this, see if he doesn't. His own daughter is leading the Charonte."

Cupid nodded, looking stiffer than usual. "This is very, very, bad."

"What does Loki have to do with this?" Cethy asked.

"And more importantly, who is he?" Missy added.

Hippolyta was incredulous. "How do you not know of Loki?" the Amazon queen queried. "He was a trickster god of the North. For the most part he was a harmless prankster until he murdered another god and was sentenced to an eternity of imprisonment. Even now he is laid out on a table, bound and chained, with the Midgard Serpent's venom falling onto his face. There he will stay until the end of the world when the Fates weave him free."

"Oh," said Missy. "You guys don't fool around with punishments do you?"

"So what we have here is an underworld goddess, the goddess of war, and the goddess of discord all working against us," said Cethy thoughtfully. "Great."

"I'm not so sure that this is bad as you think," Missy said. "This Loki is chained to a table and not our problem as of yet. Cethy and I can handle Erin and I don't think that the other two would have the same kind of fire power under their belts. What possible punch can Bave possibly throw at us? She can't do anything to me that the Androktone haven't done already."

Hippolyta had her head in her hands. "No one can fight like Bave can. She's a Celtic war goddess, Nemesis. She lives for blood. Is that enough of a punch for you?" Missy fell silent.

"What about Hel?" Cethy asked.

Cupid let out a heavy sigh. "She has only the most basic powers left from the Fall. For now she can only move through space and briefly stop mortal time. But once she starts gaining power, we have to worry. Hel has complete dominion over the dead. If we are fighting against her, we are fighting against the entire underworld."

"Oh, snap." Missy's mouth was open. "I'm sorry but aren't there other underworld rulers who could stop her? Who was that guy on that lives down there? Hades?"

"He's missing," Cupid answered immediately. "And has been since the Fall. He was the next to disappear after you."

"Is there any chance we could have support from that end?" Hippolyta asked. "Are there any in the underworld who might want to help keep Erebus where it belongs?"

"It doesn't seem likely," Cupid said. "If the Charonte succeed and take the Fates, Erebus will consume the other realms. The underworlders would love that extra room. They won't help."

"So then let's do something about it." Missy jumped out of her seat, a resolute expression on her face. "Let's stop talking and start doing. You're wasting time just telling us that we are going to fail. Let's get this Circle made so that we don't have to worry about Erebus or the end of the world. No more messing around, let's just do this."

Cethy got to her feet behind her friend. "Let's do it," she agreed.

Hippolyta frowned. "But you don't know what you are up against. There are powers at play that you don't understand yet."

"Most gods were weakened after the Fall," Missy pointed out. "Why not try to get as far as we can before we have to worry about their powers returning. Maybe by then our powers will be strong enough that we will be able to stand our ground. Let's do what we can before we are forced to fight."

"You want to just move on?" Cupid said. "If you get into a confrontation with the Charonte you will lose, make no mistake about that. You aren't a full set of Norns yet."

"We aren't collectables, Cue," Cethy said. "And we'll be ok."

"Prometheus is looking for the last two Norns, isn't he? Come on, Cue, we can't do anything more from here," Missy pointed out. "It's time to take what we've learned and make the Circle. Let's accomplish all we can before it comes to war."

A small smile appeared on Hippolyta's face. "Well spoken. When you are ready to fight, the Androktone will be behind you." She clutched Missy's forearm in a sign of kinship and the small girl returned the gesture. Hippolyta had noticed that Missy had darkened the tribal marks under her eye, and the small gesture meant much to the ferocious queen. "We take care of our own."

"Well, Cue?" Cethy turned to the winged god. "Where to next?"

Cupid cleared his throat. "We go after the Aegis," he said. "It's time to get Athena's shield."

—Chapter Nineteen—

"Try again."

"I've *been* trying again. It isn't working." Crossly, Cethy dropped Missy and Cupid's hands. "Never in my life have I ever shown even the slightest inclination for teleporting. You can't just expect me to do it now." The small group stood on the same cliffs where the Androktone had captured them three weeks ago. They had said their goodbyes to the Amazons, though out of the corner of her eye Missy could see a few hidden in the trees and brush, watching the botched departure. No doubt they were betting on how long before Cupid lost his patience and just left them there.

"I'm not interested in your excuses, Cethy," Cupid said through gritted teeth. "Don't tell me why you can't. Prove to me you can."

Missy growled. "What's gotten into you?" It was true that the god had never had a kind word for her, but he had always treated Cethy with a small amount of condescending respect. Now he seemed equally disgusted with them both. "You can't goad her into doing it."

"I don't think that either of you understand that you need to be working at full capacity before you get near the Charonte," Cupid said angrily. "Cethy, you need to be able to bend and actively use your luck. Not to mention working on your telekinesis. Nemesis," Cupid snarled at Missy impatiently. "I am tired of your temper tantrum pyrotechnics. I want to hear a little less talking and see a little more magic. You are supposed to do more than just feel others. You are supposed to sway their choices, act as a conscience. You should be able to change your shape. If you don't get a grip on your magic by the end of the week, so help me I'll..."

"You'll what?" Cethy snapped. Her eyes were on the quiver of black arrows that were slung over Cupid's shoulder. The Sight played in her memory showing

Missy falling over and over, impaled by those very arrows.

Cupid's eyes narrowed. "I remember when you were the quiet one," he said snidely.

"I can change my shape?" Missy asked. The enthusiasm in her voice was unmistakable. "Forget bending, teach me how to do that!"

"One disaster at a time, please." Cupid said impatiently. "Now try again."

"It's alright, Cethy." Missy took her friend's hand and gave it a squeeze. "You can do this." She looked at Cupid. "Is there anything I can do to help?"

"You can be silent." Cupid took one of Cethy's hands. He refused to touch Missy and stood as far from her as he could without walking clean off the cliff. "Clear your head, Cethy. Think about what you need and why it's important. Focus on Athena's shield. Focus on what we need. This is what your gift does. You should be able to find it just like you find anything else."

"I feel stupid standing here chanting 'shield' again and again in my head." Cethy complained.

"I know." Missy agreed. "I almost feel like you should click your heels together three times and say 'there's no place like the Aegis.'"

Cethy choked back her giggles and tried to keep a straight face. "Alright." She emptied her mind and focused on everything Cupid had told her about Athena's shield. According to legend the shield was made of bronze, inlaid with gold with a horrible figure painted at its center. Nothing could penetrate it. The mere sight of it froze people in their tracks. Cethy put all of her will in that image and wished herself to be with it.

Cethy had forgotten about Missy's aversion to bending until the split second before Missy gasped and pulled away from her. Cethy and Cupid both made a grab for the sixteen year old, but Missy and the rest of Tir na n-Og faded away. The two appeared on a rock surrounded by a harem of seals. As far as the eye could see in every direction was water. Cethy had brought them to the middle of the Atlantic Ocean.

Cupid was furious. "Go back and get her. Go back and get her, *now*!" he demanded.

"I don't know how to go back and get her!" Cethy snapped. "And stop yelling." Cupid's shouts were upsetting the seals that were sunning themselves in the early light. Cethy's skin prickled. She looked closer... Those were not seals. They weren't animals at all.

"I told you that she would betray us!" Cupid railed, oblivious to Cethy's appalling discovery. "She let go so that she could run off to the Charonte and tell them about the Aegis. And on top of that, you dropped us in the middle of the ocean. I hate water. I hate it!" Cethy could not find her voice so she just pointed at the unnatural creatures that surrounded them with a shaking hand. "What?" Cupid finally caught sight of the monsters. Sleek seal bodies mixed with humanoid faces and arms that ended with webbed hands. "Oh. Selkie."

Cethy was at a loss. "Selkie?"

"They are water dwellers like mermaids or sirens. They can control weather and are harmless for the most part," Cupid said anxiously. "And don't change the subject. Get us out of here."

"I don't know how!" It was practically a whine. Cethy didn't want to be stuck on a rock in the middle of nowhere any more than Cupid did. She just wanted to go home. Believing that she could do this had been a mistake. Cethy wasn't the adventurous type. She'd done nothing but mess things up since she'd agreed to find the Fates. She'd been knocked unconscious by

Anubis and if it hadn't been for Missy and Cupid the quest would have ended right in the Mayan. Cupid had saved them both and Missy had convinced Niamh to trade with them while Cethy had gotten herself thrown into a prison pit. Now Cethy was lost somewhere in the Atlantic Ocean with a deity that she didn't trust and without her trusty best friend to bail her out.

Somehow she had botched it again.

"What are they doing? Why are they getting closer?" Her voice came out as a squeak as the selkie all shifted to get a better look at the two intruders. They blinked their massive, liquid eyes, intelligent and far from friendly.

Cupid shrugged. "They are probably just curious. Don't worry about them. You just proved that you can bend space. Now do it again!" He gripped Cethy's shirt collar and shook the girl savagely. "Get us out of here!"

"Tressssspasssserssss." A creature crept close enough to reach out a webbed hand and grab Cethy's ankle.

"Let go." Cethy howled. She was not sure who she wanted to escape first, the crazed god or the water monster. She struggled to get away from Cupid but his grip at her collar was unshakable. She flailed, kicking and shrieking, and her heel caught the selkie attached to her ankle full in the face. It let out a shrill noise like a porpoise and jumped from the rock. The rest of the selkie echoed its cry and abandoned the rock for the ocean. Startled, Cupid released Cethy and stumbled back. He came dangerously close to falling into the water but scrambled away from the ledge as though it were acid instead of salt water.

"You will pay, tressspasssersssss," the injured selkie called from the water. "We will have revenge for thissss!" It sank beneath the waves and vanished. Cethy shivered.

"Great." Cethy said morosely. How quickly things changed. A moment ago she was in a friendly, albeit strange, place, with her best friend at her side and a journey ahead of her. Now both were likely in danger. How could Missy have left her like that? What if Cupid was right and her cousin really was off with Erin, laughing at how stupid and gullible Cethy had been? Cethy collapsed onto the rock. "What are we doing here, Cue?"

Cupid was fit to panic. "How am I supposed to know? We should be within grabbing distance of the Aegis," he said. "I told you to bend to the shield. All you had to do was close your eyes and think about the thing. This should have been easy. As easy as bending a pipe cleaner."

Cethy shivered. Why was she suddenly so cold? "Next time you can do the bending yourself," she told Cupid. "I am done with all of this crazy traveling. I'll stick to the Parkway. Or better yet, I'll just stay home!"

"I'm not so sure there's going to be a next time." Cupid groaned and pointed over Cethy's shoulder.

Cethy spun around and cried out. A wall of water rushed towards them. The selkie rode the giant wave, screaming and jeering at the two trapped deities. Cethy shivered again, her breath frozen clouds in the warm air. With apprehension Cethy reached into her shirt and pulled out the amulet. It was softly glowing green and leaving little traces of frost where it touched her skin. Missy had given her Niamh's message. *It will only grow cold to warn of danger.*

At least she knew that it worked.

The wall of water drew closer. "Cue, what do we do?" Cethy demanded.

Cupid mumbled to himself. "Nope. No. I did not agree to die for this." He paced frantically on the rock. "If I lose their luck they will be furious with me...but I can't...I can't."

"Cue, we need to do something!" Cethy insisted. "This is not the time for you to have a meltdown!"

Cupid stopped pacing, his eyes crazy and his wings quaking. He looked at Cethy, weighing his options. "Perhaps it is better this way." He opened his wings and took flight.

"What are you doing?" Cethy was dumbfounded. She lunged at the god to try and keep him grounded but she only succeeded in ripping his quiver from his back. "You can't leave me here!"

Cupid hovered for a moment. "Look at me. I am all wings. If these things get wet, I will sink like a rock. I am not about to die for you."

"Don't leave me here," Cethy pleaded.

Cupid watched the wave draw closer. He shuddered violently and almost fell out of the sky. "Anything but water. I cannot be around water." He climbed into the air to gain height on the wave.

"Die, tresssspasssser!" Cethy faced the wave as it came. She cast one last furious glance at the speck circling overhead. If she survived this, she was going to kill Cupid. Foolishly, she took a breath and braced herself as the mountain of water hit the rock.

As quickly as it came, the wave was gone, swallowed back into the ocean. The rock had been swept clean, not a mark left on it. One sulking seal person returned to its sunbathing. It held a handful of seaweed over his face to staunch the flow of muddy brown blood that was coming from his nose. It leaned back and caught sight of Cupid flying overhead.

"Losssst your tiny harem, flyer!" The selkie yelled. "She's with Poseidon now."

—Chapter Twenty—

Cethy was lost in a world of blue and green. Waves lined with white foam swallowed her, tossing and spinning her like a rag doll in a washing machine. Her lungs demanded oxygen, but Cethy denied her body the air it craved. She felt her limbs grow heavy as she frantically tried to break the surface. The longer she held her breath, the heavier her arms and legs became. Little yellow and orange dots exploded in her vision and clashed with the blue-green vastness of the ocean. Cethy's chest was worse than on fire. Her heart was trying to pound its way clean out of her body.

Cethy desperately kicked her feet and tried to follow her last escaping air bubbles upward, but she wasn't making any progress. The surface stayed beyond her reach. How far down did the wave push her? Cethy's thoughts became nonsensical as her brain suffered the lack of oxygen.

"Tyche."

The ice chip had come out from under her shirt and floated on the leather thong around her neck. Cethy was looking straight through it.

"Tyche."

Images spun in the heart of the ice. Cethy's limbs stilled as she focused on the pictures filling the water around her as the amulet's power seeped into the ocean itself.

Salt water burned Cethy's eyes, but she could not look away nor could her mind make sense of what she was Seeing. It was that cursed hilltop. Metal clashed and sparked, and war cries filled the air. Over the screams and clatter of weapons, Cethy heard a familiar voice. "Tyche, Stop!"

Missy appeared running up the hill dressed in blue with that strange silver tattoo wrapped around her arm. A sword gleamed in her hand bloody and deadly. The giant wolf appeared, snarling and slobbering, just like he had in the first vision. Missy brandished her blade, prepared to face the monster, but she stopped, her eyes wide. The sword dropped from her hand. Clenching her stomach, Missy fell onto the muddy hummock, two arrows piercing her body. The life drained from her eyes as Cupid landed beside Missy in a storm of feathers, his bow in hand.

Cethy had Seen all of this before and she could not understand why she was Seeing it again, now of all times. She expected the vision to end with Cupid's arrival like it had before, but the horror continued.

Cupid bent over and roughly ripped the arrows out of Missy's still body. He grinned madly as he snatched the sword out of the mud. Cupid looked into the air and waved the sword triumphantly. "It's done!" Cupid yelled into the thick of the battle. "I have the sword!"

A shadow passed over the hill and Cupid flinched. "You're too late!" he shrieked into the air. "You're too late! She's not coming back this time!" He awkwardly brandished the stolen sword at his unseen tormentor, his face a snarl.

In a flurry of feathers, a blonde haired boy dropped out of the sky and knocked Cupid off his feet. When the feathers settled, Cethy was stunned. The appearance of this second angel baffled her. There were two Cupids, identical in countenance and fury. One was on his back in the mud sniveling and grasping for the arrows that had spilt from his quiver. The other grabbed Missy frantically and tried to slow the blood that pumped steadily from her torso.

The Cupid that held Missy keened, the sound one of despair and sorrow. Desperately he tried to wipe the mud and gore from the girl's lifeless face. He cradled the slaughtered goddess in his arms, his expression terrible. The murderous Cupid scrambled away, a handful of black arrows in one hand and Missy's sword in the other. He took to the air, laughing wildly as he vanished along with the rest of the vision.

Cethy was bewildered. Two Cupids? It was not possible. She had no time to process this new information before the tiny black spots completely enveloped her. She could not breathe. She could not get to the surface. She was so tired, so disconnected from the pain in her lungs, it no longer mattered. Cethy closed her eyes and let the ocean take her.

She was not alone in the water. Poseidon had waited for Cethy to stop struggling before he approached her. There was only so much a god could do when he no longer had form. His body had vanished in the Fall, forcing him to become one with the element he had once dominated. As the girl grew still, Poseidon cradled her in his watery embrace and pulled her further into his kingdom beneath the waves. There was much that the young goddess might be useful for.

—Chapter Twenty-One—

Pain course through her body and Missy yanked her hand away from Cethy. Just like back in Dionysus' dorm room, the sky, the trees, and the cliffs of the Valhallan Isle disintegrated around her. New surroundings took their place but the complex beauty of the bend was lost on Missy. She found herself bent over on a congested sidewalk, gasping for breath and wiping her watering eyes. No one seemed to notice or care that a teenaged girl with a sword had just materialized out of nowhere.

"Cethy! Could you have possibly made that any more painful?" When no one answered, Missy straightened up. Cethy and Cue were nowhere in sight. She was alone.

"Move it, kid." A man pushed past Missy and sent her sprawling onto the sidewalk. Missy made no motion to get up. She stared dazedly up into the overly bright sky and caught sight of a street sign overhead.

"Santa Monica Boulevard?" Missy got slowly to her feet, golden-brown eyes large with surprise. Quickly, she ducked into an alleyway and beat the gravel off of her already filthy pants. "What am I doing in Los Angeles?" she asked the garbage in the alley.

"That is an excellent question."

She spun around, hand on her sword. Missy had just enough time to see the middle aged woman that stood between her and escape before she was caught by the throat and hoisted into the air. Missy's back was slammed into the alley wall and there she hung, pinned. The people who walked past hurriedly averted their gaze so as not to be drawn into the altercation.

"What are you doing here, Nemesis?" The woman held her against the wall effortlessly. She had a pretty face that was ruined by the sour expression she wore. Her black hair was pulled back into a tight bun and her gray business suit was not at all flattering. Dark sun glasses hid her eyes. She looked mortal. Her strength implied that she was not. "What are you doing here?" the woman repeated.

"Asphyxiating." Missy gasped.

The woman pulled back and slammed Missy back against the wall a second time cracking the brick in the process.

"I am not playing games, cousin," she warned. "If you are here to cause trouble I will banish you again, damn the consequences!"

"It was an accident." Missy tried to remember how many times she had been brained in the past month. If the concussions did not stop soon, she was looking at a future with absolutely no short term memory and the notion was not an appealing one. "We were bending and it hurt. I let go. I don't know how I wound up here." Missy choked out past the hand clamped around her neck. "Who are you?"

The woman slid her sunglasses down her nose and glared at Missy with violent purple eyes. After a moment she released her grip on Missy's throat and the girl dropped back down to the sidewalk. "I'm just one more who lost everything in the Fall," the woman said callously.

Somehow, Missy knew. The name appeared in her mind, a hazy memory that felt like something out of a dream. "Hera." There was no doubt that she was speaking to the former queen of Olympus. Missy rubbed her throat. "I guess you already know who I am," she croaked. "No introduction necessary there." For the second time that day, Missy's vision failed her. Nothing came from the goddess. Not so much as an iota of color or sensation. Missy frowned, worried. It seemed that when she did not want her power to work, it charged through her in overdrive. Now nothing seemed to work properly. "Do you attack every god you meet, or am I special?"

Hera smiled, but there was no warmth in it. "Trust me. You're special." She glanced up and down the street. "Walk with me, Nemesis. Maybe we can figure out what you are doing here."

Missy felt Hera's grip on her arm and the sixteen year old was quickly lead down the sidewalk and away from the dark alley. "Where are we going?" Missy was not afraid, but she felt a certain amount of foreboding. Hera had lost everything as a direct result of something Missy had done. There were sure to be bad feelings. Feelings that, for one reason or another, Missy could not sense.

Hera pulled Missy onto West Fifth Street. "We are going to the library."

"The library?" Missy was incredulous. "But I need to get back to my friend." She paused, "My cousin needs me."

"Our cousin," Hera corrected. "Which one? Hermes? Artimas? Aphrodite? Ares?"

Missy tried to wrap her mind around the fact that these legends were a part of her family tree. "Cethy. Or Tyche, I guess. She needs me. I have to get back."

Hera paused, frowning. "So he found the luck goddess," she mumbled. "Good boy, Prometheus."

Missy pulled her arm from Hera's grip. "You know, don't you?" she demanded. "You know what we're doing."

Hera laughed coldly. "Darling, everyone knows what you are doing. Just not everyone knows that it's *you* doing it. Now, come inside where we can talk safely." Missy looked up at the magnificent white building they were standing in front of.

"This is a library?" Missy was astonished. "All we had at home was a bookmobile."

Hera shook her head. "This is more than just a library." She looked disappointed in Missy. "Honestly, Nemesis, Cupid made you sound intelligent."

"Cue was here?" Hope rose in Missy's chest. If Cupid had been here before, he might return and find her. He could take her back to Cethy. Her hope turned to confusion and then disbelief. "He said I was smart? That doesn't sound like him."

"Smart-ish. Honestly, Cupid thinks too highly of you, especially after everything you've done to him. You are just a blundering idiot with a sword and you should be treated as such. Not some dainty princess that needs protection," Hera said dryly. Missy could not imagine that anyone would think less of her than Cupid did, but she had been mistaken. Obviously the usurped queen of Olympus had no love for her either. Hera took Missy's arm in her vice grip and pulled her through the doors to the library. "Welcome to the Hub."

The Hub might have seemed like just a normal library to the dozens of mortals who moved in and out of the doors but Missy suspected that the ankle high gnomes that darted across the floor unseen by the people checking out books were slightly out of place. Missy's jaw dropped. "Are those…"

"Irritating." Hera supplied. "But necessary. The gnomes are mine and report directly to me. They run messages and notices for me. Imagine, once I was queen of the gods and now I'm queen of the lawn ornaments." Hera scowled and Missy hid the smile that was threatening to appear.

"What is this place, really?" Missy asked. "It's not just a library. I can feel it."

"Maybe she is smart." She knew that voice, as if from a past life or a dream. Both, she knew, were possible. A young man, hardly older than she was, emerged from the non-fiction section carrying an armful of books. A gnome had hold of his pant leg dragging him forward toward the two women.

"Hello, sister." He was handsome, dressed in a grey suit and black tie. Black leather gloves covered his hands. His hair was a little on the shaggy side, and his eyes were the same golden brown as Missy's. There was something in their depths, however, that Missy had yet to acquire. There was an ancient danger there, waiting beneath their warmth and his charming smile.

"Thanatos," Missy whispered. The name came to her lips unbidden. "I know you."

The teenager closed his book and nudged the gnome away with his foot. "Good. We weren't holding onto much hope that you had any memory at all. The theory is that you were worst affected by the Fall. No memory. No magic. Apparently, you got off easier than we thought."

"Cupid said she had no memory," Hera said as the two siblings stared at each other. One calm and curious. One confused and captivated. "Thanatos, be careful! That's the third gnome this week!" Hera pointed to the man's feet where the tiny creature had suddenly clutched its heart and fallen over dead.

"Occupational hazard," Thanatos said lightly to Missy, not taking his eyes off of her. "Hence the gloves. Don't want to touch anything by accident."

"And your occupation is?" Missy asked. Her throat had gone dry.

"Death." His smile was lazy, his eyes half shut. "You were right, by the way. This is more than just a library." Missy stiffened as he carefully put his arm around her and led her into the stacks. "This is the Olympian Hub. A safe place for those of our Divine Line to come and collect themselves and their memories. The more gods that surface the more information and memories are available. We have agents all over the world who nudge possible Olympians in our direction."

"You bring them home," Missy whispered. She reached out and caressed the book laden shelves. Missy turned to Hera. "If you want the gods to come here, why did you try to put my head through a wall when you saw me on the Boulevard?"

Hera busied herself with straightening her jacket. "Cupid was here a few weeks ago. He told us that you were traveling with a Norn and might decide to betray her before too long. If you came here alone, I was to detain you. It was nothing personal. It was only business." Her voice was empty of remorse or guilt for having almost cracked Missy's head open. That wasn't what prompted the hurt look on Missy's face. Cupid had been so sure that she would turn that he had left explicit instructions to confine her if she did show up in Los Angeles.

"We've been trying to keep track of the resurfaced gods," Thanatos continued on, throwing a warning look at Hera over Missy's head. "If they come through here, we teach them, give them time to relearn their past if necessary. Then we know where they are and what they are up to. At least," he added pointedly, "most of the gods are welcome. Hera's been very selective. I'm lucky she lets me stay here."

"Wait." Missy pulled away from Thanatos. "You are using the Hub to keep track of us? What for?"

Thanatos rolled his eyes. "It is not what you think," he said, sounding as if he had explained this a hundred times before. "The Hub is for our own protection. Here we can keep weakened gods safe. There are things happening out there that we are trying to prevent."

"Thanatos." Hera's violet eyes glowed as she glared at the death god. "I suggest that you don't... overwhelm the girl."

"Do you know who this is?" Thanatos asked. "She's protecting a Norn, Hera. An acting champion. I suggest that you don't forget it." Hera obviously did not like to be threatened. Missy felt her power drain from her body and paled, suddenly substantially weaker. She could see it, black and glittering in the air around Hera. She sighed with envy. That would be an amazing ability to have.

Thanatos ignored the charged feeling in the air though he looked a bit wobbly himself. "The Charonte have found a way to kill the gods and I think that Nemesis has a right to know. She's the one that has to face them. We both know that Tyche is no fighter."

Hera glared for a moment and then shrugged. The tension in the room broke as Hera released their power. Her violet eyes were emotionless. "If you really believe that she is acting as the Norns' Champion, then by all means, fill her in. I just don't want to hear your complaints when she betrays us and helps the Charonte rid the entire Mortal Realm of us."

Missy stared at Thanatos, her golden eyes filled with alarm. "Kill the gods?" she asked, her voice barely a whisper. "They can kill us?"

Thanatos's face was somber. "It has been going on for months, possibly years, and it is only now coming to our attention. I have been working to try and find some reason for this madness, but I am no closer to discovering how the Charonte are doing this." He paused. "You know about the Charonte?"

Missy nodded. "Cue told us. He never mentioned that they could kill us, though. He said we were immortal." That was not completely true, though. He had warned her and Cethy before they ever left Ithaca. *"Don't take any unnecessary risks,"* he had said. *"Especially against the Charonte."* He had known then that they could die, but had kept it from them. Was he trying to protect them or was it purposely omitted to endanger them?

"Times are different now," Thanatos said gently. "Our immortality is no longer the weapon it once was. The Charonte have found a way around it." He gestured for Missy to follow him and she did so automatically, hardly paying attention. "The Charonte are evil. They are Harvesting power and immortality from the gods somehow. Aside from a few frightened nymphs and the odd centaur, all who were Harvested were found dead. Already we have found Athena, Apollo, and our own brother, Hypnos. All were drained of their Divine essence and killed. Who knows how many others are out there that we haven't found yet?"

"But why?" Missy asked. "Why take their powers? Why kill them?"

Thanatos sighed. "I don't know. That is what is so frustrating. And now that they are gone there is no way to bring them back. Once a god is killed he drops into Erebus like a brick. It's a great loss."

"Erebus?" Missy said. "Isn't that the underworld?"

"Yes." Hera's distaste was obvious.

Thanatos nodded. "We aren't supposed to die, little sister. If we do it's not by natural means. We become trapped, stuck in Mictlan, the lowest most point of the underworld." He shuddered. "Those who go to Mictlan, stay there. It is a punishment, you see, for evading death for so long. Immortals are not meant to die, little sister, and when we do... We suffer for the privilege."

Missy was stunned. "So our immortality is useless? I am supposed to protect Cethy during this quest. I was kind of counting on the fact that I couldn't die."

Hera laughed. "Don't be foolish. The Charonte would make short work of you. You're a child."

Thanatos shook his head. "You cannot die until they take your power from you. Your immortality lies in your magic, you know. Once you become mortal you are vulnerable to death." He threw his arm back around

Missy's shoulders in a very brotherly gesture and smiled sadly. "So you are immortal, Nemesis. It just doesn't do you any good."

Missy could not help but be overwhelmed. She spent hours touring the library with Thanatos and getting acquainted with how the Hub worked. It was time wasted. She was distracted by her own thoughts and the dozens of nymphs that flounced through the aisles shelving books, unseen by the mortal clientele. They were all tall and slim, with hair that trailed the floor in ridiculous shades ranging from pale rose pink to ivy green. The gnomes, who spoke complete and total gibberish, looked like upturned carrots and carried notes and missives from floor to floor. Missy had thought they were all wearing tiny orange hats until she stepped on one by mistake one and was as assaulted by a slew of incomprehensible swear words. When she had been thoroughly scolded the little orange blighter zipped off along the shiny tile, a bizarre little blur on a mission.

It was well after midnight when Missy sat nodding off among a pile of books. A scant few other gods came through the library's doors in the time she spent in the reference section with Thanatos. Thanatos had immediately hidden his little sister in the stacks and cautioned her to stay out of sight. "You are not the Olympian favorite," he said putting yet another stack of papers down onto the table. "It is best if you just stay as invisible as possible until this whole thing is over. Once the gods are restored, and they find out your part in our Rise, you will no longer have to be afraid of them." He sat beside her, flipping through books and looking for anything that might help the young goddess and her Norn.

"I'm not," Missy said, expressionlessly.

"Not what?" Thanatos asked, distracted by a page in a thick book.

"I'm not afraid of them."

Thanatos pushed his book away with a sigh. "Well you should be," he said. "They all blame you for what happened."

Missy shrugged. "How can they blame me? If anyone should be blamed it is Zeus."

Thanatos looked sharply at Missy. "Who told you that Zeus was to blame for the Fall?"

"He told me himself." Missy had not expected her laid back brother to snap like that. "He admitted that it was his fault."

"Well, he would think that wouldn't he?" Thanatos said, settling back into his seat. "It's no wonder you aren't afraid." For a few moments the two of them sat in silence. Thanatos read through page after page, while Missy sat wallowing in the half formed story she was a part of. "I have to admit to you, Nemesis," Thanatos said suddenly, "I am surprised to see you working *with* the Norns and not against them. Saving the world was never your style."

Missy frowned. She was quickly getting tired of defending herself. "Is there a reason why everyone thinks that I'm evil?" she asked.

Thanatos's eyebrows flew up in his amusement. "I never said that you were evil. I just said that you were never one to throw yourself into a fight that wasn't yours. You liked to watch and then, when the bloodshed was over, you would deal out your punishments."

"Well, I'm a bit more proactive now," Missy said icily. "I'm doing everything I can to help Cethy, and I'd appreciate a little less skepticism. You all act as if she's your only hope when she hasn't even done anything. I do all the work and she gets the pat on the back. Everyone fawns over her and criticizes me. I should just walk away and let her fall on her face."

"That's what we all expect," Thanatos said evenly. "Cupid was furious when he could not dissuade you from following Tyche. He was adamant about keeping you out of the way. Prometheus suggested that you had a right to prove yourself."

"I bet Cue wasn't happy," Missy muttered.

"More worried, I think."

Missy slammed her book shut. "Am I so untrustworthy?" she demanded bitterly. "I understand that I did something unforgivable in the past, but I am trying to make up for it, aren't I? What do you people want me to do?"

Thanatos carefully closed his book and regarded Missy evenly across the table. "You don't like it, do you?"

"Don't like what?" Missy snapped. Thanatos's emotions were slow and calm. The opposite of her own. She could feel his eagerness for knowledge and was reminded of Erin. She could also sense his sympathy and it swarmed around her like an annoying cloud of gnats.

"Usually you are the one who judges others. Now the tables have turned and others are judging you. It must be an uncomfortable sensation." Thanatos watched Missy for her reaction.

"I just want to be judged fairly," Missy said, suppressing her anger at being so tested. She felt miserable. From the beginning of this whole ordeal she could feel their dislike. It poured from them, coating her until Missy could barely even look at herself. She did her best to squelch Prometheus's shock and distrust at her presence. She had had to force Cupid's anger and hatred out of her own emotion. Hera had attacked her. Zeus had barely concealed his distaste, sending her after Erin and away from Cethy. The Amazons had taken full advantage of the chance to beat her senseless. It was payback, she knew, for the terror she had rained down on them in a past that she could not remember. Cethy alone stood by her side and believed in her, and now Cethy was off saving the world without her. Missy hid her head in her arms, ashamed of what she felt.

She was jealous of her best friend and the love she received without even trying.

"You are not the only one that they hate," Thanatos said gently. "You and I, the rest of our siblings, we've always clashed with the other gods of Olympus. We are just too different."

"But why?" Missy's voice was muffled from inside her arms. "Why don't they trust us?"

Thanatos thought about how to answer. "We are the gods most closely related to Khaos. It is from her that our powers originate and it's our power that makes us outcasts. Hera only keeps me close so that I can keep an eye out for our brothers and sisters. I'm the one who told her you were here in Los Angeles." Thanatos reached a gloved hand across the table and ruffled Missy's hair. "I don't know how it happened, but I am happy that the Fall changed you. It would seem that you are no longer a woe among mortals," he said with a grin.

"This is a productive conversation." Hera appeared with a fresh pile of books and a small army of gnomes at her feet. She joined the siblings at the table and dismissed her messengers with a wave of her hand. "I was hoping that I could trust you two to get some work done. I should have known better."

"I don't understand how there is no material in this entire library about the Charonte." Missy complained. "If the books are the memories and stories of the gods, shouldn't we be able to find out how the Norns won last time? One or two paragraphs have alluded to a Circle of Power and a great sacrifice, but it never comes out and gives us information." Missy tipped a pile of books over. Thousands of useless pages fell to the floor.

Thanatos sighed. "The Olympian Norn refuses to come to the Hub and the other two are not welcome. We have none of their stories." He looked at Hera pointedly. "For some reason we have to be exclusive and keep the Hub strictly Olympian."

Hera scowled. "Would you rather the other Divine Lines know our secrets?"

"Better we don't know anything at all." Missy felt the familiar prickle of contempt from Thanatos as he debated Hera. "Now we don't know how the Charonte can be beaten or how they are stealing our divinity. Or why, for that matter."

"That is what is bothering me most," Missy said. "Why? Why take the powers? Is it some sort of sick trophy? Are they using it? What could they possibly do with someone else's immortality?" Missy demanded. "We know nothing."

"We know a little," Hera said through clenched teeth. "Immortality is everlasting. If the Charonte are Harvesting essence, they do not have a lot of choices. They can release it back into nature or they can reanimate it."

"Reanimate?" Missy was not as passionate about learning as Erin. She didn't read every book that was placed in front of her and she did not delight in puzzles and riddles. "The Charonte are creating life?"

Thanatos snarled. "It is far more despicable than simply creating life. Hera disagrees, but I think that the Charonte are giving the essence they steal away." Missy flinched. Thanatos's lips were curled in disgust. "Imagine two souls trapped in a single body. You have two sets of memories and emotions. Two sets of morals. Two sets of wants and needs. It's poison. It is extremely dangerous and the weaker essence is almost always destroyed."

"Who would want that?" Missy could not understand what was worth poisoning your soul.

"Who wouldn't want it?" Hera retorted. "Lower level magical creatures would jump at the chance to live as a god."

Thanatos made a frustrated sound. "What I don't understand is why we haven't heard anything. The way gods gossip we should have some information especially about a situation so dire. Each body that we have recovered has been completely mortal. No magic and no immortality left in them at all. We are dealing with something completely unheard of and no one is coming forward with so much as a hint," Thanatos ran a hand through his hair, clearly troubled. "The gods are scared." He picked up one of the books that Hera had thrown onto the table and made a face. "What exactly are we supposed to be learning from this?" he asked, waving the book. "Arthurian legend? There won't be any clues about the Charonte in here."

"This one is not about the Charonte," Hera said, sounding smug. "This one is about the Circle. Nemesis promised Cupid that she was going to be a good little goddess and help the Norns build the Moirais' Circle and I," Hera smiled, "just found the next item on his list."

She pointed to the book's cover. It depicted a falcate sword rising up from a lake, a blue-green hand gripping the glittering, silver, hilt. "Does that look familiar?"

Missy and Thanatos stared blankly at the book. "It looks like a sword," Missy mumbled. "Oooo." Her sarcasm was obvious.

"Not just the sword, Nemesis, the hand that is holding it!" Hera said.

Thanatos grinned and it brightened his entire face considerably. "Of course! Those sneaky buggers.

There never was any Lady of the Lake was there? They've had it all this time"

Hera fumed, glaring daggers at Thanatos. "Your blasted sisters. You think they would have told us they had Arthur's sword."

"Excalibur?" Missy asked. "Excalibur is real?" Her tone made it evident that she thought the two of them were crazy.

Thanatos slid the book under Missy's nose. "Of course it is real. Did you really think something so famous was just made up? Excalibur is known all over the world."

Missy rolled her eyes. "So is the Easter bunny. Is he part of the Circle, too?"

"Actually, he's in Reno," Hera said absently as she took a file from a gnome. She began to shuffle through it, making a mess on the table. "Hesperides. Hesperides. Where are they?" she mumbled to herself.

"What are Hesperides?" Missy whispered to Thanatos.

Thanatos smiled. "More siblings of ours. They are very clever, very flashy. They act mainly as guards. If there is something that you want kept safe, you give it to the illusionists. The Night Nymphs. The Hesperides are guaranteed to keep it safe."

"So these nymphs have Excalibur?" Missy stared in wonder at the picture on the book's cover. "Well, what are we waiting for?" she demanded. Missy buckled her sword belt around her waist and looked up at Thanatos.

Thanatos turned to Hera. "You heard the girl." he said with a smile. "What are we waiting for?"

—Chapter Twenty-Two—

It was just after dawn when Hera appeared out of thin air by the docks at Bodega Bay with no one the wiser. Missy was at her side, her displeasure obvious as she fell to her knees panting and gasping. "I wish I didn't have to keep doing that," she choked. "I'd rather lose the rest of my hand." She flexed her mutilated right hand, the smallest digit missing. The wound was a constant reminder that surrender was not an option.

"Hippolyta should never have done that to you," Hera said with a frown. "As useless as that little finger is, no mortal should ever go cutting away at the gods. You should not have let her exercise that sort of power over you. You have killed for less."

"I have no interest in killing," Missy mumbled.

"That is hardly appropriate," Hera scolded. "You are supposed to be the Norns' Champion aren't you? Do you intend to just walk through this mess handing out daffodils? What would your cousin say if she heard you?"

Missy smiled and rose to her feet, brushing her knees free of dirt and sand. "I hope that Cethy would be pleased that I was valuing life."

"The Charonte do not share your values," Hera snapped. "I assure you that you are in for the fight of your life. Before this is over you will kill."

"Not if I can help it," Missy insisted. "I will do everything in my power to keep the bloodshed to a minimum."

Hera ground her teeth in annoyance. "How noble. You think like a mortal, not like a god. No other god you fight will hesitate to kill or torture. Compassion is a mortal trait."

"If anyone should have compassion," Missy pointed out," it's the gods." When Hera ignored her, the younger goddess shrugged. "It's just a thought."

"Keep it to yourself," Hera snapped. "The Hesperides should be in this area. I want you to be very careful," Hera said, all business. "The Hesperides are more powerful than ordinary water nymphs and you should not underestimate them. If they are guarding Excalibur you can be sure that they are guarding it well. They are illusionists, the lot of them. They know your fears and your desires so I suggest that you do not lie to them. They will be able to sense it and it will only make them angry. If you want to keep your mind intact just take their test, get the sword, and get out of there."

Hera kept well away from the water and motioned for Missy to walk along the dock. Missy clutched the sword that Hippolyta had given her and set out. Her feet echoed on the planks with every step she took toward the Hesperides and the next item of the Circle.

A yawn burst forth against Missy's will. Had she really only left Tir na n-Og the day before? It seemed like ages ago that she had beaten Antianara in the training yard. It seemed like weeks since she had lost Cethy mid-teleport. She yawned again. She could not remember how many days it had been since she had last slept.

"Hello, sister."

Missy started. She had been so lost in thought she had walked right into the thick of a group of little girls. Extraordinary was the only word in Missy's vocabulary that adequately described the five girls. All of them had the same pale yellow hair with an unmistakable green tint to it. Their skin was an almost undetectable blue. Five pairs of intelligent green eyes were glued to her.

She hesitated, unsure of how to respond to their greeting. She opted to keep silent, merely dipping her head in respectful acknowledgement. The nymphs stared, their eyes slanted in judgment. They were all five stretched out on the pier as a few early morning fisherman walked past, ignorant of the deities surrounding them.

"They cannot see you," one of the nymphs said, reading Missy's nervous expression correctly.

"They choose not to see you," corrected another. "That is the reason so many gods have been able to hide for so long."

"A tiny mortal head cannot make sense of what we are so it simply blocks us out." A nymph giggled and splashed her feet in the bay. The Hesperides all smiled at one another, silently laughing at their little joke.

Missy wished for the millionth time that Cethy was with her. Cethy was smarter and so much better at understanding all of this godly insanity. "I'm not so sure that I make sense of you myself," she muttered. The Hesperides looked at her, their liquid green eyes bright with amusement.

"That is because you are still lost," said the one closest to her, not sounding like a child at all. "You lost your true self in the Fall. You may stand before us, but you are lost regardless."

"You are out of balance," said another. "You simply refuse to accept yourself. If only you shed this mortal act and become the Nemesis we all remember, you would be much better equipped to help the Norns. Although," the nymph amended, "the Nemesis we remember would never have chosen to do so."

"Then why would I want to be that goddess again?" Missy interjected. She thought about the way everyone had been treating her lately. Everyone was suspicious that she had a hidden agenda. They all thought she was going to betray Cethy and the quest. "I don't want to be the same person I was before the Fall," she said firmly.

"That is your humanity speaking," one nymph said sordidly as she made the water beneath her boil and spit. "As a god you are at the height of evolution. Your emotions drag you down."

"It is true," said a nymph, stepping off of the docks. She did not sink into the water, but walked nonchalantly atop of it. "Before the Fall you were exactly who you needed to be to do your job properly."

"Before the Fall everyone hated me." Missy could feel her anger rising. "I don't want that life."

"Then you will stay out of balance. You will never regain your powers." The Hesperides looked at Missy as if should have known better. The teenager held their glares, refusing to feel guilty about her new life. "It's not who you are, sister. Not at your core. You're playing make believe."

"You cling to your human name and your human values and it weakens you," said the nymph closest to her. "Until you accept who you are, you will fail time and time again. You may gain a certain amount of power but it will do your cause little good. You must recognize who you are. Only then will you make progress."

Missy was careful to keep a small amount of distance between her and her newly found sisters. "You know nothing about me."

"We know everything about you." They laughed, each throwing their heads back and letting out a bellow that seemed too large for their petite frames. "You are our sister. A child of Darkness. Erebus itself was your sire, and our mother is the Night. You are made to be feared, meant to live outside of the light."

Missy felt her stomach plummet into her sneakers. This was the first she was hearing about her true parents. Child of Darkness? The underworld and the Night? "No," she said. Her voice was a clear warning. "I am not evil."

A nymph giggled, twirling her hair. "No one said that you were evil."

"Do you think that's what the underworld is? Evil?" asked the nymph walking atop the waves that lapped at the docks. "Erebus is a necessary part of life. No mortal may live forever. Erebus embraces those who must move on from this world. It is a haven for souls with nowhere else to go. It has its sinister parts, but so does the Mortal Realm. So does Valhalla. No thing or place can be all good or all evil."

"Neither is the Night evil," added another of the Hesperides. "It is a time of rest, and healing, and reflection. Life is at its most vulnerable and real in the dark. Dreams come in the night. Love is most honest in the darkness. Justice is not truly blind, sister," the nymph winked at Missy, "You merely did some of your best work at night. The night is mysterious and misunderstood, harsh and unforgiving, but still a part of the natural order. You carry that within yourself."

"Sister?" One of the nymphs had come close to Missy. Those liquid green eyes and strange blue skin only made the whole conversation surreal. "Having such parents benefits you."

There was a murmur of agreement. "You are more than simply Vengeance. You are Reprisal. Retribution. Justice. Judgment. Until Zeus banished you, you were the only one who was able to legitimately pass judgment on mortal beings and gods alike without suffering for it. You were the hand of reckoning."

"You have allowed a truly wondrous gift to become a burden," one of the nymphs said sadly.

"Do you understand?" asked the Hesperides in unison. "Your heart might be in the Mortal Realm, but Erebus is your soul."

Missy felt cold comprehension grip her. "Am I…am I an underworlder?" she asked. It explained everything. That was why everyone treated her with such distaste. She knew the opinion that the rest of the gods had about underworlders. Why had no one told her? Many had alluded that she was fighting for the wrong side, but no one had come out and said that she was a part of the very thing they were fighting to keep in its place. She was betraying her very nature by following Cethy. The knowledge knotted her stomach. No matter which way she turned now, she was working for the enemy.

"You are an underworlder and so much more," a nymph said lightly. "You were always mother's favorite. Grandmother's too. We weren't given nearly as much power as you were."

"Grandmother?" Missy asked, uncertain. She was apprehensive about hearing any more news of her family tree. Her curiosity got the better of her. "Who?"

"More like what," a nymph said happily as the water jumped and danced at her command.

"There are things that simply are," a nymph said carefully.

"Grandmother," the Hesperides said together. A collective shiver ran through the nymphs. Missy looked at her arms. Goosebumps had broken out all over.

"What is she?" Missy whispered.

"Khaos," a nymph said quietly.

"Before there was anything, there was grandmother. She gave everything life and power, then she disappeared," said the nymph who walked on water.

"Every now and again she makes herself known by throwing the world into mayhem, but it's never anything too extreme. The realms always rebuild."

"You were one of her favorites," said the nymph closest to her. "True there were gods stronger, or better known. There were gods with whole lineages to oversee, but you were the only one with the power to keep them in line. You were always more powerful in a quiet sort of way."

"Sorry?" Missy was not sure how to respond.

"It is not a matter of apology," a nymph said with a kind smile. "We have our own powers and purpose. We do not need yours."

The nymph walking on water shuddered. "And I would not want to be in your position for all of the powers and favor in the worlds."

"My position?" Missy asked.

"Yes," said the nymph closest to her. "You may be powerful, but you have something that we would never ever want."

"What is that exactly?" Missy demanded.

The nymphs all smiled the same perfect smile at her. "You have the ability to choose."

"And before your war is over that is what you have to do. Choose."

"Are you saying that you can't make your own choices?" Missy asked. "That Cethy and Erin, the rest of the gods, don't have freewill?"

The Hesperides were unconcerned. "You make things far too complicated," the nymph on the water said. "Each god is meant for only one purpose, and so we fulfill our purpose without feeling loss or regret. We have our fun, but the Divine are defined by our jobs. Your friends' freewill is no more than a side effect from the Fall. It will fade with the rise and they will feel no loss. Only gained purpose."

"And what about me? Will I lose my freedom when the gods rise?"

"No," a nymph said happily. "You always have been, and will be, free of most godly law. That is what makes you so dangerous, so despised, and so desired. You can choose for yourself, sister, and soon you will choose for us all."

"Nothing with you people is easy, is it?" Missy said with a sigh. "Everything has to be a riddle."

The Hesperides all giggled together. "Has no one told you the rules?" asked the nymph closest to her. "The reason that these quests are so wrought with danger is so that those who are unworthy do not gain reward. The more difficult we make things for you, the stronger you will be at journey's end."

"You do this on purpose?" Missy was aghast. "I have no intentions of becoming some sort of tragic hero just to appease your ridiculous rules," Missy said through gritted teeth. "Even if our mythology is filled with little else." Missy had a tight grip on the Amazon sword at her hip. The Hesperides watched her, faces lit with impish grins.

"Your battle is not with us, sister," a nymph said. "Release your sword."

Missy sighed and slowly loosened her grip. What was she going to do, hack up the pack of unruly girls?

"It is time," they said together. "Your test is simple. All you have to do is reach Caliburn. Once you have the sword your test is over and we will release you. Or maybe you will turn back?"

"Caliburn?" Missy scanned the docks for Hera, but she had vanished. "I thought I was here for Excalibur."

The Hesperides shook their heads, their blond-green hair rippling. "Excalibur is what the sword became when mankind tried to put limitations on a Divine blade. The sword in its natural state, as a weapon of Valhalla, is called Caliburn."

"Are you ready for your test, sister?" asked the nymph on the water.

Missy nodded. The nymphs came close to her, and began stripping her of her weapons and extra layers. Soon a small heap of steel was piled as Missy's feet. One of the nymphs, Missy could not tell which, leaned close. "We want to make sure that you leave here stronger than ever."

"Yes," another nymph's voice whispered happily. Missy could feel a cool breath on her ear. "We want to make sure you have the power to succeed. I promise, wonderful Nemesis, we will do our very best to kill you."

—Chapter Twenty-Three—

Hera had warned Missy about the Hesperides. She knew that they were illusionists and yet the girl was not prepared when the dock began to slowly disintegrate under her feet. Missy braced herself for the pain that always accompanied bending but it did not come. It was an illusion.

Her Amazon training kicking in. Missy remained calm and loose, her eyes closed as she counted her breaths. "I'm still on the docks," Missy reminded herself. "It isn't real."

Isn't it? She heard the five voices of the Hesperides in her mind.

"I know about you," Missy answered aloud. "You can try to scare me all you want, but I know that it is only an illusion. It isn't real."

We shall see. Whispered the nymphs in unison. *Now open your eyes.*

Missy obeyed and surprised relief flooded her body. She stood on a sandy beach, watching the waves lap greedily at her ankles. She could hear the seagulls crying overhead and could not help but smile. She was home. The Hesperides had brought her back to Jersey.

Sunlight gleamed off of something rising from the waves. Missy squinted into the brightness of the water. A magnificent blade pierced the rolling tide only a few miles off shore. Somehow Missy did not think that Caliburn's capture would be as easy as a simple swim, but she was not about to complain. She stepped forward.

The ocean's salty spray blew into her face, and the familiar smell relaxed her. She was out to her waist before she appreciated the nymph's decision to take her weapons. Here, they would only have been an encumbrance. She stood in the waves, adjusting to the heart-stopping cold of the water. Missy took a deep breath and dove headfirst into a breaker. The icy water washed over her and Missy was thrilled that this was her test. This was as natural to her as breathing. She rose to the surface and with calm, even strokes she began to swim her way toward Caliburn.

Only a few yards out, Missy felt something pull on her leg, drawing her to an unexpected stop. The ocean under her was alive with power and it tugged at her determinedly. "I should have known," Missy muttered. She quickly filled her lungs with air and let the Hesperides' enchantments pull her under the waves. The sooner she finished this test, the better.

Missy coughed and spluttered as she broke the surface and scrambled to protect herself from whatever tricks the Hesperides had up their sleeves. She was no longer in the water, but tangled in a bright pink blanket. Missy sat up, scrutinized her new surroundings, and let out a sigh of relief. She was not in danger, but rather very confused.

She was in a child's bedroom. Shelves lined the walls, filled with books and picture frames. Stuffed animals and board games littered the pale pink carpet. Mobiles of sea shells and polished glass caught the light as they spun from the ceiling.

A picture on the nightstand caught Missy's attention. It depicted a little girl on the beach, sporting an exceedingly large sweatshirt. She was held by a woman with long messy curls and a man with mischievous eyes. A puppy was tugging on her pant leg as she laughed happily. Missy's hands shook as she picked the picture up. There was no doubt in her mind who the people were. She'd seen them in her dreams often enough. Missy also knew they weren't real.

This could have been yours. Missy dropped the photograph and the silence broke along with the frame. The nymphs were in her head. *Do you see what you have been denied? Love. Family. A real life.* Missy heard footsteps coming down the hall outside and pause outside the bedroom. *Her* bedroom. The bedroom she had always imagined was out there waiting for her somewhere. "Sweetie, are you alright?" a kind voice called through the door.

"Fine." Missy gasped. Her voice was thin and young. She looked down and her dirty t-shirt and jeans were gone, replaced by a crisp cotton dress that hung off of her skinny frame. She grabbed at her hair but only managed to get a handful of short curls. Curse those nymphs! They had turned her twelve years old again. The footsteps moved on and Missy let out the breath she had been holding.

"You might as well put me right back in the water," Missy said aloud to her empty room. "You can't tempt me with a past I know I won't ever have."

You think that we tempt you? The nymphs said. *We are merely demonstrating what being a god has cost you.*

Missy choked as sea water spilled into her open mouth. The pretty little bed room was gone and once again she was in the Pacific Ocean. There was no time to mourn the childhood she had been robbed of. She was on a mission. Missy focused her mind and continued towards the shining hilt of Caliburn, shaken. She had not gone five yards before she was pulled under the waves with violent force. There was no gentle tug on her jeans or an opportunity to breathe, only a rapid descent into the nymphs' power.

There was no transition into this new torment, just the monotone buzz of fluorescent lighting. Missy could not move. She felt woozy and light headed like the sense had been knocked from her. Her eyes were glassy as she took in her surroundings, unable to focus.

Missy was boxed in by empty white walls and the smell of antiseptic was in the air. A messy desk was in the middle of the room and cluttered file cabinets lined the far wall. There were no windows. The air-conditioning sent cold blasts down the open back of the hospital gown she was wearing. A round man with a thin attempt at a mustache stared at her, his face bored. A legal pad was in his lap. Its pages were covered with his stout penmanship and bored doodles. Missy tensed as she recognized the room and the man. She made an effort to get up, but she was unable to stand. Her hands were strapped to the arms of the wheelchair she sat in, and her muscles had no strength.

"This isn't real. This. Isn't. Real!" Missy had been cautioned that the nymphs could tell a person's fears and wants but she had not anticipated this nightmare. They had dug up the one memory that she would have preferred left buried. The Hesperides would pay for this.

"I was hoping that after all of these months you would be making improvements." The round man adjusted his white coat and fingered the base of his stethoscope. "It almost seems like you want to spend the rest of your life locked away. Well?" he asked. "Do you?"

"No." Missy's voice was horse. A side-effect, she knew, from hours of screaming. That was what she had done most when she was locked away in Westfield. She had screamed.

Missy could not look away from the man who had spent over a year of her youth torturing her. She remembered the shock therapy and the starvation she had endured at his orders. She had been injected with horrible test medications that had made her hallucinate and burn. She had been thrown into solitary for weeks at a time. No one had cared. No one asked questions when you were an unwanted ward of the state.

"This isn't real." Missy's voice was a whisper. She could feel the cold leather of the straps on her arms.

"This delusion has to stop." The doctor began to fiddle with the equipment on the tray next to her. Missy heard the clink of tools, saw the flash metal, and her body seized up in fear.

Missy felt tears slide down her cheeks. Cold sweat broke out all over her body. She was shaking, terrified. It had been three years since she had run from the mental institution and still this memory was enough to turn her into a sobbing, thrashing wreck.

Not over the past, are we?

Missy screamed as the cold pierce of a needle penetrated the back of her neck. With all of her strength Missy jerked away and hit a wall of water. Once more she was afloat in the waves. She shook as she treaded water and Missy could not help but feel like less of a goddess than ever.

How are you supposed to save the world when the mere memory of your past in enough to paralyze you with fear? asked the Hesperides. With quaking hands Missy rubbed the back of her neck where the sting of the needle still pulsed under her fingers. She would have to be careful. Apparently, the Hesperides could do more than just cast illusions.

Not as easy as you thought, is it? the nymphs said together. Their voices echoed in Missy's mind. *Do you see now the cost of your Divinity? You have no family, no home, no education, no resources, and no past. It is all a direct result of your being a god. No good has come from your powers, and no good ever will.*

She could see Caliburn ahead, its glistening hilt a beacon of hope. She was close. Missy swam on, distracted by the nymphs' cruelty. They could have chosen to show her anything else and it would not have shaken her so completely. Her mind wandered to the room and the family she would never have, and the scars that she knew would never heal. If she were a true Olympian, she would never have let those things happen to her. She would not have had to grow up without a home. She would not have been a victim for Westfield's sick science experiments. She could have protected herself. She could have risen above it.

Rise above it? the Hesperides taunted. *You know who you are, Nemesis. Everything you touch, everything you love, only gets dragged down to your level. You will never Rise.*

Missy saw the Hesperides enchantment the second before she was dragged under. She was not afraid of being pulled beneath the waves, but of where those waves would take her. Missy knew that she would be dropped into another illusion before she needed to breathe, and sure enough, the water was gone in the blink of an eye.

Missy hesitated, unsure of what to do. This vision was different. Power was settled happily inside her, familiar and natural. Magic filled the air around her as she gazed into a dark fountain. The reflection that stared back at her was not the one she expected. Her curls flowed down to her waist, bound back with thin gold chains. She was draped in flowing black cloth, her only adornment was the shiny white arrowhead that hung on a leather cord around her neck. She also had to be at least thirty. There was no rhyme or reason to the Hesperides' test. They simply seemed determined to make her lose her mind.

"Nemesis, I am speaking to you." Missy tore her eyes from the fountain and her bizarre reflection and found herself surrounded by a court of amazing characters. Only in her wildest dreams did she think that she was a part of such a world. The Olympian elite watched her carefully, waiting for her to speak. In this place, she knew her family on sight. Hera was there, but her hard face was softened by long dark curls. Her violet eyes were still quick and aware, but the crazed glint that Missy had seen in Los Angeles wasn't there. Her body language clearly said that she had better things to do. She nodded at Nemesis, smiling slightly.

She knew them all. Athena, Apollo, and Demeter sat on the edge of the fountain as far from her as possible. Athena's gray eyes were concentrating on the platform in front of them. A younger goddess with long dark hair stayed to the shadows, but gave Missy a small wave. Missy returned Artemis's wave and grinned. A light-haired man with golden sandals strapped to his feet winked at Missy as she surveyed the group. She recognized Hermes and the mischievous look on his face. He was a friend. The ever-gorgeous Aphrodite stood stoically beside a blonde man with wings that flowed down his back. There was no need to see the man's face. She knew Cupid when she saw him, no matter what age he was.

"Nemesis!" Zeus stood before her, nothing like the god she had met in the beach bar. This was Zeus in his prime. He was standing tall, his blue eyes angry. His hair was black as night itself, dignified instead of decomposing. Even the lightning that jumped and flashed in his hands seemed more electric.

"I am listening, my king. But I have yet to hear anything worthwhile." Nemesis spoke and Missy was stunned. She had not said anything at all. The words had come from Nemesis.

Surprise. The Hesperides said. *It is best if this memory is left unaltered by your current voice, sister. You are only here to watch and see what a mess you made of things. You will have no control here.* Missy was not sure if she liked being a prisoner in her own body. At least in the other illusions she had the power to control her actions and words. Here she was just going along for the ride.

What is the matter? Afraid that you won't like what you see?

"How dare you!" Zeus seemed to puff up with indignation and Missy's attention returned to the scene at hand. "Must you thwart me at every turn? I have called you here to do the very thing you were made to do, pass judgment on a criminal, and still you are a nuisance. It is your place as the goddess of retribution to punish this god for his crimes. Now do your job and stop wasting my time." The lightning in his fist seemed to glow brighter.

Nemesis rose and made her way over to where Cupid stood silently in front of Zeus. "What is his crime?" she asked quietly. She did not look at the winged man, but stood in front of him, between Cupid and his accuser. This action alone invoked the hiss of whispers from her Olympian family.

"Your audacity knows no bounds, Nemesis!" Zeus all but threw Nemesis out of the way. He gripped her shoulders and pulled her aside. Nemesis did not even wince though dark electrical burns blossomed under his hands. She merely glanced at them in slight surprise. "I have already told you! Cupid assaulted me early this morning," Zeus growled. "He thought to shoot me with one of his fool arrows, one of which you wear as a medallion around your throat. This is treachery!" Zeus had obviously only just noticed Nemesis's amulet and the discovery did not please him.

Nemesis leaned her head to the side, as though thinking. "He attacked you?" she repeated to Zeus. "This morning?" Zeus nodded impatiently, his face a twisted mask of anger. "Was that before or after you visited me?" Nemesis asked lightly. The whispers of the godly court grew louder. No one spoke to Zeus in that tone, and no one ever accused him of dalliance with Hera present. To do so was suicide, for if Hera did not punish her for the accusation, Zeus would later.

"How dare you," Zeus began but with a flick of her wrist fire erupted from Nemesis's hand. It was a clear warning to the king of the gods.

"How dare I? How dare *you*. You brought me here to condemn Cupid," Nemesis announced loudly. "But I choose who feels my wrath, not you."

The fire in Nemesis's hand dwindled out with a hiss. Hera stepped forward and the queen of the gods seemed to grow bigger as she drew the powers out of the gods around her in glittering mass of color that none but Nemesis could see. "What do you mean he visited you?" Hera demanded, her anger settling over the entire mountain top. She turned to Zeus, and this time the lightning was flying from *her* fingers. "I cannot trust you alone for a moment, can I?" There was a roar as the gods all began to yell at once. They were so busy arguing amongst each other that no one noticed Cupid open his wings and step off of the mountain. And no one noticed that Nemesis was at his side.

"He is not going to be happy about this. True you distracted him, but for how long?" Cupid asked. He adjusted his grip on her waist so that Nemesis would not fall. "He will redouble his efforts, Nemesis. Zeus always gets what he wants."

"You mean me?" Nemesis asked. She was smiling. "Let him try. There's only one Olympian I'm interested in and it isn't spongy old Zeus." Missy was horrified as her old self carefully drew Cupid into what could only be described as a loving kiss.

Missy was dumped back into the ocean. "Explain yourself!" She scrambled to keep herself above the waves that threatened to bury and spit the salty water from her mouth. "Where are you, you stupid trolls? Why show me something like that? Was that a memory, or are you just getting you jollies ticking me off!"

There was no answer. She had walked into this test voluntarily and until she took the sword, her mind would remain the Hesperides' play thing. Her head spun with everything she had seen. First they toyed with her wants, showing her the normal childhood and family she had wanted all of her life. Then they forced her to relive the darkest and most horrific time of her young life. She did not understand what they thought they were gaining by showing her this. Cupid? She was more likely to sprout wings and shoot magical arrows herself than be involved with Cupid.

Are you finished? You don't want to see any more of the truth? Can't handle it?

"I'm not finished," Missy shouted at the water. Caliburn was only fifty feet away, just waiting for Missy to swim out and grab it. Missy knew that the worst was probably yet to come but she did not hesitate. She would not let the nymphs put her through all of this for nothing.

Missy refused to take her eyes off of the sword. She could feel the current trying to push her back, away from Caliburn. Her progress was slow, but it was consistent. She would not stop. She could not stop.

The water grew thick with magic. For the first time Missy fought against the pull of the Hesperides' power. She did not want to see anymore. None of it made sense. Nothing they showed her would make her want to turn back. Nothing they showed her would make her quit. Each memory, each desire, each fear only made her want to succeed all the more. She would reach Caliburn, and then she would make the nymphs pay.

The Hesperides won the tug of war for Missy's attention. She was once more sitting by the black fountain, its dark water shimmering in the evening sun. This time, there was no Olympian court. Zeus stood before her alone, powerful and threatening. Unconsciously lightning crackled and popped around his hands and head. The king of the gods looked down at her. There was lightning in his eyes as well. "Well?"

"Well what?" Nemesis snapped. It seemed that Missy would have no voice in this illusion either.

That's right. Watch, the nymphs' voices lilted with laughter. *Watch what you have done.*

Zeus circled Nemesis, his blue eyes popping with anger. "I'd like you to explain how you expected to get away with not only causing a riot on my mountain, but disappearing with the god on trial. I'd also like to know how long you two thought you could sneak around without my knowing."

"Me? And Cupid?" Nemesis said calmly. "Seems a bit farfetched, don't you think?"

"I think," Zeus said tightly, "that when the most reclusive goddess in Greece finally comes out of hiding, it isn't for nothing."

"Why do you worry so?" Nemesis demanded. "Just pick someone else. There are others who would be thrilled to have you. Your wife, for one."

"You think to judge me, even now, when you stand accused of treason?" Zeus was disbelieving.

"Telling you no is not treason," Nemesis said. "You are like a spoiled child throwing a tantrum because you haven't gotten the sweet you asked for."

"Do not flatter yourself," snapped Zeus. "The very thing that makes you so desirable is what makes you odious. The chaos in your blood calls to all of us. You should be hanging off of the mountain right now, but the other gods will not allow it. You have them all wrapped around your finger. Tell me, have you won them over in the same way as Cupid?"

Nemesis rolled her eyes and got to her feet. "Your choice of words show your weakness, Zeus. We are finished here."

What happened next came so quickly Nemesis had no time stop it. There was a flash of lightning and when the dust cleared there stood Zeus, clutching three feet of Nemesis's smoky, beautiful curls. Nemesis felt her head and sure enough, only a few inches of curls remained. Missy sighed inwardly. So that was what happened to her hair.

"This is your shame." Zeus spat, throwing the armful of hair at Nemesis's feet. "It is less of a punishment than I would have liked, but it will have to do. Don't forget who rules here, Nemesis."

Nemesis seemed unconcerned by Zeus's actions and his speech. She glanced at the pile of hair and she smiled. Her eyes were cold. "Imagine being judged by the king of the gods," Nemesis said softly. "Consider this moment a gift, Zeus. You will not have another at my expense." Nemesis turned away.

"Wait, Nemesis." Zeus's voice was harsh. "There is still the matter of the love god."

"The matter is settled," Nemesis said evenly. "We will stay out of your way, and you will not look for us."

"You presume to order me about?" Zeus seemed to glow with his rage and power.

Nemesis was not intimidated. "I will presume much more than that if you don't heed me, Zeus." Fire drew up around her body, turning her into a walking inferno. "If you do not leave us be, I will take everything from you. If you interfere with me again, I will see to it you lose your kingdom, see if I don't. You will fall, and I will celebrate it."

Missy slammed into the water hard enough to knock her senseless. She had not even enough time to fill her lungs with air before she was ruthlessly towed under again. She watched with mounting horror the suffering of the gods as one by one they vanished. Their faces as their plight flashed before her eyes amid a tumult of magic were twisted with confusion and fear. Tears, prayers, and curses did nothing to save them from their fates. One by one, the gods Fell.

Do you see what you do? The nymphs asked as Missy struggled to move on. The Hesperides' power beat at the girl, dragging her back. They were doing everything in their power to keep her from reaching the shimmering sword cutting through the waves. *You hurt people, Nemesis. You are toxic to everything that you touch. Look at their faces, look at the pain.* The Hesperides forced image upon image on Missy and the tortured faces of the Fallen bombarded her.

Missy could not keep going. Tears rolled down her cheeks and mixed with ocean water. *You see now why you are hated.* The nymphs continued their torment. *You are not trusted. You are alone. What do you think to gain from killing yourself here? This is not your quest. This is not your responsibility. When the Norns fail and the Moirai weave the world away, they will leave you unharmed. You will live the rest of your days in Erebus, where you belong.*

The waves grew larger, rising over Missy's head. Caliburn slipped away.

Give up, Nemesis. Give up.

Missy floated well beneath the surface, unable to move. The truth of it all simply weighed too much. The Fall was her fault. Not Zeus'. She had cursed him, and so had cursed them all. She had destroyed Olympus and every other pantheon... And she'd done it for the love of a god that hated her.

Give up, Nemesis.

Give up? Missy stirred, her eyes cast upward to where the sun lit the surface of the water. It was just a ring of light. A circle. *Give up.* Those words meant nothing to her. She had made a life for herself out of nothing. She found a way out of the hospital. She had found a way to survive. She had managed to keep her tiny family together in the hotel room until Prometheus showed up and set everything in motion. Through all her struggles Missy had never given up. The Hesperides had chosen their words poorly.

Gasping for air, Missy broke the surface with a hiss of steam. Fire erupted from her skin, extinguishing just as quickly as it made contact with the water. Missy ignored the crushing breakers that threatened to drown her. Growing up at the beach had trained her well, and her strokes were strong and even. Caliburn drew closer as the fire within pressed her onward.

Think about this, the nymphs warned. *Think about the sacrifice you are making by helping the Norns. You are betraying everything that you are.*

"Better to betray myself than Cethy." Missy reached out and grabbed Caliburn's hilt. An electrical pulse shot through her arm, and Missy felt strength in it. She felt like the goddess from the illusion. She was Nemesis. "Rise!" Missy's voice was full of purpose and Divine power as she tugged the sword out of the water. Caliburn resisted for a moment, its hilt burning into her skin. It was almost overwhelming, but Missy refused to let go. "Rise. Take your rightful place!"

Missy threw herself back, dragging the sword with her. Caliburn came loose and immediately her power vanished, leaving her without Nemesis's confidence and strength. Missy hit the dock hard and collapsed. She was right back where she had started. The nymphs stood around her in a circle, their faces lit with pleasure.

"You are victorious, Nemesis," said a nymph knelt at her side. "And we certainly did not make it easy for you."

Another of the Hesperides knelt at Missy's side and began to wipe away the ocean water and sand away with the hem of her dress. "Indeed. It would seem that Caliburn has chosen a fearless goddess to be its wielder."

"Congratulations," said two together.

Missy was sopping wet. She shook violently, not from cold but from alarm. Caliburn was next to her, filthy from tip to hilt. It was not nearly as remarkable now. Dull and unexceptional, it hardly seemed like the Divine weapon she had fought so hard to win. It lit with ribbons of color, pride and humor...

The sword was alive.

Missy was too overwhelmed to wonder how an inanimate object like a blade managed to *feel* and shook damp curls. "Was it real?" The words were barely able to make it past her chattering teeth. "What you did back there? What you showed me at Olympus? Was it real?"

"We merely showed you the memories that you buried long ago." One of the nymphs eyed Caliburn warily, and made a point to give the sword plenty of room. "Everything that you saw was taken directly from your own head. We manipulated nothing."

"Even that child's bedroom," said a nymph with a kind smile. "You dreamt of that place, of your possible parents, so often as a child you believed that it was real and waiting for you someplace."

Missy coughed. Her stomach turned unpleasantly, its contents mostly seawater. "I thought you said that you were going to try and kill me," she said. "Not that I'm complaining, but I'm hardly even hurt."

"We never said that we wanted to hurt you physically." The Hesperides laughed in unison. "We attacked your mind, Nemesis. We attacked your heart."

Chapter Twenty-Four

Thanatos had lost all but the most basic of his powers in the Fall but there was still one thing tethering him to his glory days. As death, he was connected to all life. The only life he was interested in at the moment, however belonged to his wayward little sister. Missy's essence had vanished from his watchful eye a few hours ago, taken in and shielded by the Hesperides' power. She would be protected from his radar until the nymphs decided to release her. The trouble was he needed to find her and quickly. He had no time to wait for the nymphs to finish playing their games.

Thanatos looked horrible. He was pale and covered with soot. His suit jacket was missing and his shirt was ripped and untucked. His face was covered in dried blood, but he moved quickly and quietly, ignoring his pain. He was running from something.

Thanatos searched the California shoreline and finally felt the pull of Nemesis's immortality. He appeared in Bodega Bay in time to watch Missy yell at the Hesperides and cough up seawater between curses. The giggling nymphs kept their distance from the angry goddess and the newly freed weapon she waved threateningly in their direction.

Thanatos forgot his hurry as he laid eyes on the sword. She had done it. Caliburn was one of the few divine weapons left and after centuries of hibernation it had finally chosen a new champion. Not only was the sword necessary to create the Moirais' Circle, but it was a source of potential power for its wielder. "Nemesis."

Missy jumped at the sound of her brother's voice. She spun around and scowled at Thanatos as he approached the dock. "What were you thinking, sending me after something like that?" She drove Caliburn's point into the pier. Thanatos came closer and stared at his bedraggled little sister. Water dripped from her clothes and curls but that seemed to be the extent of her physical ailments. It was her eyes that had Thanatos worried. Glowing gold and panicked, Missy's eyes were unfocused. She was scared to death of something and her hands shook with unseen tension as she faced him.

"Nemesis?" Thanatos looked to the Hesperides. "What did you do to her?"

"We did nothing. Nemesis simply got a look at the truth for the first time in a long time," one of the nymphs said evenly. "I do not think that she likes what she saw."

"She is no good to us in the future if she is traumatized by the past," Thanatos shouted. He fell silent as Caliburn's sharp point rested against the thin flesh of his throat. He had not even seen Missy retrieve the sword from where it had been sticking out of the dock.

"Don't talk about it!" Missy's voice cracked. "Don't ever! You didn't see it! You did not have to watch them all!" Her chest heaved with the strength it took to hold her new and awful memories at bay.

"Nemesis? Missy, it is ok." Thanatos used both names to try and reach his little sister. "It is over." Thanatos could feel the sting of Caliburn's point under his Adams apple. He had no choice but to watch and wait. Missy's eyes were frightened and wild, as if she did not recognize him. He frowned. The Hesperides had done more damage than they realized. "Missy, put it down."

Missy quivered and lowered the sword. The Hesperides came forward and offered Missy a sword baldric and sheath that matched Caliburn's curved hilt. She buckled the belt across her chest and over her shoulder so that Caliburn rested comfortably across her back. "How could no one have told me?" she whispered. "How could no one have said?"

Thanatos shrugged. "Perhaps they were afraid of being shish-kabobed," he said dryly.

"Why would you send me after something like this without warning me first?" Missy demanded, pointing to the hilt sticking up over her shoulder. "I can handle any obstacle course you want to throw at me, but I won't let anyone else mess with my mind." She crossed her arms. "And you!" She rounded on the five little girls who smiled sweetly up at her. "You are off my Christmas card list."

Thanatos did not understand. "Didn't Hera tell you what they would do?" he asked distractedly. "It's not like her to leave out something that important."

"She downplayed what would happen. A *lot*." Missy shivered and wrapped her arms around herself. "Hera should have told me. I'll have to *thank* her for letting it be a surprise." The way Missy said it indicated that there would be very little thanks relayed to the queen goddess.

Thanatos gasped, remembering why he had hunted Missy down in the first place. "Where is Hera?" he said quickly. "She needs to get back to the Hub right away. We've run into a problem."

Missy looked around. "I don't know. I left her right here." She glanced at the nymphs. "You didn't do anything to her, did you?"

"It was not us," the Hesperides said in unison.

"Are you alright?" Missy had only just noticed that Thanatos was a beaten wreck. "What happened to you?"

Thanatos ran his fingers through his hair nervously, a trait he shared with Missy. "Before you left, Hera asked me to investigate a possible Olympian in Missouri. It was a dead end so I came back, but when I got to the Hub," he paused, distressed, "everything is destroyed, Nemesis."

"What is?" Missy asked alarmed. The Hesperides looked at each other with concern.

"The Hub. All of the books that we have spent years collecting have vanished. All of those memories are gone. The files, the notes, the lists, and the research have all been cleaned out."

"Someone took our books? Our memories?"

Thanatos nodded miserably. "What's worse, everyone thinks that we are responsible."

Missy's mind was tense and tired from her ordeal with the Hesperides and so could not make sense of what Thanatos said. "Everyone thinks we are responsible for what?"

Thanatos sighed. "They think that we ransacked the library. Half of the gnomes are dead in a heap. The files on the gods and their whereabouts are gone. Our records are completely destroyed. This is a very serious blow to the Norns, Nemesis, and a huge opportunity for the Charonte. If they get their hands on those records the gods and their powers are sitting ducks. The Norns won't stand a chance."

"They think that we did it?" Missy was incredulous. "How exactly was I looting the Hub when these five were torturing me?" She glowered at the water nymphs.

"You don't know how their minds work," Thanatos said bitterly. "They need someone to blame and we are better scapegoats than most. They think that I raided the Hub while you kept Hera distracted. That is why I need to find her. She can tell them the truth." He fell silent. "I have never seen Prometheus so angry. And Zeus! It might have been better had you not reached the sword. The instant you touched Caliburn the gods felt it and the power you released made Zeus his old self again. Truly, the Rise has begun and at the worst possible time." Thanatos turned and showed Missy a blistering wound that crawled up his back through the rip in his shirt. "Lucky me," he said sarcastically, "his aim is as good as ever."

Missy had thought that after the Hesperides' test she would never be horrified again, but she was wrong. The skin on Thanatos's back was blackened and oozing. "Zeus did that? The last time I saw him he could barely stand, let alone strike someone. Believe me. He tried."

"Things are changing," Thanatos said. "Your quest is giving the gods back their strength. You must feel it."

In fact, Missy did feel something, but it was not power as Thanatos suggested. It was a quiver in the air, a stench of fury and disappointment. "I think we are about to have company," Missy said tensely. "Very angry company."

"It must be Zeus and the others!" Thanatos turned and looked up and down the street. People walked past oblivious to the powerful charge in the air. There was no hint of an immortal mob in the street. "How close are they?"

"Closer than you anticipated." Prometheus stood behind them at the end of the dock. His hands were folded and his eyes were narrowed in disappointment. "I had hoped that you would prove us all wrong about you, Nemesis," he said looking angrily at Missy. "And Thanatos, we trusted you. We left you in charge of one of the most important components of Olympian history and you betrayed that trust. How could you do this?"

"But I didn't do anything!" Thanatos said. "Hera can straighten this all out, if you just wait, we can find her."

"There is no longer time to wait. The Hub and its purpose are destroyed, the Charonte have taken a significant lead over Tyche and Cupid, and you have led Nemesis to Caliburn." Prometheus gestured to the sword hanging on Missy's back.

"Of course! She is helping the Norns!" Thanatos insisted.

"If you don't believe us, then take the sword," Missy said. "Give it to Cethy. Don't accuse me of being dishonest." Missy undid her baldric and offered Caliburn's hilt to Prometheus. The Titan looked taken aback.

"I cannot touch it," he said finally. "No one can. It has chosen you and will be yours until you breathe your last breath. Since you are a god, you can only imagine how long that will take." His eyes were intense as he stared at the two shaking and wounded young gods. "What is the truth here? What have you two done?"

Thanatos lowered his head, miserable. Missy remained silent and returned the belt back over her shoulder. If Prometheus thought she was guilty, there was nothing she could say to change his mind. Olympus already had her pegged as an underworlder. They would never trust her no matter how much good she did.

"We saw into her essence," the Hesperides said together. "Nemesis is not the betrayer. She has done nothing but help you and your cause."

"Nemesis helps only herself." Zeus appeared in the street with Hermes and Dionysus at his back. D winked at Missy and Hermes barely concealed his toothy grin. Missy reached out tentatively with a thread of her power. Her Empathy sorted through their feelings and she sighed with relief. She sensed mischief and their satisfaction in a joke well played. It seemed that duplicity was the fashion of Olympus. The king of the gods had no idea that both Dionysus and Hermes were on good terms with the vengeance goddess.

Missy gathered all of the emotion very quickly, and returned her attention to Zeus. She could not help but be impressed. The Hesperides' illusion did not do Zeus justice. Returned to his former glory, Zeus crackled and popped with undeniable power. He wore regular street clothes, but there was no mistaking him for a mortal. His eyes landed on Caliburn strapped to Missy's back and his anger became palpable.

"Put down the sword, Nemesis," Zeus demanded. "It does not belong to you."

"It does," said the Hesperides in unison. "Caliburn has chosen Nemesis to wield it. She is the first in over a thousand years to champion the sword, and the first god in history to be chosen. Caliburn belongs to Nemesis, and Nemesis to Caliburn. So long as she breathes, the two cannot be separated."

Lightning struck the dock, leaving a burnt out vein in the wood. The Hesperides fell silent but did not retreat. Zeus glared at nymphs. "So long as she breathes," he conceded. Electricity crackled in his hands.

"Don't threaten me!" Missy had not anticipated her outburst, but she was tired and she was sore down to her very core. She had been dragged through the darkest and most horrible parts of her past. She had been abandoned on an island with giant women whose pleasure came only from causing her pain. She had been chased from her home by a monster. She was separated from her best friend and among people who did not trust her or want her company. How much further could they possibly push her and expect her to remain calm?

"Return what you have stolen, and threats will not be necessary," Zeus shouted back.

Missy drew her sword. She could feel Caliburn trembling in her left hand and knew that it was not she who was shaking. The sword was alive and could feel the tension in the air the same as she. It itched for the opportunity to show her how skilled it was in battle. Slowly it swayed at her side, deciding how best to neutralize the enemy.

"I have stolen nothing!" Missy said through clenched teeth. "The Hesperides tortured and tormented me so that I could *earn* Caliburn! I saw things," she paused, the memories haunting her, "I won this thing fair."

Another flash of lightning hit the pier and an explosion of splintered wood pelted the unlucky group of siblings. The Hesperides let out a squeal. All five of them leapt into the water and vanished. "I do not care how you tricked Caliburn, I care only about the records you had stolen from the Hub. Return them immediately or face your death."

Thanatos and Missy looked at each other. Thanatos was not afraid, but he was in no condition to protect Missy or himself. He had not been as lucky as Zeus was to receive his full powers back. Missy was hardly able to stand, let alone fight. Her breath was still harsh in her throat, her mind preoccupied by information she had not yet had time to process.

Zeus took advantage of their momentary weakness. Streetlights nearby broke sending startled mortals scurrying away as Zeus pulled electricity towards him. An electrical current so large that the great Zeus buckled under its weight was launched through the air. There was no time to do anything accept sit back and embrace the speedy death that seemed inevitable.

Caliburn swung through the air and cut into the current, biting through the godspell that Zeus had hurled. The sword moved of its own accord, dragging Missy along after it. It cut and jabbed, a silver blur in the blinding lightning storm. Caliburn thrust one last time and the electricity was absorbed into its blade.

There was silence on the pier as the sword became lifeless once more. All of the gods, even Thanatos, stared at Missy. Disbelief and shock were written on their faces. Hermes and Dionysus no longer smiled. They watched Missy with fear on their faces. Caliburn's true purpose had been revealed.

Missy was terrified by what the blade had done. "It wasn't me," she stammered. "I didn't do anything." She tried to explain, but Zeus's expression was closed.

"Very well, Nemesis," Zeus said. His anger made him trip over the words. "May you be so lucky in our next encounter."

One by one the gods bent, leaving Missy and Thanatos alone on the dock. The sun was just starting to set when Prometheus spoke up from behind them. Missy had forgotten that he was even there.

"You claim that you are a changed god, and yet you make enemies when you could be making friends," Prometheus said evenly. "I suggest you think about what you want, Nemesis." With a pop, he vanished as well.

"We need to get away from here," Thanatos said after a few moments of silence. "Once the shock wears off Zeus will come back and I don't think that you can handle another hit like that."

Missy swayed on her feet and sheathed Caliburn with shaky hands. "I'm fine," she muttered doggedly.

Thanatos knew better. "Oh, really?" He pointed to Missy's shaking hands.

Missy looked down and gasped. Her sword hand was covered in blood where the electricity had all but fused Caliburn into her palm. Little shocks of lightning jumped between her fingers, left over from Zeus's attack. The electricity moved down her fingers and collected on the back of her hand. It became a swirling line of silver, inching its way along her forearm, across her hand, and ended where it wrapped around her left pointer finger. From elbow to fingertip the creeping silver light stretched and spun like an eerie tattoo.

There it stayed, glowing happily, a blinking, crackling, part of her.

It was all too much. Missy had not slept in three days. In that time her body and mind had been pushed to the breaking point, and so she was not surprised when she felt herself getting lightheaded.

Thanatos had not expected Nemesis to faint. With a sigh the god scooped her up, taking care to not let their skin touch. He did not want to risk releasing death on the girl. He hesitated. They could not return to the Hub and there was nowhere else two teenagers could go without arousing mortal interest. Besides, someone would be waiting for him. There was only one thing to do for it. Thanatos bent and left behind the California shore, the limp form of his sister in his arms.

Chapter Twenty-Five

Dionysus sat alone in his room and watched the numbers change on his football clock. His fingers drummed on the desk impatiently. He dearly wanted to pop open a can or bottle of whatever was on hand, but he restrained himself. He glanced around the messy room. Cupid had not returned while Dionysus was away with Zeus. He frowned, an expression completely foreign to his usually jovial face. This mission was ruining his good time, and that would not do at all.

There was a soft pop and two figures appeared in the tiny dorm room. Dionysus nearly jumped out of his skin. Thanatos stood by the door with Missy thrown over his shoulder. He dumped the girl into a pile of dirty laundry and feathers and stretched his aching back. "What took you so long?" Dionysus demanded. The moment he recognized Missy his smile returned. "You should have been right behind me."

"Prometheus had a few parting words of wisdom," Thanatos said. "Told her to be a good little goddess and play nice with the rest of us."

Dionysus laughed. "That's Prometheus. Always thinking ahead," he said. "What's the matter, Than? You look like you need a drink."

Thanatos made a face. "Concentrate. I have bigger problems. Zeus chased me right out of the Hub. Almost split me in two." Thanatos tried to reach around and see the blackened burn between his shoulder blades. Dionysus made a face. The wound stretched from Thanatos's neck down to his belt. Most of the skin was black and dead and flaked away like an overdone sunburn.

"That's gross," Dionysus said wincing. "Rub some dirt in it."

Thanatos plucked a stone beaker from the baldric that was still buckled over Missy's shoulder. "If this is what I think it is, I won't need dirt." Thanatos was unable to keep the sarcasm out of his voice. Water from the enchanted spring would do the trick. "Just a drop." Carefully he pulled free the stopper and dabbed the cork against the oozing burn. The skin bubbled like melted wax and slowly crawled back together. Muscle rewove itself whole. In a moment Thanatos was whole again and without even a hint of pain. "Not bad. At least she was good for something." Thanatos returned the beaker to the sword baldric and flexed, enjoying the freedom of movement his back now allowed.

"Don't act like she didn't hold her own against Zeus today. Saved your life, too. What did you do on the docks again? I think it was a lot of wah-wah-wah," Dionysus said mockingly. He decided that he had waited long enough. He went to the mini fridge and pulled out a cold bottle. Thanatos glared at him but Dionysus shrugged. "What do you want from me, man? This is who I am."

Thanatos rolled his eyes. "An age old excuse. Now what do we do with the girl? I certainly don't want to keep babysitting her. She's going to get me killed."

"That is a bit cold, man," Dionysus said. "And he told us to watch her."

Thanatos made a face. "I don't want to watch her. Just because she has a death wish doesn't mean I do. The little idiot almost got herself killed. Imagine trying to use that sword in her condition. She's reckless with her life." Thanatos shook his head. He was not a bad person, but rather an underworlder who knew what waited on the other side of life. He was in no hurry to face Mictlan and that was the direction Missy was headed in. "She needs to learn caution. She's no good to anyone dead."

"Please," Dionysus said with a loud exhalation. "Don't be so dramatic."

"That's rich coming from you," Thanatos said dryly. "I thought you were a patron of the arts."

Dionysus grinned. "Good art. There is nothing entertaining about you whining. Don't you think you ought to get her off the floor?"

"She's fine." Thanatos dismissed Dionysus's request with a wave. "I'm done carrying her around. It's your turn. I cannot do this. He told us to watch her. He'll hand us our throats if he finds out we failed in keeping her properly in hand..."

"No one has ever kept Nemesis 'in hand'. She's outside most Divine expectation." Dionysus smiled. "She certainly has the whole intimidating champion thing down. She scared us all to death on the docks. Hermes almost swallowed his tongue. Neat trick with the sword, though."

"Yeah, neat." Missy uncurled from where she had been dropped on the floor. "The laundry, Than?" she asked her brother coldly. "I'm not a dirty shirt."

Missy held more than her temper back. A whimper threatened to erupt from the depths of her throat. She had woken up in excruciating pain. Every movement of her arms and legs sent lances of agony through her shoulders and down her spine. She bit back a yelp and stared at the two men. Her brother and her friend were covered in the brown spots of guilt and Missy shook the vision away. She had caught them talking about something they did not want her to know.

"Welcome back, beautiful," Dionysus said grandly. "It's just not a party without you."

Thanatos made no pretenses. "What did you hear?" he demanded.

"Enough." Missy's golden eyes were like chips of frozen topaz. "Who told you to watch me? Prometheus?" she demanded. "Zeus? Or is there someone new who doesn't trust me enough to do my job?"

Thanatos and Dionysus exchanged looks. "You took that out of context," Thanatos said.

"Sure I did." Missy whimpered and leaned against the wall, panting. "Everything is just a big misunderstanding. I don't get it, right? Because I'm," she paused, "what did you call me, Than? A little idiot? I *am* an idiot. I thought that I could trust the two of you."

"Missy," Dionysus began but she cut him off.

"Save it!" she ordered. "You people, you *gods*, have made me feel like I have something to apologize for, like I did something wrong when I defended myself. You've blamed me for everything, when you are just as much at fault as me!"

"The Fall was your doing and yours alone. You did not have to stand against Zeus," Thanatos snapped.

"But he was wrong!" Missy yelled. "I am not the only person to blame. You put the Fall on my shoulders and expect me to carry all that weight around. Well, not anymore."

"The burden of what you did cannot be cast away by mere words. It was your actions that ruined us and it is your responsibility to fix it. I told you that you would be blamed, so just deal with it."

Missy shook her head in disbelief. "Deal with it? That's the best advice you have?" Missy forced herself to her feet. "You want me to just accept all of the hatred you people are throwing at me? No wonder Nemesis was a monster. You turned her into one." She turned on Dionysus. "And you were spying on me?"

Thanatos scoffed. "Yes we were told to watch you, but only because you cannot be trusted." Golden eyes bore into golden eyes as Thanatos and Missy glared at one another.

"I'm untrustworthy?" Missy demanded. "I have been nothing but honest with all of you. Who is really untrustworthy, Than? All you have done since I met you is lie to me and keep secrets! The day I ruined the gods, I did the worlds a favor!"

"You're bleeding," Dionysus said when she had finished.

Missy's shirt was half soaked with blood. Her energetic rant had sent piercing pain into her back though in her rage she had ignored it. Missy rolled up her shirt and looked at her back in the mirror. A horrible disfiguring burn ran from neck to hips, black and open. It was identical to the oozing injury that Thanatos had born from his run in with Zeus. Missy cast her brother a look laced with fury. Her fingers immediately dropped her waist where the stone beaker was secure on her belt.

"That's just perfect." Somehow seeing the source made the pain that much worse and Missy shot one more furious glare at her brother and supposed friend before she turned on her heel and left the dorm room. She slammed the door behind her. Dionysus and Thanatos sat silent and still after she left, each one thinking their own thoughts.

"Tell me if I'm wrong," Dionysus said opening a new bottle for himself. "But that looked an awful lot like…"

"Yes. It did," Thanatos interrupted. "I wasn't expecting that."

—Chapter Twenty-Six—

Poseidon watched and waited patiently. There was no sun beneath the waves. No cool breeze to tempt Cethy back to consciousness. It had been over two thousand years since he had last seen another Olympian and he would wait as long as necessary for the luck goddess to wake up.

The sea god would have smiled if he had still had a mouth. The day after this surprise fell into his lap he had felt things changing again above his watery domain. There was a call in the wind. *Rise*, it whispered. *Rise. Take your rightful place.* Now he had an Olympian resting comfortably in the air bubble he had created for her. If only she would wake up.

As if she heard his thoughts, Cethy opened her eyes. The darkness that surrounded her was complete and terrifying. The only sound was the deep bone-shaking bellow of the ocean. The last thing she remembered was that treacherous angel abandoning her and now she was waist deep in something cold and wet. What had happened?

"It is good to see you awake. I was worried."

Cethy flinched. The voice was a whisper, but so low and big she could *feel* it. She twisted in her liquid prison, but there was nothing to see, simply darkness.

"Do not be afraid," the voice said quickly. "It was never my intention to frighten or imprison you. Understand if I let you out of that air bubble you would be most uncomfortable. You are at the very bottom of the Atlantic Ocean."

"The Atlantic?" Cethy repeated. Something bumped her arm as it floated in the air bubble with her. Cethy shrank away from it but when nothing started nibbling at her, she groped in the darkness and felt Cupid's quiver. Cethy had managed to hold onto it when she lost consciousness. "I'm at the bottom of the ocean? For how long?" She was fighting down the panic that was swelling in her chest. There was not much she could do if what the voice said was true.

"I am Poseidon," the voice continued. "You have been asleep in my waters for a week of mortal time."

"A week?" Cethy was stunned. "I've been here a week? I've got to get back to the surface!" She paused. "Where are you?"

"I would show myself to you, but the Fall was not kind," Poseidon said.

"Not kind?" Cethy asked. "How so? You still have your power. At least, you have enough to keep me here."

"I have not had a body since the goddess Nemesis unleashed her fury on Zeus. Foolish creature. There are always consequences."

"And the selkie?" Cethy questioned.

"They are not gods," Poseidon said simply. "The little monsters. They go untouched while their lord suffers."

Cethy had heard enough. "Well, thank you for the air and all, but I really shouldn't be here. Can you take me back to the surface?" The water around her rippled in what could only have been laughter.

"I could have taken you topside at any time," Poseidon said. "I have kept you here for a reason. You want something, and I want something. It is only right that we help one another."

"I don't want anything from you," Cethy said. "I just need to get back to land."

"I see. I was under the impression that you were here for Athena's shield. My mistake," Poseidon said lightly. "I just thought that the only thing that would draw the luck goddess so far from her natural element would be the Aegis."

Cethy could have cursed. That lousy shield. "And what do you want in return?" she asked. The redhead knew perfectly well that there was nothing freely given when it came to the Divine. "Keep in mind I have nothing. No control over my powers, no one to help me, and no way to get you your body back."

The water rippled in Poseidon's sad laughter. "I will have no body until the gods further their ascent to power. Until I have back what is rightfully mine." Cethy stumbled as the bubble began to move upward. "I was once guardian of this great ocean. There have always been other water gods, but while I was strong I had a way to keep them at bay." Poseidon chuckled. "Sorry, small water joke." When Cethy did not share in his mirth he cleared his throat and continued his tale. "Soon after the first gods and goddesses began to disappear, I made the mistake of leaving my trident behind while I investigated an object that had appeared in my kingdom.

"Athena's shield had plummeted into my waters, immediately becoming my property. I can only assume that she lost it as she was lost herself, spinning off through time and space because of that fool, Nemesis."

"Don't talk about her that way!" Cethy yelled.

The water grew cold around her, as did Poseidon's voice. "Nemesis deserved her fate," Poseidon rumbled. "There was no need for the rest of us to share it with her." Cethy was given the distinct impression that if Poseidon had had eyes he would have been glaring at her. "Insolent youth. I returned here to find my trident gone, most of my powers along with it. I had the shield to protect myself, but no trident to protect my people or my ocean. Before I could go on a campaign after my weapon, the Fall's curse hit me, and I was stripped of my body."

"That is awful," Cethy whispered. "I had no idea that the Fall was so horrible."

"Then you are fortunate," Poseidon said sadly. "Now, we come to the bargain. I will give you the shield. All I need is my trident back first. Bring my trident from the god who stole it and the shield will be yours."

Cethy could not ignore the sense of foreboding that was stealing over her. "Who took the Aegis exactly?"

"Sobek." Poseidon's voice was so full of venom, it made Cethy shudder. "The Egyptian god, Sobek. You must go to the Nile where he lurks and you must get me back my trident!"

Cethy went blind as the air bubble broke the surface and sunlight filled her world once again. She was slouched over in her liquid enclosure, her face covered with her arms. It had been a week since she had had a breath of fresh air and the moment that Poseidon set her free, she gulped oxygen greedily into her lungs.

The selkie stared at her as she tried to pull herself, sopping wet, onto the very rock she had been swept from a week prior. One dragged itself over and helped pull her from the water. Cethy could not help but notice its swollen nose. "I am ssssorry," the selkie hissed sulkily.

"Me, too," Cethy said, trying not to stare.

Cethy wrung out her red hair and stood dripping. A small wave beat itself against the rock. "Luck goddess!" Now that she was above water Poseidon's voice felt less like a bellow and more like a whisper seeping up through her feet.

The eighteen year old dropped to her knees and rested the quiver at her side as the water pooled in a crevice in the rock face. "You must remember not to get too close to Sobek," Poseidon warned. "He is a fertility god, and he takes his responsibilities seriously. And do not be fooled by his appearance. Get back that trident and you will have the shield. Now, go." Cethy could feel a blush rising in her cheeks. "What are you waiting for? Go."

"I can't," Cethy said miserably. "I don't know how. I've only bent once and that was to get here. I'm not sure how to do it again."

The pool of water by her knees rippled with frustration. "Focussss." The selkie was at her side. "It issss what your flyer did. He focussssed his thoughts and vanished."

Cethy stared at the eerie sea creature. Her blood ran cold in her veins. "Vanished? Cupid bent?" she asked, her voice a whisper. "Are you sure?"

The selkie nodded his brown eyes sincere. "He flew far above my wave then vanished."

Cethy pulled her amulet out from under her shirt. The ice chip glistened in the sunlight, casting little rainbows on the rock. She brought the enchanted ice to her eye and cleared her head of distraction the way Niamh taught her. Somehow she was able to ignore her pounding heart and heavy breathing.

"Show me." Cethy muttered to the amulet. "Show me the past."

A single color appeared in the depths of the ice, joined quickly by others. As the image expanded, Cethy recognized the very rock they were standing on now. She saw herself yelling angrily into the air as a massive wave rose up to wipe the rock clean. She watched as the selkies jeered at Cupid, mocking his loss and his cowardice. She watched as the love god rose into the air, carried by those great wings. "I have to tell Bave," he muttered. With that Cupid vanished into nothingness.

Cethy dropped the amulet. Rage swelled in her chest. She didn't need to look into the ice to see that day on the cliffs a month ago. Missy stood between

Cupid and herself, wheezing and gasping from their recent journey to Tir na n-Og.

Those who were not granted wings with which to travel were given the ability to move through space. I can fly.

He said it himself. Cupid could not bend space.

Cethy felt sick to her stomach. She did not understand how she had missed the clues before. Cupid returning to Tir na n-Og a full week early, and abandoning Cethy to the selkies' wave. Even Cethy's visions of the future suddenly made sense. There had been two Cupids. Two of them.

"What's the matter with you girl?" Poseidon had obviously been talking and was displeased at being ignored. "What's wrong?"

"It's Cupid," Cethy whispered. "He's a fake!" Cethy's blue eyes were cold. Something was growing inside her chest, expanding with power. "I'm sorry. There's something that I must do." She hardly had to try this time. Her mind was completely focused as she disappeared from the rock. Cethy had found her inner goddess, and it was furious.

Poseidon poured himself back into the ocean, heaving a great sigh. "She'll be back." he said to the selkie. "Of that I have no doubt. Soon she will return. Soon, the gods will rise."

Chapter Twenty-Seven

Cethy came out of the bend emanating raw power. She did not recognize where she had emerged, but Cethy followed her luck. For years her ability had led her to silly things that she did not need or want, but now it was leading her exactly where she wanted to go. Her mind was wholly focused on the Cupid in her vision and her search for his essence had led her here.

Cethy's dusty blue eyes swept her surroundings. Rolling green hills surrounded her. A country road wound off into the distance. To her right was a rickety wooden fence enclosing a grove of apple trees. Her quarry was there, hidden from her. It knew she was coming. It was afraid.

For the first time in her life, Cethy felt no limitations. No fear. *Tyche.* She thought to herself. *Not Cethy.* And so she was. Gone was the self-conscious, frightened little girl who needed Missy to keep her safe. Gone was the junk collector. Gone was the victim. Tyche had at last emerged.

Tyche lazily flicked her hand at the fence and the wood collapsed into a pile of splinters. She smiled. The false Cupid had said that she was telekinetic, able to move things about with her mind. It would seem he had not lied about that. She stepped into the orchard, her eyes boring through the grove of apple trees. "I suggest you come out." Her voice rang out through the silence, authoritative and severe. "And no tricks. I do not feel forgiving." Nothing moved. There was not a sound except for Tyche's slow deliberate steps. "Suit yourself." she growled.

The newly awakened goddess pointed to an apple tree in the grove and let pure Divine energy spill out of her fingers. The ground shook as the tree uprooted and flipped over in the air. Dirt and fruit fell to Earth as Tyche used her mind to shake it all loose. With a bellow, something small and gray-black dropped from a leafy branch and rolled into the grass. Tyche released the tree, letting it land in a confused pile of earth and wood.

"Mercy. Mercy!" A filthy animal crawled from the debris. "Goddess, I had no choice! Please, show mercy!"

Tyche stared down at this new enemy, unsure of what to think. The shaggy gray monster might have been an extra furry cat if not for the thin membrane that stretched between its front and back legs like that of a flying squirrel. Its coat was grubby and matted. The tiny face was dominated by a pair of gigantic yellow eyes. She had been looking for the false Cupid and had been led here. This was not a new enemy, but an old one in a new form.

"You had no choice?" Tyche's mind gripped the little animal and lifted him clean off of the ground. "You had no choice but to leave me to die?" She bounced the shaggy cat into the grass. "And I suppose that you won't have any choice but to kill Missy when the future comes? I won't let that happen!"

"Kill Nemesis? I would not!" Those large yellow eyes filled with tears. "I *could* not! Cupid was too strong to let me so much as touch her, let alone kill her! I know you're displeased that I left you behind but I had to. I can't bear to be near water and you dropped us in the middle of the Atlantic. A wet pouka is powerless pouka, goddess."

Tyche tightened her invisible grip on the creature. "I suggest that you start answering some questions," she snarled. "Starting with what you are and what you did with the real Cupid."

The animal moaned. "I will not tell you. It is not worth the punishments that Bave will inflict upon me."

Tyche was stone faced as she drew the animal close through the air. His words were as hoity as his tone despite the terror that shook his small frame. "Then pick your poison because if you don't answer me, I'll kill you myself." The animal's enormous yellow eyes grew even larger in fright. "Now, what are you?"

"A pouka," it said wretchedly.

"A what?"

"I am a pouka," the animal wailed. "A shape shifter. A creature of Irish folklore. My kind are in allegiance with the Charonte. They give us Divine essence and in return we pouka do their bidding. I was supposed to lead you through Circle. You and Nemesis were to do all the work while I spied on you as Cupid. As soon as you collected the items, I was to steal them and bring them to Hel. I had no choice."

"You keep saying that," Tyche growled.

"It's true." The pouka struggled in Tyche's grasp. "The Charonte kill the gods and give us the essence they steal. Powers. Immortality. It's a drug to our kind. We don't come by such things naturally and so long as we do what they say, the Charonte let us pouka keep the Divine essence. All we have to do is hold the shape of the body they show us."

"Body?" Tyche listened closely to everything the pouka was saying and tried to hide her confusion. The little monster was just like all the other myth units she'd come across since Prometheus knocked on her door. Riddles and cryptic nonsense spun through her mind while she processed his grand way of speaking. The only thing that was clear was that the Charonte were behind this. She should have known. They had found themselves a tribe of shape shifters. Who knew how many of them had flawlessly taken over the lives of the originals? It was lucky that Cethy had caught the little imposter before he had been able to unload the precious items of the Circle from the Norns' hands. The water, soon to be the shield... Tyche started, and glared at the shaggy beast. "Wait. What body?"

"The bodies that the Charonte show us." The pouka gave up his struggle and hung limply in the air.

"They show us the gods they kill so that we can mimic them."

The pouka let out a shriek of fear and pain as Tyche shook him with her mind. "You lie," she growled.

"Mercy!" the pouka squealed. "I cannot!"

"You can't lie?" Tyche demanded. "You lied your fluffy tail off on Tir na n-Og. You were pretending to be Cupid!"

The animal howled in terror. "I was a free beast on Tir na n-Og but once a pouka is captured it cannot not speak false! You have caught me, goddess, and until you free me I cannot so much as utter a dishonest word. Please understand. Hel will kill me for this! Do not ask me anything, do not make me answer!"

"Cupid is..." Tyche's voice was hard. Her hold on the pouka tightened. "The real Cupid? He's gone?"

"Yes," the pouka yowled. "Yes, Cupid has been delivered to the underworld. I saw the body myself. I carried his essence! Bave gave it to me."

The power in Tyche snuffed out like a candle in a hurricane. Cethy gasped and collapsed into the debris. The pouka let out a frightened squeal as it was suddenly released and dropped to the ground. It started to scramble away, but Cethy's heart-wrenching whisper stopped it in its tracks. "Cupid is dead." It was not a question, but a stunned admission.

The pouka inched toward Cethy. "Only in the mortal sense. His strong emotions and memories are still in his essence. Cupid lives on in his Divinity."

"And where is that now?" Cethy whispered. "If he lives in his essence, then give it back. Save him."

The pouka chattered nervously. "I fear that I cannot. When I left you, I failed. The Charonte extracted Cupid's power again." The pouka had crept close to try and comfort the goddess and so was horrified when the girl burst into tears. Frightened, the small animal let out a chirp of alarm and bent space to escape the girl's forlorn cries.

—Chapter Twenty-Eight—

It was hours later before the pouka plucked up the courage to reappear silently in the orchard. The small animal was anxious, his senses on alert. Every shadow was menacing, every sound threatening. The pouka inched forward. Hidden somewhere in the debris of the fallen tree was a goddess gone mad. Slowly the pouka crept closer. That was the downfall of his kind. They were constantly curious. It froze. There she was.

Cethy was still, her tears long dried. She sat among the wreckage of the uprooted tree, hugging her knees, her eyes unseeing. She had a lot of information to wrap her mind around. Not only had she misplaced Missy, but her guide was dead, the Charonte were stealing abilities from the gods, and an entire tribe of shape-shifting monsters was running wild with Divine power. If she had any luck at all, it was all bad. On top of that she was stranded and without any active power of her own. The last several hours Cethy had been trying to bend, but to no avail. She could not concentrate long enough to focus her thoughts. All she could think about was the mistake that had started it all.

"I should never have left the Mayan," Cethy muttered to herself. "Why did I think that I could do this?"

The pouka crept closer. Something glittered in Cethy's hand and the shape shifter could not look away. Cethy's face was a frustrated scowl. "Work. *Please*, work!" A shiny talisman dangled between her fingers, catching the light of the sinking sun. "Why won't you show me what I want to See?"

Cethy drove her fist into the grove's soft earth. She had failed. Prometheus had set her on the right path and explained what needed to be accomplished. All she had done was make a mess of things. It was good that she and Missy had been separated. Missy would be better off without Cethy dragging her down. From the very beginning it was Missy who got the job done. Missy had faced Erin and Anubis in the hotel while Cethy had gone out the window to escape. Missy had trained with the Amazons and earned the water for the Circle. Missy had stood up to the false Cupid.

The amulet burst into light in Cethy's hand, colors swirling in its center. Cethy fumed. She had no control over the talisman or the visions that came to it. The images in the ice chip came of their own accord, heedless to her demands. She held the amulet up and immersed herself in what it held.

It was Missy. She was half drowned, shivering, and standing next to a strange man. Neither of them looked especially happy. Missy clutched a sword in her hand and swayed on her feet, weak. Lightning erupted in the image and Cethy dropped the amulet in the dirt.

That was not what she had wanted to See.

"Shiny."

Cethy almost jumped out of her skin. The pouka had come back and had snuck up next to her. It was lying on its stomach, its black nose quivering with apprehension. It pawed at the silver chain resting in the upturned earth. "Look."

Cethy glared at the pouka, but its attention was on the amulet. She picked the ice chip out of the dirt and wiped its surface clean. The redhead hardly even set eyes on the amulet before it pulled her into its depths yet again.

The image was as cold as the ice it appeared in. Cethy didn't even recognize the beach out back of the Mayan. It was empty and still. No waves lapped against the sand. There was no wind to shape the dunes. Even the sun gave no warmth. Something was horribly wrong.

The pouka crept closer to Cethy. Slowly, it climbed into the girl's lap. It never took its eyes from the vision.

"Erebus." Its fur stood on end as it hissed the word. The vision showed them only one thing. Emptiness. Emptiness covered her entire world.

The ice went dark.

Cethy was stunned. "What was that?" She couldn't shake the chill that the vision had given her. "What happened to everything?"

The pouka stayed curled up and shivering in Cethy's lap and the girl did not try to displace it. "That, goddess, was the soul of underworld free in the Mortal Realm. Erebus. It takes the life from everything it touches. Sun, waves, wind, people... All overwhelmed and drained by the Void."

Cethy shook her head. "I was supposed to stop this from happening," she muttered, absently she drew the pouka up under her chin for comfort. "I'm the one who was supposed to prevent this."

The pouka glanced up at her, its yellow eyes massive. "I am well aware, goddess. I was charged with foiling your attempts at success but so long as we are being truthful with each other, I'd much prefer to help you stop that vision from ever coming to pass." The pouka climbed up onto the girl's shoulder, its squirrelly tail wrapping around her arm for balance. "You cannot let Erebus rise to the Mortal Realm. Erebus consumes all life. It spares nothing."

Cethy rubbed her head with her free hand. From the beginning it seemed that one problem after another was stacking itself at her feet. She had to find Missy, stop the Charonte from finding the Fates, and stop the Fates from weaving the end of the world.

"But I can't stop it. I'm all alone and my powers won't work. How can I to do this without my abilities?" she asked. "How can I do this without Missy?"

"Nemesis will take care of herself, goddess. But I can help you. I'm more than capable of bending and I had Cupid's memories long enough to know what you have to find." The monster's tail tightened around Cethy's arm. "The Charonte might have reclaimed Cupid's power but we pouka have skills all our own. I can still shape-shift and spy. I'm not without uses." It twitched with nerves and excitement. "I will help you win, goddess, I promise. And no pouka would dare break its word."

Cethy shook her head and the pouka gnawed on one of her earrings. "Why do you suddenly want to help me?"

The pouka released Cethy's earring. "This is my world, too. If it falls so do the pouka."

"And you cannot break your word?" Cethy asked.

The pouka showed its teeth. "Never. If I did I would get stuck in a single shape. No pouka wants to get stuck."

Cethy contemplated her future. She certainly couldn't stay in the lonely orchard. And she couldn't fight the Charonte and secure the fates all by herself. The pouka had Cupid and perhaps had the guide's memories. The strange creature could know where the remaining items of the Moirais' Circle might be. It also had magic, and that was something Cethy sorely lacked. "I hope for all our sakes that you're telling me the truth, pouka." Cethy's voice was not as strong or as sure as she would have liked it to be.

The pouka resumed its attack on her earring. "Why would I lie now? I am helping you this time, goddess. We are now on the same side."

Cethy stood, careful not to expel the pouka from its place on her shoulder. "What do I call you? I can't just call you pouka all the time, can I?"

The furry animal moved to Cethy's other shoulder, its tail looping around her neck for stability. "My kind do not have names. Pouka are just... Pouka."

"But won't that get confusing? What if I'm taking about your family?" Cethy pulled her earring from the animal's grasp. "Stop that."

"You may call me whatever you like, goddess." The pouka pouted and hid beneath Cethy's hair. It flicked her earring with its paw. "I have always been partial to a winged shape. That was part of the appeal in becoming Cupid. My favorite form is a gull. You may call me that."

Cethy nodded. "Gull it is. Let's do our best then, shall we? Can you take us to the trident?"

"We shall not let Erebus rise." The newly named pouka clutched Cethy's shirt with its little paws and pulled the goddess into a bend.

Even with her amulet, Cethy had no idea what the future held. There were so many things that did not make sense, and not nearly enough time to ponder it. She was already moving through the fabric of space, towards the unknown with Gull perched on her shoulder. She couldn't be sure if the pouka was a friend or an enemy and for the moment it didn't really matter. For now, at least, Cethy wasn't alone.

Chapter Twenty-Nine

Cethy wasn't convinced that Gull was completely trustworthy. Earlier that week he had left her for dead in the middle of the ocean so she had plenty of reason to be skeptical. She was even more uncertain of his loyalties when they appeared in the middle of a loud and unfamiliar place. The smells and noise were overwhelming. Gull had brought them right into the middle of a busy market place. Cethy was sure that they would be discovered, but no one seemed to notice that she had materialized out of thin air with a small monster on her shoulder. People moved past them in large groups, speaking quickly and in a language that Cethy did not understand.

"Gull, where are we?" Cethy shrunk back against a stall selling vegetables. Adventure was not her forte and the unfamiliarity of the place was very quickly giving her a panic attack.

Gull stuck his head out from under Cethy's hair, his nose quivering. "Egypt. It smells like Kom Ombo. I lived here long ago. Lovely place."

"We're in Egypt." If nothing else this quest was making her well-traveled. Cethy peeked her head out of the shadows and frowned. They needed to find Poseidon's trident. To do that, they needed to find Sobek. "I thought you were going to bend us to the trident." Cethy hissed. "So far you aren't helping."

"Sobek is a Nile god, is he not? So it stands to reason that Sobek should be by the Nile." Gull tugged on Cethy's hair, forcing her to turn and look. He was pointing down the narrow lane, his tiny claws extended in excitement. "Look there!"

A sturdy stone structure stood not twenty feet away, separate from the market. It was a shrine and if the bronze statue out front was anything to go by, it belonged to the crocodile-headed Egyptian deity. Cethy grimaced and stepped back into the crushing mass of the market. Gull hugged the back of her neck and tried to stay hidden beneath her short hair. She could feel the small animal pulling on her earrings in his excitement. Only a few more steps would take them into Sobek's temple. Cethy hesitated outside the building. Anything could be waiting for them inside.

"Why do you hesitate? Go in and fetch your trident so that we may extricate ourselves from this location."

Cethy did not want any more surprises. She reached into her shirt and pulled out Niamh's amulet. "Show me." she commanded. "Show me what's inside."

The amulet seemed to heave a sigh as pictures appeared inside. Cethy brought the small ice chip to her eye and was dazzled by a brilliant blue sky, and dark water. Waves lapped against a small bit of rock as Cethy appeared in the image, a fluffy tail wound tightly around her arm. She was leaning on a bone white staff tipped with three sharp points. The trident.

Cethy smiled and stuffed the amulet back into her shirt. "You ready, Gull?" she asked. "Finally, something is going to go right." Cethy gave Gull a scratch behind his ear and stepped into the temple.

Inside it was empty and dark and smelt of incense. Candles flickered on the altar and along the walls. There were life-sized crocodile totems propped up behind the altar, their mouths forever open in a toothy gape. A heavy velvet curtain hung behind the altar. It heaved slowly in the breeze from the open door.

Gull's tail tightened around Cethy's arm. The air in the tiny shrine was oppressive and heavy, though not as heavy as the sense of foreboding that settled in Cethy's stomach. Horrible things had happened in this ancient place. Cethy could hear the screams, the pleading, coming from the pendant around her neck. Cethy's stomach clenched. "I don't like it here," she whispered. "This is a bad place."

Gull agreed and his tail tightened around Cethy's neck. Cethy was already backing out of the temple when Gull tugged sharply on her hair. "Do not run. Be as Nemesis is. Brave. Strong."

Cethy did not want to be brave or strong. She wanted to run. She wanted to tell Poseidon thanks but no thanks. She wanted to wake up from the nightmare that had become her life.

"Why are you here?"

Cethy let out a half strangled scream. A man stepped out from behind the velvet curtain, his face hidden by a veil that obscured the bottom of his face. His eyes were blank. "Why have you come here?" he asked, his voice as empty as his eyes. "Sobek does not converse with your kind."

"My kind?" Cethy asked shakily.

"Olympians." the priest said. "He has no fondness for your pantheon. You should leave. Now."

Gull's hair was on end, his sharp little teeth barred. "He is not right, goddess. Look at his eyes." Cethy could feel it, too. The priest's voice was too slow, his movements jerky. It was as if he were a robot being controlled by someone who wasn't quite sure how to work the remote.

"I'm not leaving until I speak to you face to face, Sobek," Cethy said to the priest. She tried to keep the fear out of her voice, but to no avail. "It will not take long."

The priest was silent for a long while. Indeed, Cethy thought that he was not going to respond at all. "Very well," he answered at last. "I am in the Nile, waiting for you. Come to me, Olympian."

The famous river that carved its way through Egypt gave Cethy the willies. Its water was dark and murky, hiding its horrors beneath the surface. Every ripple, every wave, seemed like a crocodile's wake. With each movement of the rushes, Cethy was convinced that evil was lurking towards them.

"So what's the plan here, Gull?" Cethy paced the banks, her eyes on the water. "I don't have an active power, you know. If he doesn't like what we have to say, we're in big trouble." Gull chittered on her shoulder, laughing. "It isn't funny, Gull. You are the only magic we have."

"My tricks won't be a match for an angry god," Gull said. "It's in our best interest not to tell Sobek that."

"What aren't you telling Sobek?"

Cethy shut her eyes in irritation. That was the second time in an hour that someone had snuck up behind her. Cethy turned and cocked her head in confusion. A boy stood among the reeds, eyes as yellow as Gull's though they had none of the warmth. He came forward, his hands webbed, his fingers clawed, and his teeth sharp, yellowed, and horrible. He was only a child. A cruel-looking child.

"Sobek?" Cethy did not know whether to be frightened or sympathetic. "What happened?"

The boy snarled. "Olympian foolishness," he said. "The Fall. One moment I'm the Nile god as I have always been, the next I'm on the wrong continent and I'm, I'm..." he faded off.

"Twelve?" Cethy supplied, hoping that she was being helpful.

Sobek glared at her. "Yes, twelve. Thank you," Sobek snarled. "I was going to say hideous. Look at me! I could pass for human! It's sickening." Cethy wasn't entirely certain that Sobek would pass for a human but she thought it best to hold her tongue. Sobek bared his horrible pointed teeth. "This isn't natural. It isn't who I am. I'm supposed to look like them." He pointed into the river where a small legion of crocodiles floated in the shallows. "What is that thing draped over your shoulders?"

Gull stuck his head out from Cethy's hair and bared his teeth. "I beg your pardon? I am not a *thing*! I am a pouka!"

"The pouka are returned now too? Wonderful," Sobek's voice was thick with distaste. He sat down in the dark soil and sighed unhappily. "You wanted to talk, Olympian. So talk," he ordered. "I have things to do."

Cethy opened her mouth, but no sound came out. She hadn't really thought about what she would say to Sobek when she found him. What could she say? *I need the trident you stole to save the world?* She didn't think that that would go over well.

"Have you noticed anything unusual, lately?" she asked lamely.

Sobek snorted derisively. "Well it isn't every day that my shrine is sullied by an Olympian and a Celtic monster."

"That's not what I mean." Cethy felt like she was arguing with Missy. She would have to choose her words carefully just to get anywhere. "Have you felt stronger? Sensed anything?"

Sobek looked at her with those angry yellow eyes. "Is that what brings you here? The Rise?"

Cethy hesitated. "Actually, I'm here about the Circle."

Gull let out a shriek into Cethy's hair. "Goddess, why would you tell him?" he moaned.

"The Circle," Sobek repeated. He put his chin in his hands, thinking. "So you are a Norn. Since when do Norns travel alone? That's not very bright. Anything could happen to you all by yourself."

Cethy did not like the look in the god's eye. Neither did Gull and the pouka chirped angrily from her shoulder. "She is far from alone, river scum. The goddess has me!"

"And little protection you would be if anyone decided to do her harm," Sobek said carefully. "You chose your companion poorly, luck goddess." Sobek stood and inched forward.

"You'd do well to keep your distance!" Gull screeched. "Or Nemesis will hunt you down. She is the Norns' Champion and if you are fool enough to threaten her cousin, vengeance will find you swiftly, make no mistake."

Sobek froze halfway through his advance. "Nemesis is back, is she?" the little boy asked. He smiled. "I always liked her. She wasn't nearly as foolish as the rest of you except at the end. I offered to share my river with her once." The little god took a few steps back. "Very well. Nemesis can exercise her wrath elsewhere. Still you are here, and that warrants answers."

Cethy's heart was fit to pound its way free of her chest. Once again, Missy had saved her and she hadn't even needed to be present to do it. "I already told you that I am here about the Circle."

"Nothing I have can be used to build that tragedy of an enchantment," Sobek said trickily. Cethy's eyes narrowed. She knew what Missy would have said. Technically, Sobek had not lied. He did not have any of the items for the Circle. "I'm afraid I can't help you, though I would if I could."

"You could give me the trident." The words were out of Cethy's mouth before she could stop herself. Gull made a frightened sound and hugged the back of her neck. Cethy's stomach dropped as Sobek's uncanny eyes burned into her.

"What does a Norn need with my trident?" Sobek demanded. For a child he was terrifying. "The trident isn't a part of the Circle or any enchantment that you would be interested in."

"Poseidon has the Aegis. If I want to build the Circle I'm going to need to get the trident for him. If you return his trident, he will give me the shield."

Sobek smiled, his jagged teeth a clear threat. "No."

"No?" Cethy repeated.

"No. That trident is the only power that I have left. Who will protect the crocodiles or flood the river if you leave me here powerless? Without it I am little more than a human child. An ugly human child. No mortal would show me mercy. I won't help you."

Cethy could not believe her ears. "But if you give Poseidon back the trident, I can build the Circle and the gods will rise. You'll only be without power for a short time."

"No," Sobek said. He was getting agitated. Gull peeked out from Cethy's hair. Behind them was the bank of the Nile. The pouka let out a frightened chirp. Dozens of crocodiles waited for them there. The water surged with scaly backs and snapping jaws. The water was churning and vibrating with the beasts' unease. "I will not subjugate myself for any god, for any reason. The answer is no, idiot Olympian. No."

Cethy had not expected Sobek to just hand the trident over, but she had thought that if she explained how important it was, that she was trying to save the world, he would comply.

"You don't understand," Cethy whispered. Her body buzzed with barely contained anger and bitter disappointment. Missy would have convinced Sobek to do the right thing. Why couldn't she? Cethy tried to appeal to Sobek again. "Without the shield, the Circle will be incomplete. The Moirai will weave destruction of the Mortal Realm. That includes your river, Sobek. If you want to protect it you need to help me!"

Sobek shook his head. "No."

"I am not leaving without the trident, Sobek," Cethy said, sounding braver than she felt. She froze, a chill plunging into her chest. Her breath came out in frozen puffs of air. The amulet.

"Then I suppose that you aren't leaving." Sobek waved a hand and a white staff appeared in his chubby fists. The trident was magnificent. Made from the bone of some underwater giant, it dwarfed the Nile god. "I am truly sorry about this, but I cannot part with the trident. If Nemesis comes to avenge you, I will let her know that you are no real loss. To think that you are a Norn," he shook his head. "Your venture must have been doomed from the start."

Sobek pointed the trident at the reeds that grew along the river and the ground began to shake. Cethy screamed as the reeds pulled themselves from the damp ground. She and Gull were trapped in a cyclone of swamp grass. It twisted around them, weaving together into a cage. "Maybe after a few days in the Nile you will see my point of view." Cethy could hear Sobek's voice on the other side of the reed wall. "Don't worry. It shouldn't leak too much. And I wouldn't try to escape. You'd never make it past my brothers." There was a great vibration as though a hundred great beasts were laughing. The crocodiles were thrumming.

"Leak?" Gull's fur was on end, his slight frame shaking.

Cethy felt the reed box moving and suddenly her feet were wet. She moaned. "He's putting us into the river."

Chapter Thirty

Hel shivered and hugged her arms about herself. After hiding for so long in the Mortal Realm she was ill prepared for the eerie cold of the underworld. It sunk into her bones and made her tremble uncontrollably. There was no natural light, no warmth, in the Erebus. An eerie blue glow cast a dim relief of the desolate, gray landscape. Everything looked the same, but Hel knew better. This was once her kingdom, her domain. To think the realm harmless would be a grave mistake.

Hel paused to listen. She had been in the Void for several hours and had not yet adjusted to the stillness. "Should have worn a coat," she muttered to herself. Her voice was the only sound in the smothering silence. That was the Void. Cold and silent. Her resolve was solid. Hel refused to turn back empty handed. For now the pouka were in league with the Charonte but the lot of them were tricksters and irritably moral. The Charonte would not be able to manipulate them for much longer. Eventually, they would lose interest or worse, realize the unique position they had in the war to come. Nothing was worse than a pouka who knew too much. Hel was not about to let a herd of flying squirrels ruin her plans. She was going to secure a Charonte victory, one way or another. Even if it meant she had to break the very laws of nature.

She had left Bave sitting in the Mayan with Eris and a significant job to do. Piles and piles of books and files littered the floor of Eris's room. The location and powers of most of the Olympian gods were in those files. The histories and secrets of Olympus were at their disposal. It had been too easy in tricking the foolish Olympians into let their guard down. One well-placed spy had undone centuries of work. Still it was no time to celebrate.

Hel had put on a joyful face when she felt her powers grow stronger, but upon closer inspection the underworlder was grim. Hel had returned to her kingdom but she did not feel the relief or familiarity she had anticipated. The Void no longer felt like hers. It wasn't enough. Somehow she had become a stranger in her own empire. It was the Mortal Realm that called for her rule now but to accomplish that Hel needed to push herself deeper into the bowels of Erebus.

She blamed the Norns for her foul mood. Earlier that morning Hel had heard a whisper in the wind. *Rise,* it had called to her. *Rise. Take your rightful place.* The voice was one that she had known a lifetime ago. Nemesis. Hel had been about to fly into a rage, but then she felt the rush of power that accompanied the ghostly call. Far from bettering her mood, the power boost only darkened the underworlder's mood all the more. It meant that Nemesis had gotten her filthy hands on an object of the Moirais' Circle. It was Nemesis's strength, her determination that had carried her voice to the gods hidden around the world. The Olympian was pulling the Norns ahead of the Charonte and it could not be tolerated.

"Well, well, well. Look who has come home."

Hel's skin crawled at the sound of a silky voice in the darkness. Hel was careful to stare at the ground as a shadow approached through the dim blue mist. At last. Hel had been on the hunt for a monster most foul that had long since been vanquished. It was among the most fearsome creatures in any mythology. Its devastation had reached far and wide, leaving none unscathed. It was the ultimate weapon, and Hel had to have it. "Come forward," the goddess commanded.

There was a hiss and a snake slide over Hel's foot. An incomplete figure stepped into the dim grey light. Her scaly, green skin was washed out in the poor light that Erebus offered. Most spectacular, there was nothing on her shoulders. Her head was cradled in her arms. Snakes were tangled in the monster's pale blonde hair. Every few seconds one would spill onto the dark, indistinct earth and slither away.

Hel reached into her cloak and pulled out a pair of sunglasses and presented them to the monster. "Put them on. I don't want any accidents."

The impossible creature ignored the glasses in Hel's hand. "I brought the great and powerful queen back into the Void?" Her voice was little more than a whisper. "I cannot believe it. What warrants such an honor?"

Hel shook the glasses and begrudgingly the wicked beast took them and placed them on her face. "I have an offer for you." Hel said. "Things are getting complicated in the Mortal Realm."

"Things are just as complicated here, Hel." She paused and pointed to her head. "Would you mind? This is uncomfortable." Hel sighed and flicked her hand over the creature's severed neck. She wasn't a healer by nature but it stood to reason that the better she understood something as complex as the human body the more effectively she could torture it. The monster's head rose up and reattached itself, sinews, arteries, and flesh knit together. The fearsome figure moved her neck from side to side, getting used to being whole once again.

The gorgon eyed Hel with interest from behind her shades. "It is…appropriate that you are here. Those of us in the underworld can feel the instability topside. Erebus is just itching to get up there and spread its tranquility." Medusa said the word as though it left a bad flavor on her tongue. "If you are here, then you are recruiting for the war that we all know is coming."

Hel drew herself up and glared at Medusa. "I might be recruiting, but it isn't for the war. Before we end the insipid Mortal Realm, we need to conquer it. The Moirai are awake, and the Norns are moving ahead in the race to win them."

"And you need me." It wasn't a question. Medusa could feel the strangeness in the air. She could feel Erebus, eager to rise, to be free, and it was making the underworld's inhabitants antsy.

"The Norns have found themselves a champion to help them on their quest. They do not deserve such an edge. If they have a warrior fighting for them, I feel that the Charonte should have one as well."

"Is that why you were looking for me?" Medusa's smile was coy and foul. "I am fascinated by your idea, Hel, but I can have no impact in the Mortal Realm. I have no body. I am simply a shadow, a spirit trapped in the Void. How can I help you?"

Hel smiled. "My powers are enough to give you life once more, but there is a condition, Medusa."

"I expect nothing less from you." Medusa tried to keep her eagerness in check. She did not want to show Hel how badly she wanted to escape the grip of Erebus. It did not do well to let an underworlder know how much power they truly had over you. They had a tendency to take advantage.

"Here is my offer," Hel said, coldly. "I will bring you back to the Mortal Realm. You will have a body. You will have your powers. You will fight for us. If you do your part, then at war's end I promise to reverse your curse."

Medusa snarled, baring her pearly teeth and viper fangs. "That is not something I would joke about if I were you. Aphrodite laid this curse on me, only she can lift it."

Hel knew Medusa's legend. She had watched the poor, vain, girl's sentence carried out. It was cruel and without mercy. It was exactly what Hel would have done.

When the gods were in their prime, Medusa had been beautiful and young. She was so beautiful that men had stopped worshiping Aphrodite so that they could worship Medusa instead. Aphrodite did not take kindly to such an infringement and so cursed Medusa with hideous features. Green, scaly skin. Hissing, spitting curls. But even such brutal vulgarity was not enough in Aphrodite's eyes. So determined was the love goddess to destroy her competition that she added a little extra something to Medusa's punishment. Medusa was forbidden to love. If she were to lay eyes on anyone, they were instantly turned to stone. Most of the statues in the Metropolitan Museum of Art were Medusa's handy work. Eventually the loneliness had driven her mad, made her a monster, and led to her death.

"Aphrodite will lift the curse." Hel held up a crystal vile filled with swirling red essence. "This is her power. This is her Divine essence. If you manage to remove Nemesis from my path, it's yours. You help me secure a Charonte victory and you will be alive and beautiful again. Permanently."

Medusa grinned her horrible smile. "Hel, I do believe that you have a deal."

—Chapter Thirty-One—

It was dark at the bottom of the Nile. Dark and *wet*. There was no way to know how much time had passed while Cethy and Gull sat in the reed bunker at the bottom of the river. It felt like days. Water dripped into the tiny prison intermittently in annoying little splashes. Gull was miserable. All pouka hated water and he was no exception. Water revealed pouka for what they really were. He clung to Cethy's shoulders in a vain attempt to keep dry. Cethy was forced to sit hunched up, her knees jammed under her chin. The filthy water covered the bottom of the cage up to her ankles. Every now and again the cage would rock, caught in the wake of a crocodile. More than once the entire enclosure simply capsized and sent them head over heels coated in the muddy river water.

Cethy was even more miserable than Gull. This was just one more failure. Prometheus had said that it would be impossible for her to fail this quest. She was the luck goddess. She was unstoppable. "I'm sorry, Gull," she whispered. "I never meant to get you into this."

Gull tried to shake the water from his fur. "I would forgive you for getting me into it if you would only get me out again." His snooty little voice came from under her ear.

Cethy closed her eyes tightly as the entire crate tipped. "I don't know how to get us out or I would do it."

Gull blinked his giant yellow eyes in confusion. "Goddess, you are a telekinetic, are you not? You move things with your mind. Can you not simply move *us*?"

"Well, technically that's true but I haven't been able to use my power since the orchard," Cethy said, wretchedly.

"Well you must," Gull said with a shiver.

That was that. She must. Cethy leaned against the side of the reed prison and ignored the water trickling down her back. What had set Tyche off before? She had found out that Cupid had been a fake. That he had lied to her, tricked her and Missy into trusting him. Even thinking about it made her furious. Cethy had never been anything but honest with the people around her. She couldn't understand. Gull pretended to be Cupid. Erin pretended to be her friend. Missy pretended...well, she was not sure what Missy was pretending to be and she did not care. Always Cethy had to rely on others to protect her. Always she failed to keep the people she cared about safe. She was a disappointment. Useless. She was unworthy of the quest that had been bestowed upon her.

Gull twitched as the crate swung in the water. The pressure changed suddenly and his little ears popped, his stomach plummeting into his paws. They were moving upward. Cethy sat beneath his paws, her eyes shut and a furious look on her face. The cage rocked and the reeds bent inward as the crocodiles tried to stop their ascent. The cage rocked again and more reeds broke sending a wave of water over the two of them.

"You're doing it, goddess!" Gull cried. "Don't stop. We're moving."

The crocodiles attacked the cage, splintering the reeds and shaking its inhabitants. "Enough," Cethy muttered, angrily. "Enough!" Her voice was like a sonic boom. She threw her hands out and the reed enclosure exploded sending crocodiles scattering in every direction. No water touched them, no teeth closed on them. Cethy grinned, no, not Cethy. Tyche. Tyche kept the muddy river at bay with her mind. They rose through the water, the crocodiles unable to get close enough to stop them. Tyche set down on the bank, Gull chittering excitedly on her shoulder.

"It is anger!" Gull yelled joyously. "Anger is your trigger, goddess. How fortunate that you have so much to be angry about."

Tyche threw a croc into the water, its mouth sealed shut. "Yes." Tyche's voice was low and smooth. "I think that we should ask Sobek about the trident again," she said. "I think that we might get a different answer this time."

"What makes you think that, goddess?" Gull asked.

"Because," Tyche grinned but it was void of anything even vaguely reminiscent of Cethy, "he will not have a choice."

With Gull perched on her shoulder Cethy bent, leaving behind some very confused and cranky crocodiles. They reappeared inside of Sobek's temple. A woman leapt up from where she knelt and fled from the temple, screaming about demons as she ran down the street.

"Sobek," Tyche called. "Come."

"I am not a dog." The boy appeared on the altar. "Got out, did you? I'll have to be more creative next time. Maybe remove a limb or two."

Tyche smiled and ignored the boy's question. "I have decided to give you two last opportunities to hand over the trident willingly," she said. "Fair is fair."

Sobek liked the change that he saw in the goddess. There was a destructive look in her eyes that matched his own. "No," he said lightly. "I cannot give you my trident. However, if you wanted to share my river with me, I would not object. It seems that Nemesis is not the only true goddess on Olympus." Sobek was knocked from his altar with a flick of Tyche's finger. He hit the wall of the stone temple with a sickening crunch.

"Don't make me put you in time out, little boy," Tyche scolded. "You just used up one of your chances. I was hoping that I wouldn't have to do this. People only seem to get upset, but you don't leave me any other option." Tyche reached into her filthy shirt and pulled out the amulet. "Now, you horrible little thing, show him. Show him what happens if he doesn't help."

The ice turned gray in Tyche's hand. She let it go and it floated across the altar to rest in front of Sobek's face. She restrained him with her mind. The child kicked and clawed at her power with his sharp little nails, but she forced him to See all that the amulet held. She waited until she was sure that every cold, desolate, empty moment was forever transfixed in his mind.

When the ice finally emptied itself of vision, Tyche called the amulet back and tucked it under her shirt. Sobek shivered on the floor, his eyes wild. "What was that?" he asked, his voice splintering. "What did you just show me? Was that my river?"

Tyche shrugged. "I don't know what you Saw," she said. "I only know that if everyone keeps worrying about their own agendas, we won't have a shot at stopping Erebus from sucking the life out of everything. It will be bye-bye Mortal Realm, hello eternal torment." She looked down at the boy quivering on the ground. "Which will it be?"

The trident appeared in Sobek's hands. He looked at it longingly and Tyche was given the impression that he had to force his hands to release the weapon. "Do whatever you must," Sobek said softly. "Keep Erebus out of this world."

Cethy shook away the goddess inside and accepted the trident from Sobek. Gull had watched from a perch on the altar, impressed. "That was certainly lucky," he said, his small voice filled with laugher. "Time to fetch the shield, goddess!" Gull leapt onto Cethy's shoulder and bent, taking them far from Sobek. The river god frowned before he disappeared as well. He had to have a word or two with his least favorite people.

—Chapter Thirty-Two—

Missy had no idea how she was going to get back to the Mayan. She was stranded in Ithaca and the college town's few cab companies demanded far more money than she had to part with. Grumbling and discontent Missy wandered around the campus and quickly grew tired of being at the receiving end of puzzled glances from the students. They were clearly unused to wild girls covered in blood that wore swords strapped to their backs.

"What are you staring at?" Missy finally snapped at a group who watched her unashamedly. She stormed away but not before she overheard one of them tell the others, "Chick must be going Greek." Missy had to repress the hysterical laughter that threatened to overwhelm her. Going Greek. They didn't know the half of it.

Darkness descended before Missy realized what trouble she was really in. She was far from home and all alone since she had abandoned Thanatos and Dionysus. Part of her had expected them to come after her but the campus was almost deserted as she crossed the quad. She needed to do something soon. She was hungry, and lost, and exhausted after three days with no sleep. Burning pain lanced through her back with every step. "I just want to go home." Missy sat on the steps in front of the library, her head in her hands.

"Quitting? I made you better than that." Missy felt goose bumps spring up on her arms. The voice was like a thunderstorm and the sixteen year old clapped her hands over her ears as the voice echoed on in her head and made her muscles feel like Jell-O. "Open your eyes, you silly girl." She obliged. The library and all of Ithaca was gone. Missy was sat in the dirt in a too bright world, surrounded by impossible creatures and monsters. A centaur crept close and sniffed at Missy's hair before it made a face and sauntered off. Missy's mouth fell open in stunned appreciation. She had no doubts that she was in Valhalla. The question was: How had she gotten there?

"You're right. This is only a part of Valhalla." The woman who had dragged Missy between worlds had clearly been rather rudely snooping in Missy's thoughts. She stood beside her, fierce and smiling. She was young, if dressed a bit old fashioned. Missy was wary but her caution turned to curiosity. The resemblance between the two of them was unmistakable, the differences, subtle. The woman's black curls were clipped away from her face and long down her back. Her nose was a bit too pointed, her cheekbones too pronounced, almost animal like. She leaned toward Missy eagerly and her chic sunglasses slid down her nose. Missy caught sight of eyes as golden as her own before she backed away angrily.

"Whoever you are, whatever you want me to do, forget it," Missy said.

"Forget it? I think not. I put too much work into the worlds just to let them fail now. You have to fix them."

"Why? Because I broke them?"

Amusement crossed that familiar yet unfamiliar face. "Listen to you! What makes you think you are important enough or powerful enough to break what I have made?" the woman asked, sincerely. "I only want you to fix them because you are the only one so capable."

"Lady, I've tried to fix them and have gotten nothing for it. I'm done butting in where I don't belong and where I'm not wanted."

"Did you expect them to say thank you?" the stranger asked. "The gods appreciate little, Nemesis. They are certainly not going to appreciate you, whom they were taught to hate and fear. They will condemn you even if you are their only chance at survival."

Missy turned away. She didn't want to hear anymore. "Just let me alone. I'm tired and I don't want to do this anymore. I just want to go home." She ran. Missy ran as the Amazons had taught her, quickly and quietly. She ran for what felt like miles. The miles stretched into hours, and the hours turned into a gasping, weak collapse. Missy fell into the cool crisp leaves panting and stared at the shiny boot that was tapping under her nose.

The woman looked down at her, eyes empty of sympathy but bright with understanding. Unlike Missy she was neither out of breath nor had a single hair out of place. She simply stood by patiently and left no doubt in Missy's mind. This was yet another god come to torture her.

"You wish to go home? Child, you no longer have a home," the powerful voice bruised her ears and Missy curled up in a futile attempt to escape the sound. "The Charonte have taken it over. You have nowhere else to go. You might as well continue on."

"You want the world fixed, go do it yourself. I'm tired," Missy said crossly.

"Then you will just have to carry on tired, won't you? There is no rest for the weary, or for the condemned, child. You must see this through, to the very end if necessary."

"Lady, this is the end," Missy mumbled.

The woman laughed. It was a terrible, thunderous noise. "You get that mouth from me," she said. "Your hopelessness, you get from the other side of your family. I was never much one for moping, but Erebus? It is his bread and butter. I think there are more things to wonder at than despair at. I made it so."

Missy felt her stomach sink as the pieces fell into place. "Grandmother?" she asked, hoping against hope that it was not.

"Very good. You are not as smart as some of the other ones, but you get there eventually, don't you?" It was not an insult, but a statement of fact. Missy remained silent. This was the ultimate power that the Hesperides had been so in awe of. Khaos looked over Missy with a critical eye and the air of someone who came home to find their prized sports car smashed to pieces. "You have been through the mill, haven't you? I can help with that."

Khaos did not ask permission. She pulled Missy out of the leaves and reached around the girl in the semblance of a hug. Her nails bit deeply into the girl's back and Missy felt a white hot flash of pain that made her weak in the knees. As suddenly as it started, the pain was gone. Her back was whole and unblemished, no sign of the electric burn that Thanatos had accidentally transferred to her. Even the gash on her arm from her match against Antianara was gone. There wasn't so much as a mark left on her.

"What did you do?" Missy demanded. Her mind raced. If it was water from the Fountain then she was as good as human and useless to Cethy. Her fingers flew to the stone beaker on her belt, but it was still there and stoppered. "How did you heal me?"

"Calm yourself," Khaos said. She dismissed Missy's panic. "I did not use the faerie witch's water. I would not endanger your quest, child. Not when I need you to succeed. However, in the future, I would not let others take such advantage of you. Such a healing comes with great sacrifice from the healer. Thanatos should have known better."

Missy scowled and Khaos smiled. If it was meant to be kind, it failed. The grin was animalistic and Missy could not look at it for long. "I would not be too cross at them, my dear. They only have the world's best interest in mind. Would they be caught with Vengeance otherwise?" she asked.

Missy snorted her disbelief, "What about my best interest?"

Khaos laughed again. "Your best interest is unimportant in the grand scheme of things. You are but one. I suggest that you forget your anger. Or better yet, put it to good use. The quest only gets harder from here, and you need no more distractions. That includes what the Hesperides showed you. Troublemakers the whole pesky herd of them. Always they try to stir up what is best left settled. That part of your past is long gone, Nemesis."

"Don't worry. I'd happily forget what they showed me if I could."

"Don't be so sure. You will have the opportunity to lose your memories soon enough. We will see then what parts of your past you cling to. Besides, we have more important things to worry about. Firstly, how to get you back on the right track? Perhaps it is time for you to go home after all. It will not be long before dear Cethy returns to look for you. You should be there to shoo away the Charonte before she gets there. Now, don't look at me like that. You knew that you would have to be the strong one the second Prometheus knocked on the door. You are the Norns' Champion, aren't you?"

"Yes," Missy said dully.

"Now, let's see. I suppose since you *are* my favorite, I should give you a little gift to help you on your way." Khaos held a finger to her lips while she thought. "I know just the thing." Khaos presented Missy with her open, empty hand.

"Air?" Missy asked. "Thank you, grandmother, but I have plenty."

"Save that mouth for someone who is interested in such things," Khaos commanded. "Just take it." Missy reached out, feeling foolish, but her hand came in contact with something very solid. Missy caught the oaken puzzle box before it fell from Khaos's hand. It was beautifully made and intricately carved with a twisting maze on each side. Each detail was minute, and perfect, and inexplicably familiar.

"What is this?" Missy asked. Her wonder brought a smile to Khaos's inhuman face.

"It is a token." Khaos sounded pleased with herself. "Keep it on your person at all times. You don't want to find yourself in need of it and unable to reach it." There was a hint of warning to her words. "And one last gift, possibly more valuable. Knowledge."

Missy almost flinched. "Knowledge?"

Khaos nodded. "It is about time that someone answered some of your questions. I think that three would be an appropriate number. We like things in threes."

Missy's excitement vanished. "Only three questions?" she asked in dismay.

"Yes," Khaos said. "Now you only have two."

"Unfair!" Missy yelled. Khaos smiled and waited for the girl's next question. Missy thought hard. "If I only have two, they need to be important. Where are the Fates?" she asked.

Khaos smiled. "I'm glad you did not waste that one as well. The Fates have been separated for a long time, unable to collaborate. There is one in each world. The decider is in Valhalla. The weaver, in the Mortal Realm. The cutter is in the underworld. They seek each other even now. It is your responsibility to bring them together. You have one question left."

Missy made a face. "That wasn't very specific," she said. "You cheated me out of one question. You could at least give me a little more than that. States? Towns? I'll take their addresses if you've got them."

"I do not know everything," Khaos said crossly. "I am not omnipotent. I do the best I can, just as you do."

"Fine. Then why are the Charonte stealing Divine essence?" Missy asked.

"It is a distraction," Khaos said. Her golden eyes grew dark. "They go against nature and use the power of the gods as a means of creating pandemonium and subterfuge. They've turned a breed of monsters with the power to shift their shape into cheap mockups of my gods. They spy and create disorder. You have already met some such imposters."

"I have?" Missy stopped. Fear gripped her stomach as comprehension dawned on her. "Do these fake gods... Do they lack real emotion?"

Khaos looked down at her granddaughter. "You are out of questions, Nemesis." The struck look on Missy's face made her sigh. "Their emotions are real enough, but less complex than you are capable of perceiving. You cannot sense them. They are only animals, tricked to walk upright and speak like the Divine." Horrible thoughts went through Missy's mind. She knew two gods who had given her no vision, no sense of them at all, and she feared for what that meant to Cethy and the rest of the mission. "And now our time together is over. I suggest you go home, Nemesis. You have a room to clean." Her voice sounded softer, farther away.

"But I can't bend," Missy said. She stared at the puzzle box in her hand while her mind worked on the new information she had received. "How do I get home?"

Her words were answered by silence. While she had been distracted, Khaos had simply sent her back to Jersey. Missy had not even felt the pain of bending. She stood on the beach, a filthy, ragged creature among the seagulls and the horseshoe crabs. Missy clipped the small, oaken treasure to the sword baldric that was settled across her chest and smiled. The puzzle box nestled at her hip beside the stone beaker. Missy breathed in the salty air that meant she was home.

"Hey!"

Missy instinctively fell into a defensive crouch and drew Caliburn over her shoulder. The blade flashed in the fading daylight. It was unnecessary. "D! What are you doing here?" Missy demanded, lowering her sword. The irritation she felt was all her own as Dionysus charged across the sand to meet her.

The party god was out of breath by the time he reached her. "You left me behind," he said. He pouted, hurt that she had bailed on him and Missy scowled.

"It wasn't an accident." Missy growled. "You lied to me." He didn't look at all abashed and she just turned her back on him. "Just go back to Than and Cue. I really don't want you here, D. I've got something I need to do."

"Then I can help."

"No. You can't." Missy's golden eyes were cold and appraising as she turned back to face him. Dionysus wobbled slightly in the sand, his face covered by an inebriated grin. "D, you can't even stand up straight."

"That makes me useless? Believe me, I have been in my fair share of fights. I can handle myself."

"This is not a drunken brawl. I have to face the Charonte and I can't worry about you on top of everything else. Go back to the dorm."

"Nope. I've got to keep an eye on you. Boy did I get it when you took off at school." His words ran together into a slur of gibberish. "And then we couldn't find you for four days. Where'd you go?"

"Valhalla." Missy said tiredly. "I guess time moves differently between the worlds."

Dionysus nodded energetically. "Should have figured as much. Still, better if you let me tag along. I promised Prometheus that I wouldn't let you blow yourself up. And Cue. He was worried sick when we found you here last month."

"Afraid that I'd ruin the mission?" Missy asked bitterly.

"Afraid that you would get hurt," Dionysus mumbled. He belched and the force of it tipped him over. There he lay, passed out and drooling in the sand.

Missy refused to let the god's words mean anything to her. Khaos was right. That life was over. Missy had to concentrate on the life she had now, or she would lose it. She was about to throw herself headlong into a battle that she unlikely to win and distractions were not welcome. The Mayan loomed up ahead, casting a dark shadow over the sand.

Missy tried to calm her mind and her body. She let her muscles relax and held Caliburn loosely out in front of her. The weight was perfectly balanced, the motion of the blade, smooth. Missy grinned. Caliburn was an extension of her arm that she had not realized she had been missing. With the sword in her hand she was complete at last, their collective minds joined in the glory of the upcoming battle.

Missy left Dionysus and the beach behind as she climbed up the dunes to the boardwalk. The Mayan beckoned to her, calling her to free it of the evil within. She let Caliburn's blade glow blood-red in the last rays of the sinking sun. No more time could be wasted. She had work to do.

Chapter Thirty-Three

Erin moved around room two-eleven nervously and kept her eyes on her feet. More than once she walked herself into a wall because she refused to look up and see where she was going. Bave, Medusa, and the pouka found it highly entertaining.

"What's the matter, Eris?" Medusa jeered. "Afraid to look at me?" Medusa marveled at how much had changed in only a few short days. She was returned to life and the Mortal Realm, free to prey on all who crossed her path. Her pale green scales itched slightly from the salty ocean air, but it was a sensation that she welcomed. Her only disappointment was that she had not found a way to steal Aphrodite's essence from Hel yet. The underworlder kept a close eye on her growing collection of Divine power. Each was carefully labeled and stored out of reach of Medusa and the other Charonte. Not surprisingly, trust was an issue between them.

Hel stood by the window, a fluffy pouka on her shoulder. Her arms were crossed and a frown darkened her young face. Something had changed recently. She could not put her finger on it, but with every moment that passed more power was released in the world. The Rise was already set into motion and there was no stopping it now. Hel grinned slowly, catching her reflection in the glass. It was a horrible smile.

The left side of Hel's body was as beautiful and young as ever. Her blue eye, her flowing brown locks, her creamy complexion were all the same. Her right side had become a different story. Flesh hung loose and rotten off of Hel's face. It had the blue-green tinge of meat that had been left out too long. Her hair was thin, gray, and sparse on half of her decaying scalp. Her right eye had lost all color as it festered. Once again Hel was the garish goddess of legend, divided in body, though not mind. Hel's mind was still overwhelmingly vulgar and dark. She remained dangerously out of balance and already too powerful to be reined in.

Bave was pleased with what she saw in her companion. The war goddess had never really suffered from the Fall as Hel had, and now that the Charonte were together and slowly Rising, she could not help but enjoy herself. Gone were the days of hiding. The three of them were now a force to be reckoned with. A force free to move about the Mortal Realm and cause whatever destruction they pleased.

"Hey guys, when are we going to go for the next bit of the Circle? I'm tired of waiting around doing nothing." Erin leaned against the marble statue of the delivery boy. He had been turned to white stone, courtesy of Medusa, for being late with their pizza.

"Nothing?" Hel turned and faced the youngest Charonte. "You think we do nothing? There are still gods out there, you realize. Each has the power to stop us. We have to remove the roadblocks before we proceed." The pouka chittered and scampered under the bed, lest Hel's anger be taken out on it instead of Erin.

Hands up in submission, Erin pouted. "All I'm saying is that Missy and Cethy won't be wasting time tracking down gods who are irrelevant to the quest. They will be getting it done. Missy doesn't know how to pump the breaks, I promise you that."

Bave pounced on Erin and her feet left the carpet as the Celt gripped her collar and hauled her up to her own eye level. "Are you a Charonte or aren't you?" she demanded. She gave Erin a shake. "I suggest you stop thinking like a Norn or we'll start treating you like one."

"Put her down."

Bave dropped Erin, thinking that the icy voice had been Hel's, but a fifth person had joined them in the room. Missy had climbed up the side of the Mayan and come in the open bathroom window. She quickly took stock of her surroundings and her opponents as the Amazons had taught her. She was outnumbered, and out powered, but she stood firm as the Charonte and their monster formed a half circle around her.

Caliburn flashed in Missy's hand, a clear warning to keep away. "Erin," she said politely. "Who are your friends?"

Erin wrinkled her nose. "Missy, you reek. What have you been doing? Rolling around a barnyard?"

Erin had not expected such an unkempt version of her old roommate to appear before them. Missy was covered in dirt, and her shirt was the dark, crusty brown of dried blood. A belt was strapped across her chest, obviously meant to hold the blade that she handled without fear. She looked terrible.

Hel saw a very different goddess than Eris did. She looked at the crinkled picture that lay on the floor. The wild woman brandishing the sword looked nothing like the smiling girl in the picture. The goddess before her was fierce and cold as ice. The look in her eyes was more than just a warning. It was a promise to inflict harm on anyone who got in her way. Hel frowned. Eris had said that Nemesis was nothing to worry about. Hel would have to reeducate Eris as to the definition of the word 'nothing'.

"Now, Eris. That is no way to treat your guest," Hel said. Missy glanced at her and held her sickening gaze. "You know Eris," she said to Missy. "This is Bave. I am Hel." Bave dipped her head. "And this is our champion."

Medusa grinned at Missy from behind her sunglasses and waved. "Hi."

Missy nodded her acknowledgement. "Medusa, right?" she asked, regarding the scaly woman with the snakes falling out of her pale blonde hair. "And you're their champion?" she verified. Medusa nodded.

"Whatever they have on you it isn't worth it. Go home before you get hurt."

"Alas, I owe them my allegiance, if only for the time being." Medusa fingered her glasses, eager to win her freedom and regain her beauty. "And you are no Perseus, little girl. You're the one who will be hurt."

"This is your only warning," Missy said calmly. "Leave. All of you. You are not welcome here."

Bave laughed, as oblivious to the danger as Erin. "Did you hear that?" she said to Hel. "We are not welcome. I guess we had better run along then."

Hel frowned. Her good eye did not miss much. "I think that this battle, at least, is over. Bave, Eris, we should take our leave." Hel was annoyed at her lack of foresight. She should have sent Medusa after Nemesis as soon as they returned from the Void. Instead she had waited and now Nemesis had come for them. Even outnumbered Nemesis would not go down without a fight. She was prepared to cause real damage to the Charonte. Hel saw no hesitation in those golden eyes. Still, better to test her than to do nothing. "Medusa, why not show Nemesis a true champion?"

"No." Erin scowled and stepped between the eager Medusa and Missy. "I'm not running from her. Not when I can face her." Erin had spent the last month under Bave's supervision, learning how to harness her true power and use it at will. Not just her simple hostility trick, but one that she had been waiting to show off. Erin reached out her hand to Missy, as if expecting her old roommate to accept it. "Sword," she said, clearly expecting something to happen. Erin's hand remained empty as Caliburn swung in a circle, cutting down the summoning magic that Erin had tried to call on.

Missy grinned. She felt the godspell rush through Caliburn's blade and race up her arm. The silver swirls that crept up to her elbow like pale ivy glowed as Erin's power was added to what Caliburn had already gleaned from Zeus. "Neat trick," Missy said coldly. "Somehow I was expecting something bigger."

The charge in the room was unmistakable. Missy was somber as she held Caliburn out in front of her, prepared for the inevitable fight. The only way out now was the way she had come in, but it would not come to that. Missy would not retreat. The month she had spent away from the Mayan had changed her undeniably. The emotions of the other girls in the room did not overwhelm her as they might once have done. Instead her mind was crystal clear, and now, thanks to Caliburn and the strange silver tattoo, she had Erin's ability to summon. Her attention wasn't on her new power, however, her old roommate, or even the killer gorgon lounging casually on the bed.

Her eyes were glued to Bave.

"What?" The Celtic goddess was unnerved. Missy stared at her with the strangest look on her face. It was a cross between anger and confusion. "What is that?" Missy finally asked. She pointed to Bave's throat with the tip of Caliburn's blade.

Hel, Erin, and Medusa all turned and looked at Bave, unsure of what could be important enough to so completely distract the girl from the impending fight. Bave fingered up the white arrow head that hung around her neck. "This?" she asked, confused. "It's just a trinket. Why so interested?"

Erin tried again to call for Missy's sword while the girl was distracted, but Caliburn greedily attacked her godspell and nothing happened. Missy tore her attention from Bave's pendent and glared at Erin. "Really, Erin? If it were that easy to stop me, would I have come in here alone?"

"Well, you've never been the smart one, Missy," Erin said nastily. "It would be just like you to wander into a fight unprepared."

Missy was ready to end the banter. She was notorious among the Amazons for her distaste of idle battle chatter. Missy was one who liked to get right into it. "Tell me, Erin. Was this what you were going for?" Missy switched Caliburn to her right hand and her spinning silver tattoo seemed to pulse as she held out her hand. "Glasses," she whispered heatedly, and then quickly got out of the way.

Medusa's sunglasses vanished from her nose and reappeared in Missy's hand. Total chaos took over the room and Missy suspected that her grandmother would have been rather proud of her. Missy ducked into the bathroom to avoid danger from the gorgon that stomped blindly through the room with her eyes closed. Missy watched Medusa stumble past and leapt from her hiding spot.

"Hey!" Medusa turned just as Missy swung Caliburn at her head. The monster tried to lean away from the bloodthirsty blade, her mouth open in an angry hiss, but she moved too late. Caliburn cut through her open mouth and sliced through her cheeks. Missy cursed and dove out of the way as Medusa screamed and opened her eyes.

The Charonte all ran for the door, but Missy tackled Bave. The two goddesses tumbled to the floor out of Medusa's sightline. "Where did you get this?" Missy demanded. Bave tried to crawl away but Missy pounced and knelt on the Celt's chest. Bave thrashed, bit, and clawed at Missy. Her nails raked cruelly across the girl's face and left a trail of blood along Missy's left eye and cheek. With a snarl, Missy half lifted Bave and then slammed her back to the floor harshly. "Enough!" She grabbed Bave's pendent and stared at it, her mind working furiously. "Where did you get this?" she growled. "Where? This is mine!"

Missy felt several emotions wash over Bave. First fear, then confusion, and comprehension. Finally gloating triumph lashed out at Missy's Empathy. "Trust me, little Nemesis. You don't want to know how I came across this worthless bauble. If you knew I pulled it from Cupid's corpse after I killed him, you might lose that champion focus of yours."

Bave could not have been more wrong. Missy's eyes narrowed with fury, her focus wholly on Bave. With no regard for Bave's comfort, Missy jerked the arrowhead free. Her hand was numb from the static shock the necklace gave her, but she held on regardless. "Understand this," Missy hissed, sounding more like Nemesis than herself. "You are marked for death at my hand. There is nowhere you can go, nowhere you can hide, that I will not find you. You sealed your fate the moment you sealed his." Caliburn was far too long to use at such close range, but that was what magic was for. Missy still had Erin's summoning magic quite literally, up her sleeve. The silver glow brightened into a pulsing white light as Missy tapped into the Divinity that Caliburn had collected for her. She could feel Erin's power coursing through her, dark and foreign, and it gathered in her palm, a pool of molten silver.

"Eyes," she whispered.

Bave screamed in fear and pain. Hel grabbed her mutilated comrade's arm and dragged Bave out of the room, Erin on their heels. The Charonte disappeared into the night bewailing their fear and fury that their champion and their powers had been turned against them.

Missy let the foul orbs drop and they splatted, soaking the carpet while Missy wiped her hands. She felt ill. She hadn't planned on that. It was too extreme, even she knew that, but Missy felt no remorse. She felt completely validated in her violence and that alone was enough to terrify her. She'd let Nemesis influence her again. She had to stop letting the goddess seep out. Missy had to keep control.

She was scared of what she'd become if she didn't.

Missy hefted Caliburn over her shoulder, her expression severe. Her night wasn't over yet. One silent feet she walked across the destroyed room and waited until the injured gorgon stopped thrashing and wailing. Medusa crawled along the filthy carpet, cursing in tongues that Missy had never even dreamed of.

Missy was careful to stay at Medusa's back, her sword at the ready. "I could kill you now, you know?" Missy said, her voice cold. "Or I could take your eyes, like I took Bave's. That should keep you from hurting more people." The snakes in Medusa's hair all hissed defensively and Missy paused. "But you aren't like them, are you? You didn't choose this. You're just a product of a curse."

"Able to see that, are you?" Medusa's voice was thick with bitterness. "You are the only one."

"I see a lot of things that others don't see." Missy had not realized how true it was until she said it. "How can I blame you for being a monster when my people are the ones that made you this way? I'm not going to punish you for what you've done. I think that life is to be valued, not wasted." Caliburn's tip rested at the base of Medusa's skull. Missy could feel the blade humming in her hand. It shared her indecision and Missy took a great deal of comfort from that. The sword really was an extension of herself. "Still, if you want to live, you need to start making the right decisions." She removed her sword and stepped away from the gorgon. "Get out." Missy ordered. "And try to show others the same clemency that I showed you. You won't get another chance."

Medusa snatched up her sunglasses from where they had been discarded on the rug and returned them to her nose before she faced Missy. Her face was ruined, her cheeks little more than bloody flaps where

Caliburn had bit into her face. The two champions stared at each other for a long while.

"This is not how I would chose to return to life," she said finally. "But I am indebted to Hel. She is my mistress until one of us dies, Nemesis, and I will have my freedom."

Missy shook her head. "This is why Hel is evil," she said. "I am sorry for you, Medusa. If I could give you your freedom, I would do it happily and without condition."

"You could let me kill you, now," Medusa said. She smiled and revealed her viper fangs.

Missy grinned in return. "I think not. Neither of us will die tonight," Missy offered.

Medusa came forward and Missy lowered her sword. They gripped arms in an accord and Medusa gave a curt nod. "Until next we meet, Norns' Champion." Medusa turned away and left the hotel to search for her masters.

Missy collapsed on her bed and ran a hand through her matted hair. "Piece of cake." Missy wanted nothing more than to curl up and sleep, but first things first. She cleaned her sword, and watched in wonder as ribbons of contented, peaceful blue snaked along the blade.

"What are you?" she whispered, fascinated by her weapon. It hummed in her hand and she placed it back into its sheath with deliberate care. She needed a shower and a month's worth of sleep. The arrowhead that was cradled in the hollow of her throat got tossed into the pile of junk in the corner. She didn't want to look at it. She couldn't bear to think about what it meant.

Bave's eyes were shooed out the door and over the balcony. By morning the seagulls would have gotten rid of them. Missy moved as one in a trance. Now that the battle was over she was completely drained. She simply pushed her emotions away and took advantage of her few moments of down time to work the knots out her curls and scrub the muck and blood from her body.

Not once did she think to look under the bed.

—Chapter Thirty-Four—

Cethy appeared on the rock with Gull on her shoulder and the trident in her hands. The selkie was sunning himself and looked up at her, a webbed hand held over its eyes to block the sun. "Back from Nile sssso ssssoon?" it asked. "And you brought the trident. I thought for sure you would be lunch for Petsuchossss. How are my crocodile brotherssss?"

"I didn't hurt them too badly," Cethy said happily, hugging the sea creature around its sleek body. "Go and get Poseidon, please. Quick, like a bunny!" she said when the selkie took its time dragging itself to the edge of the rock. It shot her a nasty look as it plopped into the water and descended out of sight.

Cethy practically danced with happiness. She had successfully gotten her hands on the trident, and the Aegis was within her grasp. "What's Petsuchos?" she asked Gull as the little pouka groomed her.

Gull squeaked. "Petsuchos is the reincarnation of Sobek. He is supposedly a rather massive, mean, ravenous crocodile that is best not bothered for any reason."

"Sobek isn't dead," Cethy pointed out.

"Sobek's followers don't know that," Gull said with a chitter of laughter.

The water at the edge of her rock rose up into the rough shape of a man. Poseidon emerged from the waves, a liquid god, with a distraught fish swimming about in between his nonexistent ears. "You found my trident." Poseidon's voice was sad. "I only wish that I still had the shield to trade with you for it." Poseidon reached out to touch Cethy, but his watery hand only passed through her, splashing gently against her cheek.

Cethy was speechless. Gull hissed from under her hair and his giant yellow eyes peeked out. "So you lied to her?" he asked. "Lied and sent the goddess straight into danger? I ought to bite you!" Gull nipped at the wet hand as it pulled away. The little monster got a mouthful of saltwater and shrieked his displeasure at his wet fur.

Poseidon shook his head and the distressed fish darted back and forth with no way out. "I would never do such a thing. Maybe the gods on land have forgotten it, but there is no honor in trickery. I meant what I said when I told you that we would trade, trident for Aegis." The selkie appeared from the waves and pushed a copper shield up onto the rock before hauling himself up after it. "Take a look," said Poseidon. "It is the Aegis no longer. Its power is gone."

Cethy knelt and pulled the shield into her lap. It was just a copper shield, inlaid with gold. Pretty, yes. But it was not magical. "What happened?" Cethy asked. She ran a hand over the once mythical weapon. "It's," she paused trying to figure out exactly what the shield was. "It's empty."

Poseidon nodded, driving the poor trapped fish into a frenzy. "It happened but a few days ago. I regret this, Tyche, I truly do. I only hope that you see it was not a deception, but a horrible twist of fate."

"Fate," Cethy said bitterly. She had been so close to victory only to have it snatched away at the last moment. "Already, it seems that they play games with me."

Poseidon shook his head again and the troublesome fish fell out with a noisy splash. "All is not lost, Tyche. See? My body begins to return, along with your powers. You could not have gotten the trident from Sobek by any means other than magical. The Rise has begun, cousin, and we will all be swept up in its awesome current. You are even beginning to speak like the goddess you are, and not the ruffian you were."

Cethy had noticed the change in herself, but resentment at yet another failure took what pleasure she might have felt and poisoned it. The Rise had begun, but it was not by her hand. At least now she knew that Missy was safe and alive. Somewhere the sixteen year old was making her way through the Circle, doing Cethy's job, and bringing the gods back to power.

Cethy stood up, her face an expressionless veil. She tugged the worthless shield over her arm. It was no longer the Aegis, but she had fought hard to win it. She was not about to abandon it, just because it was useless.

"Come on, Gull," she muttered. "Let's go home." The pouka brushed Cethy's hair with his claws in an attempt to make her feel better but it did little good.

"Don't forget your quiver," Poseidon said. "I certainly have no use for it." Cethy accepted the quiver of arrows that she'd torn from Gull's back when he had been playing at Cupid. Strangely, without Gull's influence, the arrows had turned from black to white. Cethy looked inside the quiver, and grinned. The enchanted water that Missy had received from Niamh rested unharmed at the bottom. At last, there was some good luck. Cethy shouldered the quiver and Gull climbed inside it. She bent from the rock, her mind only on her room at the Mayan and a good night's sleep. She left the trident behind for Poseidon, unable to go back on her promise.

Cethy appeared in her old room at the Mayan and Missy tipped backward off of her chair at the breakfast table. Missy landed with her limbs helter-skelter but quickly found her feet and launched herself at Cethy with a shriek of glee. Cethy felt the air go out of her lungs as the smaller girl caught her up in a rib crushing hug.

"Where have you been?" Missy demanded. "I've been here four days already waiting for you." She dragged a giant marble statue out from the corner to make room for Cethy's chair. "What happened to you? You smell like raw sewage. Is that the Aegis?"

Cethy was not in the mood for Missy's questions. "It *was* the Aegis," she said miserably. She put the shield on the table and let Missy inspect it.

"Was? Why was?" It seemed like a perfectly nice shield to Missy. Not too heavy. Solid. She would have been happy to wield it in battle, but as a magical artifact, it was lacking. "It's blank," she said. Missy pointed to the center of the shield where the ancient Greeks liked to place their coat of arms or some fearsome painting. The Aegis was bare.

"I know all about it, Missy. Something happened in the last five days to take the power from it, I just don't know what. Medusa's image should be right there." Cethy pointed to the shield's center.

Missy closed her eyes. "Medusa?" she asked. "Oh, Red. I think you should sit down." And so Missy told Cethy everything she had been through since their parting only days ago. Cethy stopped her constantly in an effort to drain every bit of information and detail from Missy's rushed story.

"Thanatos?" Cethy asked. "You met the god of death?"

"Yeah, he killed a gnome. It was awesome." Missy's voice was bitter at the memory of her parting from Thanatos.

Missy left out what the Hesperides had shown her, deeming it too private even for Cethy. Instead she drew Caliburn from its sheath and placed it on the table next to the ruined Aegis. "It's Celtic," Cethy said immediately. "Look at it, it's curved, and it doesn't have the crossed hilt. It's nice." Cethy reached out to touch the shining blade. Missy moved to stop her but was too late. The blade flew across the room to avoid the girl's grip. It plunged deep into the wall where it stayed, humming angrily.

"No one is supposed to touch it but me," said Missy sheepishly, retrieving Caliburn. She showed Cethy the swirling tattoo on her arm, silver and intense against her pale skin. She even showed Cethy the puzzle box that Khaos had given her. Finally, to stop Cethy from examining the curious gift, she pointed to the marble statue she had dragged over by the dresser.

"Medusa was here, Red. That's why the shield is no good. Her image must have left it when Hel brought her back to life."

Cethy shook her head. "No luck at all," she muttered. But now it was her turn, and Cethy did not leave out a thing. She told Missy what happened after they had parted ways. "Cupid was a fake," she snapped but, of course, Missy had already known somehow. "A pouka."

"A what?" Missy demanded.

Gull stuck his head out from under Cethy's hair and blinked his large yellow eyes. Missy reached for Caliburn and Cethy cuddled Gull protectively. "No. He's a friend, Missy. Aren't you, Gull?" She was startled by how dramatically Missy's face had changed. "He promised to help us, and he cannot break his word. If he does, he'll be trapped in one shape forever." The little monster shuddered on Cethy's shoulder.

"Red, I'm allergic to cats," Missy warned.

"Cat? A cat? Have you ever encountered a feline that was capable of this?" Gull jumped from Cethy's arm and glided to the floor. The pouka seemed to grow and in only a moment, another Missy stood in the room. They were exactly the same down to the swollen scratches that traced down Missy's left eye, courtesy of Bave.

"Ok, so it's a very cool cat," Missy said with a smile. "And so pretty." She pinched the pouka's cheek and Gull returned to his natural state. He hid his eyes with his tail, bashful.

"Well, I'm certainly glad that I did not kill you when I had the chance, Nemesis. I am pleased that Cupid was too strong to overpower." Missy scowled and Cethy continued with her tale, ending with when she appeared in the room.

"It has been one heck of a month," Cethy said.

"Yeah," Missy said sardonically. "I have never been so thoroughly beaten by a month in my life. I feel like I could sleep forever. I guess that's a no-no?"

"You know that it is," Cethy said. "We cannot rest until it is over. Until we succeed or fail."

Missy looked up at her friend, her cousin. That was more or less what Khaos had told her. There would be no stopping until this was over. Missy tried to smile. "I'd rather succeed, if you don't mind. So what do we do now?"

Cethy counted on her fingers. "Well, thanks to you, we have the enchanted water and Caliburn."

"And thanks to you when I kill Medusa we'll have the Aegis." Missy realized how hard Cethy had worked for the shield, and did not have the heart to tell her it was useless. "So, three of the ten are ours. What's next?"

"I think that we should go for the venom," Cethy said logically. "It shouldn't be too hard to get our hands on, and a nice simple assignment is what we need right now."

"Well, what do we have to do?" Missy asked. "You know I don't bend well, so if we have to fight, I suggest that we show up someplace safe and walk. I'm not about to pop into someplace risky, gasping and panting for breath. I'll be a danger to myself and you."

Cethy waved Missy's concern away. "There shouldn't be a fight. Do you remember what Hippolyta said about Loki?" she asked. "He's a Norse god, I think, and he is chained to a rock. Venom from the Midgard Serpent will drip onto his head until the Fates weave him free."

"And then the end of the world, right?" Missy asked, tired. "It's always the end of the world."

"Ok, so all we have to do is sneak in and catch a little of that venom. No big deal."

"What are we going to catch it in, Red? Tupperware? I have to image that it is going to be a little harder than that."

"Well, do you have a better idea?" Cethy demanded. When Missy was silent Cethy smiled. "Good. We'll leave in the morning."

Missy was quiet for a long time. She stood up and began her exercises with Caliburn. The blade became a blur as she spun and dipped, sparring with an invisible opponent. She had just executed a low sweeping block when she gasped and ran out of the room. "D! I just left him on the beach!" When she returned, she supported the aching god against her shoulder.

"What's been going on, ladies?" Dionysus said as he rubbed his pounding head.

The girls looked at each other. "Nothing," they said in unison.

Missy and Cethy went to sleep that night relieved to be at home and together again. They had a plan, now, and an actual shot at success. Their sleep was far from untroubled, but they were safe. Even Gull slept peacefully, curled up on Cethy's pillow.

Long after darkness fell, a pair of large eyes opened and glowed yellow from beneath Missy's bed. The pouka had seen her opportunity to spy on

Nemesis and so had stayed hidden for days. At last, with Cethy's arrival she had what she needed to return to Hel. She knew where the Norn and her champion would be the next day and with any luck Hel would repay her with some of that yummy Divine Essence. The pouka bent with an indiscernible pop.

Missy sat up in bed, her warrior ears alert. She thought that something might have moved inside the room. She listened carefully but the only sounds were Cethy's soft breathing and Dionysus's raucous snores from where he was asleep in the bathtub. Missy collapsed against her pillow, already back to sleep.

—Chapter Thirty-Five—

The next afternoon was bright and clear. Missy stood on the balcony outside of her room's front door and watched the waves pound the beach. She loved the water, loved the way it smelled and felt against her skin. She even loved how it tasted, salty and alive. She had woken up that morning with an eerie feeling, a deep fear that had rooted itself in her being and refused to be ousted. After her exercises with Caliburn, Missy had wandered onto the balcony for one last look at the beach.

"Last look?" Missy asked herself. "Why did I think that?"

"Think what?" Cethy lounged in the door frame, clean and ready to travel. She was dressed in a simple white sweatshirt and blue jeans, and her red hair was pulled away from her face.

"Nothing," Missy mumbled. "What are you wearing?" Missy had grown tired of ruining her clothes and had settled on black under armor and a pair of black pants. The only color on her person was the blue scarf that she wore to keep her hair back. She had weaved her dark curls back into one giant plait down her back, but already flyaway curls had wriggled loose. "We're going to train you in camouflage when we get back, Red."

"I'm not the warrior, Missy. You are." Cethy could not help but think about how different her cousin had become. She hardly even looked like the loud, laughing girl she had lived with. Now she was just a cold, solemn veteran. Every inch of her was the warrior that the quest needed, but not the Missy that Cethy wanted.

"Ready to go?" Missy asked. She walked back into the room and checked her baldric. Caliburn, the stone beaker, and the puzzle box were all secure. She slung the belt across her back and sighed. "Off to battle we go," she said to Cethy. "Ready when you are."

Dionysus watched the two of them with mounting concern. Missy had forbidden him to travel with the pair of them. He had to wait until they came back. "*If* you come back," he said. "But hey, you're Nemesis, right? You don't need Dionysus hanging around, ruining your battle buzz." He waved his hands in her face and Missy had laughed and hugged him around his broad chest. Dionysus closed his arms tight around her and squeezed until her feet left the ground.

"I just want you to stay safe, Dionysus," she told him honestly. "I don't want to have to worry about you as well as Cethy." That had kept him happy all morning, but now he was worried again. And there was not even anything to drink in the room since he had cleaned out the mini-bar the night before.

The girls gripped hands as Gull scampered over to sit on Dionysus's shoulder. The small monster had been ordered to stay behind as well and he was not at all happy about it. With a smile and a wave the girls vanished from the hotel room. Dionysus had nothing to do but sit back and wait for them to return. He hoped that there was something good on television. He lounged on Missy's bed and flipped idly through the channels. He had just turned up the volume on some music channel when Missy and Cethy came hurtling back into the room.

"I warned you!" Missy snarled between her clenched teeth. "I warned you that it wouldn't be that easy! Nothing on this quest is going to be as easy as just showing up and *asking*."

"It would have been that easy if they hadn't been waiting there for us to show up!" Cethy shrieked back. Her hands were balled into fists furious ribbons of bright red swirling around her in an aggressive dance, flickering in and out of Missy's Empathetic vision.

Dionysus lost all interest in the television and stood between the two girls before it came to physical blows. As it was, Missy's fists were up and Cethy was using her sneaker to furiously pummel the younger girl. "Knock it off, the two of you! What happened?" he demanded. "Who was waiting for you?"

"The Charonte," Missy said angrily. "There was an ambush waiting for us in the cave. Somehow they knew that we were coming." She marched over to the bed where Gull watched the pair of them and grabbed the pouka by his fluffy tail. "What I want to know is how you did it. I ought to wring your furry neck!"

Missy was suddenly heaved off her feet and hurled against the dresser. The poorly made piece of furniture shattered beneath the force. Slowly Missy stood up and shook herself free of debris. Splinters and blood fell to the floor as she surveyed Cethy coldly. "I suggest you not do that again."

Dionysus's mouth was open in horror. Cethy had used her telekinesis to launch Missy across the room. "Cethy, why would you do that?" he whispered. "She's on your side. You never use your powers against a friend."

"Are you sure?" Cethy snapped. "It was awfully convenient that the Charonte knew we were coming, and I know that Gull didn't tell them." Missy shook her head in disbelief and the redhead glowered. "I can prove it," she insisted. "Gull? Shift for me, would you?" Gull immediately did Cethy's bidding. He turned first into Cethy and then into Dionysus. He finished by turning back into his own shaking form.

"See? He couldn't have broken his promise," Cethy said. "He can still shift, and that just leaves you, Missy."

"You think I told them that we were coming?" Missy demanded. Her voice quiet and she struggled to keep the hurt out of it. "You? I thought if there was one person I could count on to trust me, it was you."

"One person foolish enough, you mean!" Cethy snapped. "You almost got us killed!"

Missy was very still. She didn't trust herself to speak or to even move. The two girls just glared at each other, their eyes hostile, their powers barely controlled.

"I am uncertain of what took place." Gull climbed up Dionysus' back to perch on his shoulder. "Even after Nemesis found out that I was masquerading as Cupid she did not attack me. I thought her most gracious. What happened while they were gone to so anger the goddess and her cousin?"

Cethy collapsed on the bed. Missy said nothing but stood still as a statue, covered in wood dust and stray socks from the wrecked dresser. "The Charonte were in the cave when we got there," Cethy explained. "Missy practically clubbed me over the head with that sword of hers."

"It was either that or pose pretty for Medusa," Missy snapped. "The gorgon was there, Red, and Caliburn could hardly keep up with all the magic they were throwing at me. I mean, I'm good, but I'm still new at this whole power absorption thing. If we hadn't gotten out of there when we did..." Missy did not finish the thought. The silver swirls on her arm still stung with all of the godspells that Caliburn had gobbled up. Luckily Bave had stayed mostly out of the skirmish. She was still not completely recovered from her previous run in with Missy.

"Well," Dionysus thought it important that he find out. "Did you get the venom?" He immediately regretted asking. The looks he received were all the answer he needed.

"So what now?" Missy asked. "Trying again seems like a suicide mission to me."

Cethy did not answer right away. Her face was screwed up in displeasure. "I don't think that you should go back, Missy," she said. "Ever. I don't want your help anymore. All you've done is cause trouble."

"All I've done is *cause trouble*?" Missy repeated, taken aback by Cethy's declaration. "All I've done is *your* job. Everything you were supposed to do, I did for you. You needed to get water, I got it. You needed the sword, I got it. The one thing that you were left to do was find the shield and you couldn't even do that."

"I have the shield!" Cethy protested.

Missy made a frustrated sound. "What you have is a worthless antique. The shield is useless so long as Medusa is alive."

"Then," Cethy paused, trying to outthink her cousin. "Then I'll find Medusa and handle it. I'm the Norn, Missy."

"You're a joke!" Missy snapped. The silence that settled atop of that statement was beyond tangible.

"Is that what you think?" Cethy asked. "Is that why you betrayed me?"

Missy shook her head. "I never betrayed you, Red."

"You're jealous that Prometheus chose me and not you. You're jealous that I'm wanted and no one can even stand the sight of you!" Cethy didn't seem able to stop herself and Missy's jaw tightened in anger.

Missy stormed to the door, glaring around the room at the people who she had thought were her friends. Her family. "You deserve everything you get," she said to Cethy as she passed. "And next time I'm not going to protect you from it." With that, she left. Dionysus and Cethy stood in the smothering silence, sure that she would come back. She never did. Nemesis was gone.

Missy wandered the boardwalk for hours. She had no desire to go back to the hotel or to see Cethy. She just wanted to put as much distance between herself and her treacherous cousin as possible. Is that what she had been like in the Divine heyday when her powers were out of control and she had been a part of the Olympian court? Had she snapped on her friends and her family? Cethy's accusation rang between her ears.

Is that what had really caused the Fall?

The night erupted with bright, blinking stars and Missy lay on her back in the sand, her head cradled in her arms. When she had lived on the beach, she loved to look at the stars. The thought of something so vast and magical had always humbled her but now the glittering nightscape only made her feel alone.

"We all serve our purpose," she said. She thought of the Hesperides. The small girls were trapped in their purpose. They did not play, like normal children. There were no soccer games or ballet recitals for them. There was only their power, and what they could do with it. Thanatos had been a victim of his power as well. She could not imagine a life where she was unable to touch another living person. Dionysus showed his Divinity. The boy was charming, fair, and very sweet, but he was a stumbling, sloppy drunk every hour of every day. He had no shot at true happiness. He was as bound to his own mythology as the others were.

Even she had traits of her old life. Missy had been the law on the Island for as long as she could remember. She had felt ill will and she had dealt with the problem before it turned into ill deeds. "I judged them," she realized. She had not escaped Nemesis. Not completely. The goddess was there somewhere, waiting beneath the surface to consume what little humanity Missy had gleaned from her life after the Fall.

For all her faults, Missy was not stupid. She was not a blundering idiot with a sword as Hera had suggested. She was as sharp as Cethy and Erin, if not as eager to waste her time with learning. Missy learned by doing and experience. Her mind sifted through Cethy's tale as well as her own, trying to put the pieces together. When pieces did not fit she cast them aside only to scramble for them again a moment later when she worked a new theory. One thing was painfully clear. They were all in way more trouble than she initially anticipated. The gods were being murdered. The pouka were tricking themselves to look like gods. The Charonte were giving out the power they had stolen. Missy put two and two together.

Hera was the one who had ransacked the Hub. From the moment Missy met Hera, she should have known that something was horribly wrong. She had felt no emotion from the woman. No matter how carefully or determinedly she tried to force her magic on Hera, Missy had gotten nothing in return. The woman Missy had met was a pouka. The real Hera was dead.

So was Cupid.

Gull had taken Cupid's power and shape. Dionysus had not seen Cupid for weeks. Bave had confessed to murdering him. There was no getting around it, Cupid was dead. He died hating Missy for things she couldn't even remember. He died thinking her evil. Like Cethy, he probably believed her a traitor.

Missy was not one for theatrical displays of feminine emotion, but this was all too much. She hugged her knees and hid her face from the night and the stars shining unconcerned overhead. Once the first tear fell, it was impossible to hold the rest back. Missy sobbed. Her whole body shook with emotions that were too big for her. She was wracked with guilt and frustration that she had caused all of their troubles and was useless to stop it. She was furious that she had not been there to protect Cupid, cantankerous though he was. She was grief stricken that there had been no reconciliation between the two of them. Not even so much as a begrudging peace. There had only been hatred. That was why Missy lamented her loss and her hopelessness into the night.

After all, she was only sixteen.

"Don't cry. Please, don't cry."

Missy looked up. Her eyes were puffy and her lip quivered under the stress of her own misery. Cupid stood on the beach behind her, his blue eyes concerned, his wings twitching. For a moment Missy felt wonder at his presence, but it was quickly replaced by anger. Thanatos's words replayed meanly in her head. *Those who go to Mictlan, stay there.* This was not Cupid, no matter what he looked like.

Missy stood slowly. She drew Caliburn and leveled the fearsome blade at the false Cupid. "If you ever take his shape again I will kill you, Gull." It was a promise.

The pouka melted back down to his true shape. His giant yellow eyes were sad. "I thought perhaps you would want see Cupid. One last time," he said. "Is that not why you were crying?"

Missy lowered her sword. This pouka, at least, was not her enemy. She was embarrassed that she had been caught mourning and she collapsed back into the sand and wrapped her arms around herself for warmth and comfort. Summer was almost over. The nights would be getting cool again, and now she had no place to live. Not that it would matter. Erebus would be in the Mortal Realm soon enough, and then the cold would be the least of her problems. That was where Missy belonged, anyway. Erebus was in her soul. The Hesperides had said so. She was a part of it.

A part of the problem.

Gull crept closer to Missy, his fluffy tail straight up in the air like a banner. "You'll come back now, won't you?" he asked tentatively.

"No," Missy said. "I just want to be alone, Gull."

"Dionysus said that's what you'd want," Gull said sourly. "But you must come or the goddess will die."

Missy rubbed her eyes. "Gull, what are you talking about? Red is fine. She's in the hotel with Dionysus, safe and sound."

"For now." Gull's fur stood on end and made him seem larger than he truly was. "But the goddess wants to go back for the venom and prove that she deserves to be the Norn. She is not like you, Nemesis. She isn't strategic or quick. She's no campaigner. If the goddess goes without your help, she will die."

Missy swore. "Why didn't you tell me that before?" Her mind raced. She couldn't just go back to the Mayan, but if she had help she could beat Cethy to the cave, and maybe have the Charonte subdued by the time her friend showed up. Then she could just hide and let Cethy have her small victory. "Gull, I need a favor." she said, chewing on her thumbnail. "Promise."

Gull breathed a sigh of relief. The hard young goddess was going to help him save his goddess. He would have promised her anything in that moment. "You have my word, Nemesis. What do you need me to do?"

Missy wasted no time. "I can't bend alone. You have to take me to the cave. Just a little outside, though. Someplace safe where I can catch my breath. I don't bend well. I'll clear the way for Cethy."

Gull's yellow eyes filled with tears. "No! I wasn't suggesting that you go and die in her stead!" The little monster wailed and climbed up Missy's pant leg. "Just stop the goddess from going. Protect her. Don't go running off and getting yourself slaughtered to prove a point."

"You gave your word, Gull." Missy said through a clenched jaw. She knew her chances. They weren't so good. "Do you want to be a squirrelly cat forever?" She had not wanted to trick Gull, but time was of the essence. She needed to get to that cave and quickly. Cethy might be insufferable, but Missy was not going to let her stumble blindly into her own demise. "Let's go, Gull."

The pouka let out a forlorn wail and pulled Nemesis into a bend. He had promised.

—*Chapter Thirty-Six*—

Missy and Gull were not alone when they arrived in the cave. Gull had brought them into a tiny chamber some twenty feet below the main cavern and given Missy a moment to regain her composure. The pair trekked upward to the main level, where Loki was to spend an eternity of torment. The cave was not as small as she had originally thought. Without the Charonte and their champion, the cave was actually very spacious. The high ceiling was covered in stalactites and as Missy watched, a massive drop of a toxic, yellow goop dripped down from the ceiling. The droplets were spaced out, one drip every thirty seconds, and Missy followed their descent to the center of the cave.

An impossibly tall, thin woman was hunched over a stone table, her arms outstretched. In her hands was large stone bowl. Deftly, the giantess moved the bowl to catch each drop of poison as it fell. Not once did the sticky liquid slosh over the side, proving the woman's centuries of practice. Every few minutes the giantess dumped the bowl onto the rocks where its contents hissed and bubbled.

Missy stepped out of the shadows. "Are they gone then?" she asked. She hoped she sounded nonchalant, but it was difficult to tell. She probably sounded more like she was ready to wet herself. Gull clung to her sword sheath and she could feel his small body shaking against her back.

Sigyn had been in the cave for what felt like several lifetimes. It was her job to catch the poison, to try to offer her husband some relief from the venom's bite. She looked down at the prostrate god that was chained to the stone table. Loki. She glanced at Missy over her shoulder. "You again? I did not think that you would return. Be wary. Those others have not gone far." Sigyn turned her attention back to Loki and the stinking poison that had ruined his face and his mind.

Missy nodded. Slowly, cautiously she approached the stone table. So this was the fate of those who crossed the gods. Missy could not help but think that she had gotten off easily. Her banishment was nothing compared to this cruelty. The giantess glanced sidelong at her and Missy felt the fierce, protective aggression that colored the tall woman with a deadly red ribbon of emotion. "Come to gawk at the great Loki, have you? I'll not let him be humiliated further." Sigyn's warning was clear.

"No." Missy's voice was soft, respectful even. "I am here only to protect my friend."

"There are no friends here." The man on the table spoke at last. "Those who come here are duty bound to do so. Sigyn is bound to me by the duty of marriage. The Charonte are bound by their duty to their own greed. What binds you, young one, that you are drawn to Loki's Despair?"

"Friendship has its own duties," Missy whispered. "My cousin is on her way here and there are evil beings loose in your caves. I won't let her get hurt. Not if I can stop it."

Loki's laugh sounded as if it had not been used for some time. The loud, wheezing rasp echoed off the high stone. "You would die to save your cousin?" he asked. "I would also have died, if it meant that I could have saved my nephew, but my sincerity fell on the deaf ears. I caused his death instead of saving him and the gods judged my act so heinous that this is my eternal punishment." Loki's voice was bitter. "I deserve worse, but I also deserve mercy."

"Hush, Loki." Sigyn's voice was gentle for one so large.

"But I will have my revenge," Loki said. "One day I will be freed and I will punish the gods for this."

Missy shook her head. "The venom warps his mind," Sigyn whispered to her. "It poisons his blood, even his very soul. He is mad, I'm afraid."

"I am so sorry," Missy said, and she meant it.

Sigyn watched the tiny girl who had appeared in her prison. "Your sincerity is refreshing, little goddess. There are usually naught but lies told here in the Despair. The venom is yours, if you want it. You should take it now and go. No need for there to be any more trouble here today. That a battle raged here at all is not right. This is not some glorious field of war. It is a dark and unfeeling place. Go. Go before it consumes you. Stop your cousin from coming, and keep her safe."

"Safe? There is no longer such a thing as safety. The Charonte are creating danger and trouble in all the realms. The concept of peace is more mythology now than your husband, Sigyn." Missy closed her eyes and prayed that when she opened them the gorgon would not really be there, watching from the darkness. Medusa glared at Missy from behind her sunglasses, barely visible in the shadows. Medusa stepped forward and Missy caught sight of the brittle scabs on Medusa's cheeks. The marks only added to the gorgon's frightening appearance. "So we meet again, young Nemesis."

Sigyn's face twisted. "Do not fight here," she ordered. She thrust a bowl into Missy's hands and quickly grabbed up another one before the next drop of poison fell. "Leave now," the giantess ordered. "Do not bring yet more evil to this place. Take your poison and go."

"Perhaps you should leave before the Charonte come back," Medusa said. "I do not feel like killing you today."

Missy tried not to let her relief show. She accepted the bowl of venom and began to back away from the stone table and those who crowded around it. There would not be another battle today. There would be no more grief. Missy and Gull had almost made it out of the chamber when there was a flurry of movement. Missy felt herself pitch forward and the bowl of venom left her hands. Instinct told Missy to roll out of the way and to drag Gull with her. The last thing either of them wanted was to be covered in that venom. Sticky and foul, even its touch caused suffering. Loki was proof of that.

A howling, pained scream filled the cavern. The agonized shriek echoed loudly as it bounced off of the high ceiling and stone walls. Medusa hissed. "They will hear that! They will come back! You must run."

Missy took stock of herself. She wasn't injured. The venom was gone, but more could easily be collected. She glared at the one responsible for her fumble. Someone had bent into the cave and destroyed her only shot at escaping with the venom and without a fight. Missy felt her heart break.

Cethy knelt on the stone floor and stared down at her hands in terrified anguish. The skin bubbled and smoked, the toxic sludge that clung to her hands and arms eating away at flesh and muscle. She had caught the bowl upside down, not realizing the danger that it held. The sleeves of her sweatshirt were already burned clean away as the thick venom dripped down her arms.

There was a clatter of footsteps and Missy heard Medusa hiss, "Flee!" as the Charonte filed into the cavern.

Sigyn added her voice to the bedlam of the Charontes' surprised and angry shouts. "Leave! All of you! Get out now lest you wake up Jormungand!" The giantess pointed upward to where the venom had come from. "You dare fight here! Get out!"

Missy cursed. Her advantage was long gone now and there was no time to treat her injured friend. Instead she propped Cethy up against a wall of rock and slapped the older girl roughly across the face. "Snap out of it, Norn. Now is not the time to lose your mind! Gull, do something!" The pouka leapt onto Cethy's shoulder and began to whisper furiously into her ear in a desperate attempt to sooth Cethy's mind.

Missy drew Caliburn slowly and faced her enemies. The Charonte spread out around her and Cethy, advancing on her menacingly. Hel had not expected a second attack on the venom so soon, but she was pleased to see that the Norn had been hurt. *Badly* hurt. That was a nice surprise. The Norn's arms were swelling up into foul, popping, blisters, filled with some sort of black ooze.

"Aw, poor Cethy," Erin sneered.

"Shut up, Erin."

"Or what?" Erin demanded. Missy was too furious, too desperate to think straight. She lunged at Erin, her sword flashing. Erin held out her hand and a long sword appeared in her fist just in time to block Caliburn's downward chop. Missy cut under Erin's sword then slid back, aware of the other blade's longer reach. Caliburn demanded that Missy attack, heedless of the other weapon. The girls circled each other and Missy could not help but smile. Erin had none of her training. She was clumsy and slow. She was even holding the sword wrong.

Missy advanced slowly. "Don't do this, Erin," she said. "I don't want to hurt you, but I will."

Erin only laughed and charged the smaller girl. Missy had no choice. She parried Erin's blow and used the older girl's momentum against her. Missy brought her sword up under Erin's blade and felt Caliburn plunge deep into flesh, cutting bone and muscle with sickening ease. Erin staggered, pierced through the heart by Caliburn's hungry point. Her eyes grew confused and unfocused.

Missy tugged her sword free with a whimper and wiped Caliburn clean on her pant leg. She looked away from Erin, unable to face what she had just done. She was supposed to be better than Nemesis, but she was just as bad. Murderer. She was a murderer. Missy could not help it. She stumbled back and emptied the contents of her stomach onto the stone. She was still heaving when Erin's cold laughter filled the cave.

"Oh, Missy. That wasn't very nice." Erin got back to her feet. The blood that pumped steadily from her chest seemed of little consequence to her. Missy watched in disgusted horror as Erin's skin stretched back together leaving nothing behind. Not so much as a nick or bruise.

"Impossible," Missy whispered.

"Not so impossible," Erin snapped. "I drank the water, remember. You can't hurt me. I'm invincible, Missy."

"But you're not." Missy had not even noticed that Bave snuck around behind her. Missy gasped, a stabbing pain erupting in her side as Bave twisted something sharp into the flesh between her ribs. "You see, Nemesis," Bave said as she pushed her weapon deeper into Missy's body, "no one knows how we've been taking the essence from the gods." Missy wanted only to scream, but the sound was lodged in her throat. "Some months ago I took something from Morta. Do you know who that is?" Missy made some guttural noise in her throat, and Bave took that as an attempt to answer. "Very good, Nemesis. Morta is one of the Fates. She is the inevitable, the end. The cutter of the thread of life. And these," Bave pulled her weapon free with a jerk and dangled it before Missy's face, "are the scissors she uses to cut the thread of life."

Missy's blood dripped from the pair of rusty sheers that Bave held before her face. "One cut lets me in," Bave said. "The second, lets me take your power." Bave gripped Missy across her shoulders and swung the sheers down toward the girl's chest. Missy saw the blades heading for her heart and let her legs buckle. Missy collapsed well under the sheers and Bave never saw them coming. The war goddess screamed as the blades tore into her own chest while Missy crawled back to Cethy and kneeled at the girl's feet.

"You've got to bend, Cethy," Missy gasped. She touched her side and winced at the throbbing pain. Missy's hand was dark with her own blood but she wiped it on her jeans and tried to keep herself upright. "You have to get out of here. Now."

"It is over, Nemesis," Hel laughed. "Soon your Norn will fall to the madness of my brother's poison." She paused, enjoying the effect her words had on Missy. "Oh yes. It is quite the family reunion today. The Midgard Serpent is my brother. And my father is the man on the table, the very man that you once helped to pass judgment on, Nemesis. But it all comes full circle today. Today you pay for what you did to the gods. You should never have joined this fight, Vengeance. It is not your place." Hel turned to her own champion, her blue eye cold. "Finish it, Medusa."

There was little choice left. Missy pushed herself to her feet, Caliburn in her hand. Medusa slowly removed her sunglasses, exposing the cave to the fatal harm her gaze inflicted. Medusa stared at her own feet, not yet ready to do what was necessary. Nemesis was no friend, but there was a resentful respect between the two of them. They were in the same boat, Nemesis and Medusa. The only way they got what they wanted was if they fought and helped their own side to win. Medusa wanted her beauty back, but what did Nemesis want? Only to right the wrong she had done so long ago. Medusa pitied the goddess. Someone would not leave the cave alive. One of them had to fail.

"You will not die today, Nemesis," Medusa said, her voice soft beneath Cethy's gasping whimpers. "But this must end. I am truly sorry that I cannot let you succeed. This is the only way. This is the only way we can both live."

Missy understood belatedly what Medusa was saying. The gorgon's head snapped up but her terrible gaze did not fall on Missy. Instead Medusa had her eyes trained on Cethy.

"Gull!" Missy's sharp command was enough to kick the pouka into action. His shape grew indistinct, a wave of shadow that swept around both girls as he bent, dragging all three of them to safety before Medusa's fatal stare took effect. The Norn and her small family vanished from the cave and left behind one question.

How could Medusa have missed?

—Chapter Thirty-Seven—

Cethy came out of the bend still in a dive and Gull dropped from her neck, a pile of furry limbs on the carpet. The luck goddess crash landed awkwardly, head first into a stack of books. Missy's momentum was stopped by the far bed. The girl bounced off the mattress and fell with a sickening smash into the space between the mattress and the wall.

Dionysus was on his feet and at Cethy's side in an instant. The redhead could not stop screaming. Monsters moved in and out of her vision. They tormented her with dark thoughts and darker hallucinations. She looked down at her ruined hands and screamed all the louder. Her arms were so brutally burned they refused to obey her damaged brain's commands. Jormungand's venom had done its horrible work. It disfigured her skin, and poisoned her blood. Already her mind warped and twisted under the influence of the slime that clung to her.

"Prometheus!" Dionysus's voice boomed out in the tiny room. "Prometheus! I need you! Now!" Dionysus immediately went to work. He used everything he could lay his hands on to try and wipe the tacky venom from Cethy's arms. He only succeeded in rupturing the blisters, releasing the putrid, runny mess inside. Cethy's skin shed away in great chunks of flesh and muscle, atrophied by the poison. "What happened, Cethy?" Dionysus asked. Cethy was only able to scream.

Dionysus tore away layer after layer of ruined flesh. Cethy swooned while her arms burned anew under Dionysus's ministrations. "Botched it," she muttered. Her tortured mind tried to suppress the demons that threatened to overwhelm it, but it was a losing battle. "I ruined everything again." She collapsed. Her mind retreated to what little sanctuary unconsciousness offered.

Prometheus appeared in the room, calm in the midst of chaos. "What happened?" he demanded of Dionysus. The titan sunk to Cethy's side. His face was grim as he took in Cethy's mangled limbs.

"Can't you do something useful?" Dionysus demanded shakily. He pulled a layer of Cethy's skin from the towel he was using to scour away the venom and flung it away. "Heal her." He stopped scrubbing and threw down the towel he was using. A hole had been burned clean through its center.

"I cannot heal her. At least, not physically." Prometheus shook his head at the carnage. "My power has always been rooted in the mind. In thoughts. Even so," he put his hand on Cethy's forehead. "I cannot fix Tyche. Her mind belongs to another Titan."

Dionysus grabbed a fresh towel and continued his foul work while Prometheus spoke. "Well, I suggest you get him to fix her then," he growled. Cethy's arms were eaten away down to the barest layer of muscle. Dionysus dabbed gently, but no more skin fell away.

Prometheus rested a heavy hand on Dionysus's shoulder. "You've done well," he said. "She will be scarred, but most of the poison seems to have been drained. After some time, her mind will be well again. I will see to it that she is cared for."

"You should have thought of that before," Dionysus said coldly. He scooped Cethy off of the floor and deposited her on the closest bed. She was out cold and Dionysus could not help but be relieved. Better that Cethy did not see the twisted way her skin pulled and puckered on her arms. Better that she not feel the tightness in her scarred hands. Better that she not realize that she was forever maimed. "You should have taken better care of her." He looked down at the young goddess, sympathy in his eyes and his voice.

Dionysus's expression changed from pity to terror. His eyes fell to the floor where Missy was in a heap, unmoving. For a fear-filled moment, Dionysus was afraid the girl had fallen on her own sword, but the truth was far worse. A sword wound could heal. There would be no healing for Missy.

Missy's golden eyes were closed. Her face was calm, peaceful even. Caliburn was pointed down, resting at her side in acceptance. The girl's muscles were tensed but her unencumbered palm was open in a sign of defeat. Missy had willingly stepped in front of Medusa's gaze to keep Cethy from suffering a fate worse than death. She was stone.

"No. Oh, Missy, no," Dionysus said in a heartbroken whisper. He reached down and drew Missy up, stiff and unforgiving in his arms. Even her silken curls did not move. Dionysus backed away from his fallen friend, his hand over his eyes. "Oh, no. No. No."

Prometheus reached out fearfully and touched Missy's cold, marble cheek. "This was not supposed to happen," he said, more to himself then to Dionysus. "I had thought that maybe…but no. It does not matter. Not now."

"What are you going to do?" Dionysus said from the corner. He stared at the wallpaper, unable to turn and look at Missy. "The quest failed."

"Never say such a thing!" Prometheus roared. "The two of them sacrificed life and limb for this quest. How dare you call it a failure! How dare you belittle what they have done!" Prometheus began to point to the mythical objects in the room. "We have water from the enchanted spring. We have Caliburn."

"We have a statue holding Caliburn, you mean." Dionysus mumbled, sickened to his core.

"We have half of the Aegis. And they even succeeded in getting the venom." Prometheus carefully picked up one of the ruined towels where gobs of the sticky venom clung and smoked.

Dionysus said nothing. He simply motioned to Gull. The pouka had been curled up on Cethy's chest watching everything unfold with horror. At his command the little monster jumped to Dionysus's arm and the two vanished. Prometheus was left alone with the two destroyed goddesses.

"Epimetheus," Prometheus said quietly. "You were right. I should have listened to you."

A man appeared in the room, young and smiling. "They all say that in the end, brother. Still, it is rare that I am so honored by you. What have you done?" Prometheus gestured to the unconscious Cethy and the sculpture that was Missy. Epimetheus whistled. "You've put your foot in it this time. Prometheus, the great thinker, lover of mankind, and meddlesome fool. What would you have me do?"

"Anything," Prometheus said. "Anything you can."

Epimetheus examined the two girls, careful not to miss a detail. He ran a gentle finger over Cethy's scared hands. "I can fix this one. Not her burns, of course, but her mind. She is one of mine. Listen." He gestured for Prometheus to come close. "Do you hear? Her heart is filled with regrets and my favorite words of all time. *What if.*" He tucked Cethy under her blankets and smoothed them out. "What if I had never quested? What if I had not fought with Missy? What if Prometheus had never found me? This girl's hindsight is impeccable. I will care for her. Her mind will heal."

Epimetheus turned to Missy and his gruff smile diminished. "This one is a girl after your own heart, brother. She is all yours, and unopened to my magic." Epimetheus leaned his ear close to Missy's stone mouth. "I hear her even now, but she fades quickly into the underworld." Epimetheus straightened up. "She counts on her foresight. She does not look back and wish that things were different. She has no regret, nor any 'what if's' for me to prey on. She is your girl, through and through. And now she is lost."

Epimetheus put his hand on his brother's shoulder and for a moment the Titans stood facing each other. Forethought and afterthought. Preparation and regret. Brother and brother. "I am sorry for your loss, but this blunder is all your own doing," Epimetheus said. "I am not able or inclined to fix it." With that Epimetheus was gone, and so was Prometheus's hope.

—*Epilogue*—

Lena sat in the frosty chill of her lair and watched as her breath formed little clouds that floated away towards the ceiling. She did not want to look at the ice for fear that her heart would break further. Epimetheus ordered Cethy far from the Mayan. Under his gentle care Cethy began her slow emergence from the prison her own mind had created. Lena watched with mounting sadness as the redhead stared at her useless hands with cold comprehension. Worse was when Cethy looked around her empty room. Epimetheus had explained everything to her but Cethy could not grasp that Missy was gone.

"You can go to the ceremony," Epimetheus promised. "But I will not have you upset. Your mind is still very fragile and I won't have all of my work undone."

They were doing so well, a voice said sadly.

Oh, the Fates are cruel, said another.

Lena felt one of them nudge her mind. *Show us. Please?*

Lena waved her hand at the wall and her cave lit with sights and sounds. Ten days after the failed venom heist a small group appeared on the cliffs of Tir na n-Og. Hippolyta's Amazons stood by their queen and Niamh as Prometheus lowered Missy and her fearsome sword into the enchanted spring. The crowd watched with solemn faces as the stone goddess sank beneath the clear water and came to rest at the pool's pebbly bottom.

"Here at least, she will withstand the cruel hand of time," Niamh said quietly, "guarded by her tribe and her sisters."

There was the barest hint of a splash on the pond's surface and the five voices of the Hesperides spoke as one. *We will guard her as we have guarded nothing before. Our sister is more valuable than some mere godly trinket. The Fountain shall protect her from time. We shall protect her from all else.*

The vision faded as Lena wiped the wall clean. "This is not over," she said to the Voices. "It seems over, but it isn't. It can't be." The little girl tugged on her hair in frustration. Lena felt cold, but it was not due to her frozen home. It was a deep bone chilling ache that filled the little girl with dread. This was not what she had Seen. Nemesis was not supposed to die at Medusa's hand. Something had gone horribly wrong. "It isn't supposed to be like this," Lena whispered to the emptiness but there was no response. The Voices were gone.

For months Lena watched the ice intently and without complaint. The Voices never returned to her, and Lena was left alone with no one to distract her from her visions. One morning the Oracle flinched, her eyes wide with the Sight. The future was laid out before her like a map. A map that Lena had been reading incorrectly. The little girl smiled. "I See," she said softly. "We may save the world yet."